Total

EXPOSURE

JORDAN'S GAME

HUSS

JORDAN'S GAME

BOOK ONE

Edited by RJ Locksley
Cover Design by JA Huss

For everyone who…
just didn't mean it to go down that way.
It's cool.

JA HUSS

PROLOGUE

EVANGELINE

I like winter because I can wear a scarf that covers my face. January is my favorite month. When the cold threatens to overtake most people I go outside, covered up from head to toe, and... *live*. Free from stares of strangers. Secure in the notion that I am alone and unnoticed in the city of people who are way too consumed with getting back inside to be bothered about me.

The one among many who needs to get back out.

This feeling is called many things. But I have my own name for it. It's the blur of movement. A flock of starlings forming a mass of collaborative beauty in the sky. The rush of traffic on a freeway. Headlights passing by like time. The swirl of stars overhead that remind you, every time you look up, that you don't matter.

It's anonymity. Or obscurity.

The blur. I'm part of the blur.

Secluded in the isolation of being nobody.

It's not just a fantasy of mine. This is the world I live in so completely that today is the first day I've left my penthouse apartment to venture outside in almost six weeks. This is my day because it's January and I can cover up from head to toe and live the fantasy for real.

For once. I hope tomorrow is just like today.

3

People think Denver is nothing but snow. I wish it were true, but it's not. Three hundred days of sunshine every year. Yes, it snows, and yes, there are a few weeks' worth of days like this every winter. Days when the wind is strong, and the snow falls sideways, and covering every inch of skin is normal behavior.

But it's not enough when such days are your only key to the outside world.

I spend my summers locked inside with the AC set as low as it will go, wearing sweatpants, and fingerless gloves, and hoodies. If I can muster up the will to leave my sanctuary, I wear a hat, and sunglasses, and long sleeves— though the blouse is usually billowy and thin because of the heat.

Even then, it's too hot to be outside like that. So I don't walk in the park, or go to street festivals down below on the 16th Street Mall, or eat on one of the patios of the numerous trendy restaurants.

I just watch the blur from above, wishing for winter. I have a large terrace that wraps around my corner apartment where I can be myself in the summer. So I do get out, just not... *out*.

Like now.

I breathe in the frigid air, not even minding that the wind blows down my throat, doing its best to suffocate me even through my scarf.

Maybe I want to be suffocated? Did the wind ever think of that?

There is no one on the mall with me today, though it's noon on a weekday and the shops are open. We're not going to get enough snow to shut things down. Just enough to keep the world frightened and hidden away.

And it feels good. That they're the ones hiding and I'm the one out.

I walk briskly down the mall, past the art gallery. One of the few places I actually do like to visit. Especially early in the morning when no one else has time and I have plenty. A coffee shop, a Mexican restaurant that won't open for a few more hours, and then Mott's is right there. The used book and vinyl store. I got a call last night from Dan, the owner and one of the few people I consider an acquaintance. He found the recording I've been searching for.

Mei Ling Chao. Age thirteen. Live performance number seventy-one. 1959 in British-controlled Hong Kong.

I push through the doors and the heat overtakes me. People always overreact with the heat during a blizzard. Which I hate because keeping a scarf wrapped around your face indoors with a furnace set on seventy-five is more suffocating to me than the wind blowing down my throat.

"There she is," Dan says. He's bent down behind the counter, so I can't see him until he stands up holding a stack of used books that were probably donated overnight and now he's got to sort through them.

"I got your message," I say, breathless, but not because of the cold or the wind. "Are you sure this is it?"

He looks at me from over the top of his wire-frame glasses and sets his stack of books down on the glass countertop that protects all sorts of semi-valuable trinkets. "RCA Victor."

I breathe out. A huge sigh of relief because yes, that's all he needed to say. There are many copies of this particular recording of Mei Ling Chao, but the one produced by RCA Victor is the real deal.

I need the real deal.

"That's the one," I say, my heart racing with excitement.

"Why are you so interested in this one?" he asks.

It's a loaded question. He knows nothing about me. Not my real name. Not where I live. Not even my email. He has one contact number for me and it's a digital number that reroutes to my cell phone.

"I collect," I say. "I told you that."

"Yeah," he says, looking me up and down. I haven't been in here in a long time. Not since early fall when I purchased the very first recording of Anne Akiki Meyers. It was raining that day. An unusually cold day that kept people inside. So I was bundled up in a plastic slicker wearing an overly large hat that was dripping water on his decades-old industrial gray carpet. "But it's a very... unusual collection. First and last recordings of child violin prodigies. I've never met anyone who collected those."

"Well, maybe people are boring," I say, forcing a small laugh. "I like to buck the trends."

Dan stares at me for a few more seconds, considering my answer. "Right. But you've bought every modern-day female violin prodigy I can get my hands on."

"That's what most collectors do, Dan. We buy them all."

"Except... you haven't bought them all, have you, Angela?"

"I'm well on my way."

"So let me guess who's next on your list."

"Evangeline Rolaine," I say, beating him to the obvious answer. "I have her first. But if you can find the

6

last recording of Ms. Rolaine, I'll gladly take it off your hands."

He eyes me for a moment, which is more thoughtful consideration than I can handle. But I resist the urge to check my scarf or fidget my feet. So I wait a few seconds and then say, "Can I see the record?"

Dan does a shrug with his hands, like he gives up, and then holds up one finger and says, "Be right back."

I watch him make his way through the numerous shelves of books and stacks of vinyl records, but he doesn't look back and I take that as a good sign.

He doesn't know it's me. He might guess, but that's his business. I am not Evangeline Rolaine because she doesn't exist anymore.

I busy myself looking at trinkets in the glass case as I listen for his returning footsteps. And that's when my eyes rest upon a stack of cards near the old cash register.

"'What are you afraid of?'" I say, reading the only sentence on the top card.

I pick it up and study the calligraphy. It's bold and dark, rising up from the thick paper the way one might print up a fancy business card. But it's square, the size of a drink coaster you might find in a fancy bar.

I turn it over in my hand and read the back.

Dr. Lucinda Chatwell, M.D., Ph.D., ABPN Board Certified.

And then in a very fancy script, in very tiny letters, it says, "We will conquer your fear together." And a phone number.

"Here we go," Dan says, so close he startles me. I push the card into my pocket and calm my racing heart as he makes his way around the counter and places the plastic-covered album on the glass. "Mei Ling Chao. Last live performance at age thirteen. 1959. Hong Kong." He smiles at me as he carefully removes the record from the cover and says, "RCA Victor," as he presents it for my inspection.

The picture of the dog with his ear to the phonograph makes me want to pee my pants with excitement. I actually laugh at that thought.

Which must surprise Dan, because he says, "I'll take that as a yes."

"Yes," I breathe. "Wrap it up. And how much do I owe you?"

Dan adjusts his glasses and clears his throat. "Seven thousand and fifty-two dollars."

"Wow," I say. "She's worth a lot."

"She is. You still want it?" he asks. "I know I quoted you four and change. But you have no idea what I had to do to get my hands on this."

"How did you get it?" I ask. I don't usually talk so much when I come in, but I've been searching for this recording for... hell, since I was fifteen. Twelve years.

"You're not going to believe this," Dan whispers, leaning his elbows on the glass so he can get closer to me. "But a friend of a friend actually *knows* her."

"Really?" I breathe.

"Yeah." He nods, leaning in a little closer, like we're sharing a secret. There's no one in here, so it intrigues me enough to lean forward, getting as close to him as I've been to... well, anyone since I withdrew into my own world as a teenager. "She's broke," he says. "Living in a senior center somewhere in Oregon. She had this and a few others she was holding on to. But she sold it to him for six grand." He leans back up like the secret is over. "Which is why I had to charge you seven plus."

"Is she... ill?" I ask. I don't give two flying fucks about the price of the recording. But her health...

"Dying," Dan says, doing his thing at the cash register. "Cancer, I think."

"Oh," I say, my excitement deflating. "That's... that's too bad."

"Yeah," Dan says. "How do ya wanna pay?"

"Right," I say, reaching into my pocket for my envelope of cash and placing it on the counter. I knew he was gonna charge me more than he quoted. He always does. So I always come prepared because the thought of leaving here without it, then having to wait for another cold, snowy day to come back... Not gonna happen. I brought eleven thousand with me. "Gonna take me a second to count it all out."

"No rush," Dan says.

So I count out seven thousand-plus dollars and then push the bills towards him. "Double-check to make sure it's all there."

My eyes drift over to the stack of cards next to the register. *What are you afraid of?*

"What are these?" I ask.

Dan ignores me for a second as he finishes his counting and then laughs. "Some guy came in here last summer and paid me a thousand dollars to keep a stack of those on the counter at all times. I have no clue, never called the number, but he says he'll be back every now and then to check on them, and if they're there, he'll give me another grand. So I keep 'em up."

"Do people take them?" I ask, picking one up to pretend I haven't already read it.

"Sure. Lots of people. He's been in here a few times to restock. I've made like three grand off the guy already. So fuck it, right? Free money."

"Yeah," I say, putting the card down and carefully rearranging the stack. "Fuck it."

Dan puts my purchase in a plastic drawstring bag that says *Mott's Used Collectables* on it, and then slides it across the counter. "So... Evangeline Rolaine then?"

"What?"

"Your next request," he says with a smirk. "If anyone can find Evangeline, it's yours truly."

"Sure," I say. "Good luck with that. If you find it, please call me first." I grab my bag and turn to leave, acutely aware that I've been in here far too long and said way too much.

"I'll do that, Angela," Dan calls after me.

But I'm already back out into the blissful whiteout so his words are just an echo in my head.

When I get back to my penthouse I rip off my coat and scarf, burning up inside from a combination of too many layers and the desire to hear the famous last recording of Mei Ling.

She was only two when her parents put her on stage for the first time. They did it for the same reasons most parents of child musical prodigies do it. Pride. That's always a factor. Some of them, and Mei Ling's parents were among those, also do it for fame and fortune. A way to lift an entire family out of poverty.

That's why my parents did it.

I was four, not two. But what's the difference between four and two, really? I was way too young to understand anything other than I was doing something that came naturally, something that I understood, something that I loved.

It wasn't until I was ten that I started realizing how much I'd been used. And it took a few more years, four to be exact, before I... well... let it drive me crazy. When the money ran thin, about the time I was thirteen, we were staying with friends. They weren't *really* friends. They were just rich people who wanted me to play at their parties.

By fifteen I was too old to wow crowds with my youth even at stupid rich-people parties. Fifteen-year-old violinists aren't special. They might not be typical at that skill level, but the oddity is long gone.

The money went with the fame. My parents had bought houses and cars. They'd hired housekeepers and drivers. We had parties until the very last cent was spent. Huge parties with me at the center.

That's when I'd really had enough. I'd been traveling my whole life, never had a real home, or real friends, or any of the things most teenagers take for granted. Even very poor kids had more of a life than I did.

So I rebelled.

And then the court battles began. I begged a judge for emancipation. Presented my case as methodically as I could, and came out of it free, but utterly alone.

I only had one thing left. One thing my parents didn't sell, one thing they didn't get to keep when I left. A rare violin gifted to me by an heiress after a concert when I was only eight years old. I sold the Stradivarius for nineteen million dollars at auction when I was sixteen.

I've been living off that violin for more than eleven years now. The money isn't gone, but there's not a lot left. I don't work. I don't perform. Can't perform, I remind myself. And that's not my fault. It's a sickness. A mental one, yes. But still, a debilitating sickness that I have no control over.

That's my story. I don't need to stick to it because it's true.

This penthouse was my first purchase. Bought back during the housing crash. I practically stole it from its original owner for a mere three million dollars.

Still, that's a lot of money. Especially when half of what I earned off the Stradivarius went to taxes and ten percent went to the auction house.

I can't really afford this Mei Ling recording. But why live if you can't have one extravagant pleasure to brighten your day?

So fuck it. Just like Dan said. Just fuck it.

I flip the switch on my turntable, pick up the bag, and gently remove the album from its plastic cover.

I stare at it for a moment. Enchanted by the tiny grooves in the vinyl that hold music. It's a small miracle in my eyes. I place the record on the turntable and make it turn, hesitating before placing the needle onto the edge—holding my breath, hoping I don't accidentally scratch it—and then exhale and… there is music in my house. In my head. In my heart. In my body. In my fingers. I play the air the way I used to play my instrument, wondering if that joy I used to feel as a child will ever come back to me. Or if I'll die up here in this tower, alone, empty, sad, and lonely.

What are you afraid of?

The question pops into my mind unwanted.

It's not a fair question. Not in my mind. I never asked for this fear. I never called to it the way some mad people do. I never courted it, loved it, held it close.

I want more than anything to be the girl I was before they ruined me.

But I can't.

It's a sickness.

It's a disease—not just in my head, but a part of me. Of my brain.

We will conquer your fear together.

No, I don't think we will, Dr. Chatwell.

Some people are born tall. Some people are born short. Some people are born smart and some not. Some people are born with music in their fingers and some people are born to perform that art in front of people and make millions of dollars.

I'm just not one of those people.

I can't even show my face in public. Not because of who I am. That's not really my problem. No one knows who I am anymore. No one cares.

No. The reason I've locked myself away in this penthouse is because I cannot stand to be looked at. I cannot stand to be watched. I cannot stand attention.

And isn't it ironic that my God-given talent—my *only* talent—is to play the violin? A talent that's quite useless if there's no one there to hear it.

I don't even own a violin. Haven't even played since I sold the Stradivarius.

So I play the air and wander back in time when it was all real. Before that first performance. When the music didn't come with watchers. When the performance wasn't about the money.

When I was a child.

I wish I was still that child.

I go back in time and stay there. I forget who I am, where I'm at, and why I'm even alive at all.

I drift in the blur of my own mind…

Ten hours later I wake up naked in the middle of the living room, the record still turning, the needle stuck at the end, hopping to static. My eyes burn from all the tears that Mei Ling sucked out of me. My body is sore from the sobbing, my heart empty and my head pounding.

I crawl over to my coat, discarded yesterday when I got home, and I pull out that card.

I stare at it for several minutes, wondering what it would be like to conquer my fear with Dr. Lucinda Chatwell.

It's an elusive dream… but I find my phone in the other pocket anyway. I press the numbers on the card. And when the woman calling herself Dr. Chatwell answers, I say, "I'm afraid of watchers."

CHAPTER ONE

JORDAN

One year later...

Walking past Turning Point Club is still hard. I really miss that place. Like... *really* miss that place. I thought I was OK with letting it go when I said no to Bric's offer to take it off his hands and keep the whole thing going. But even though I'm a forward-thinking guy and all the things that would come with owning an establishment like that are bad news, I really miss that place.

I like what I'm doing now. Which is... well, what to call my current line of business?

It's so goddamned innovative I'm not sure it has a label. I mean legally it has a name—Your Game—and just thinking about it makes me smile into the cold morning wind. But it's just a shell corporation. A way to receive and distribute money.

But if I had to put a name on it I'd call it a... a fantasy fulfillment service.

Sounds about right.

Which is why I don't understand Lucinda's call last night. Also why I'm walking past the defunct Turning Point and into Chella's tea room this very moment.

The door jingles when I open it. Not an annoying jingle like you might hear at a gas station or a dry cleaner.

I'd call this more of a tinkling. Those teeny-tiny bells Bohemian women sometimes wear as anklets. Something like that. So it's soft, and charming, and maybe even a little bit sexy.

"You're late," Chella calls from a couch in front of the window. I take off my scarf and coat, drape it over a large overstuffed chair as I pass by, and unbutton my suit coat as I walk over and join her. There's no one else here, since it's Tuesday, and she's closed on Tuesdays.

"You look lovely," I say, lightly kissing her hand before I sit down.

She rolls her eyes, but she doesn't bother hiding the smile. I charm the pants off Chella. Not literally. Anymore. Which makes me smile. "Why do you always keep me waiting? You know I'm obsessively punctual. And you're the one who wanted to see me!"

"I know. I'm sorry. It's just I got a call from Lucinda last night asking for... a favor."

Chella lifts up her eyebrows. It's a question mark. I know her well enough to decipher that expression. And she knows me well enough to let me continue without asking anymore. So she just pours me some tea and pushes the tiny pitcher of milk my way.

I add the milk, take a sip, and then lean back into the couch cushions, wondering how much I can legally tell her and still get good advice. "Well, I'm asking for a friend, OK?"

She smiles as she sips from her own tea cup. "OK."

"So this friend, he's sorta known for... making arrangements for people."

"What kind of arrangements?" Chella asks.

"Unusual ones," I say, wishing I could say more. Tell her everything. Chella is a fantastic fucking listener. She's not really my type as far as women go, but I think I like her better than Smith, Quin, and Bric combined. She doesn't judge, for one. She's so calm. And nothing I say ever surprises her. Chella is like everyone's perfect best friend. She's also highly discreet. If I tell her something in confidence, as long as I'm not hurting people, she won't tell a soul. Not even Smith.

"So is the problem the arrangements that need to be made?" Chella asks. "Or something else?"

I think about this for a few seconds. "Both," I finally decide. "I mean, he doesn't usually make this kind of arrangement, if ya get my drift."

"I don't." Chella laughs. "But I can take a guess if you can't say."

"My problem is... this friend usually does more of a fantasy-type thing and this new request is more of a... a medical-type thing."

"Hmmm," Chella says. "Maybe you should ask Bric? He's the doctor."

"He's not a doctor," I say. Fucking Bric and his useless medical degree. "He's a fucking psychopath."

"Not so much anymore," Chella says, blowing on her tea.

Stupid Bric. "No, I don't wanna ask Bric. I need your advice. You're good at it. Bric..." I shake my head. "He can't even make a good choice for himself, let alone give someone like me—I mean, *my friend*—good advice."

"Jesus Christ, Jordan. I know it's you. Just tell me what you need. Do you want me to agree this is a good idea so you can feel better about it? Or back up your intuition and say don't do it so you won't feel guilty for turning someone away who needs help? Just tell me what you're looking for so I know how to proceed."

Love how she always gets to the point. "I'm not sure. I mean, I can help this person. I have someone in mind who might even be perfect for it. But... *should* I help this person? And should I use the person I have in mind?" I sigh. "That's the struggle I'm having."

"Well," Chella says, taking another sip of her tea. "It's all legal?"

"Of course," I say. "I'm a fuckin' lawyer. I can't be breaking the law."

"Does it involve sex?"

"No." I laugh. "That's the problem. This is like a real... condition, or whatever. I mean, it's a weird one for sure. But this is all on the up and up and someone we both know has prescribed a treatment and asked me to deliver it."

"Someone we know, huh?"

I nod my head.

"OK," she says, taking a deep breath. "OK. I say do it then. She knows what she's doing. We've both trusted her before, right?"

"Which is why I came to you. I mean, you know her a lot better than I do. Me fucking her on her fortieth birthday while her husband watched doesn't exactly qualify as knowing her. But yeah, generally, I think she's got her shit together."

Chella goes quiet for a few seconds.

"What?" I ask. "What'd I say?"

She huffs out a laugh. "God, that night..." She closes her eyes, waits a few beats, then opens them again. "That night of her birthday... that was the first time I went to Turning Point. I was just thinking about how much has changed since then."

"Fuck, I forgot about that. You were there. Shit," I say, running a hand through my hair as I picture Chella walking down the stairs hanging on Smith Baldwin's arm, already in the game, even if she didn't know it yet.

Lucinda—the woman we're both pretending not to talk about right now—wanted Smith as her choice that night. But he was otherwise occupied, so she picked me. The new guy at the club. And that decision right there changed everything in my life.

A single moment has power like that.

"You OK?" Chella asks when my silence fills the room.

"Yeah, sure. Just thinking, ya know. How things can change so fast."

"So who did you have in mind?"

"What?"

"You said you might have the perfect guy for the job but that was also part of the problem. Who is it?"

"Oh." I sigh. "I don't know if you remember him from when we were kids, but Ixion Vanir?"

"Rings my bell, but not sure why."

"We were friends, remember? You've seen him a bunch of times, but it's been like twenty years or something. He doesn't come to Denver much."

"Ixion. That kid you were always attached to at the hip in grade school?"

"Yeah, him."

"You're still friends?"

"Well… sorta? Maybe?" But I give in and admit the truth. "Not really. But I wish we were."

"So why would he help you?"

"Normally I don't think he would. But he's been drifting for a while now. In and out of trouble for years. He needs a change, I think. This might be a good change."

That's not really the reason. I mean, it is. It's all true. But there's more to it than that. Things I don't want to get into now.

"If he's always in trouble, then why's he so perfect?" she asks. "I mean, what's he got that you think you need?"

God, that's a loaded question. "He has a very specific skillset. Something this job requires. And not many others would take the job. It's kinda fucking weird."

Chella laughs. "Everything you do is weird, Jordan. So what the fuck is going on?"

"I swear to God, it's not sex!" I laugh. "It's weird because... well the woman involved is weird, and her problem is weird, and of course, there's the whole privacy thing. She's sorta... famous. Used to be, anyway. And I need someone who can keep a secret. Not blab their fucking traps off to the media and shit, ya know?"

"And Ixion, the drifting troublemaker, is your man?" She's still laughing.

"Believe it or not, yes. He is." I sigh again. "He's kept a secret of mine for a long time now."

"You," she says, one eyebrow raised, "have a secret?"

I nod. Swallow down that memory. "Yeah. Never said a word. I would've been..." But I can't even say it. So instead I say, "I would've been in a lot of trouble otherwise. He kinda saved my ass."

"But he doesn't talk to you now?"

"Not much. No." Not ever is the more appropriate answer. "But I wouldn't mind changing that."

"And this is an excuse to bring him back into your life?"

"Not like that, Chella. I don't want to fuck the guy. I just... we were friends, ya know? And... and I wish we still were. Plus, there was this other person involved and I miss her."

"He's with her? This woman you miss?"

"No," I say, frustrated at trying to put all this shit into words. "No, forget about her. I just want him."

Chella smiles and leans back into the couch cushions. "Well, then what else is there to discuss? The request is legitimate. You have the right man for the job. And you get to help someone and make up for past mistakes with an old friend. I say do it."

Relief rushes through me.

"But you didn't need my advice, did you?" She pauses to see if I'll cop to what she's insinuating. But I don't, so she goes on. "You just wanted someone to agree with the decision you already made. Regardless of the potential fallout, you want to do this, don't you?"

I nod. "I do."

"Mostly for Ixion, right?"

I nod again. "That's right."

"Then why are you so nervous about it?"

Why indeed. But I know why. "Because moments can change your life."

"And you think this might be one of them?"

"I dunno, Chella. I just want this, right? I want to make things right between us, but it could go the other way."

"And then you lose what you've already lost."

I huff out a laugh. "Yeah, I guess that's the bottom line. I lost a lot in that... *incident* between Ix and me. And I don't want to make it worse."

"Hmm," she says. "OK. I get it. But making decisions based on fear isn't normally part of your *modus operandi*, Jordan. And as someone who did make decisions based on fear before I took that leap of faith that night you fucked Lucinda on her birthday, I'd have to say… nothing lost is gained."

"That's not how that saying goes." I chuckle.

"I know," she says, shrugging. "I made that up when I was a kid overseas with my mom. If you lose something, like one of your favorite shoes, for instance, and you go looking for that shoe, but you don't find it… well, you already lost what you don't have. So if you lose again you break even, Jordan. You don't lose it again. Failing twice at the same thing is free. Doesn't cost you anything."

I nod. And we talk a little after that as we drink our tea and eat scones.

But I leave there disagreeing with her final thoughts on my dilemma.

It's possible to lose the same thing twice and the cost is definitely not free. I know. I've been there before.

I lost more than Ixion when he took the fall for me seven years ago. I lost the other person involved. Losing both of them might as well've been everything. So getting half of them back, then losing him again… Well, that sounds like a very good excuse to get drunk and never sober up if you ask me.

I take out my phone and press Lucinda's contact.

"Please tell me your answer is yes," she says. "Do not leave me hanging here, Jordan. She needs help and she needs it *right now*."

"God, this chick must be a mess," I say back, not answering her question.

"Jordan," she presses.

22

"I'll do it," I say. "But I gotta get this guy and he's… he's been out of contact for a while. So she's gonna have to wait."

"How long?"

"Few weeks at least."

"She has a concert in six weeks. She needs to be ready. She needs to—"

"I understand that," I say, cutting her off as I pinch the bridge of my nose, staving off a headache. "But this isn't normal, OK? This is weird. And I need *this* guy. Plus we gotta get it all set up. So she's gonna have to deal until it's done."

Lucinda sighs on the other end of the phone. "OK. I can wait. But this guy? He'll do it?"

"Yes," I say. Not sure. Highly unlikely unless I go in with a plan. No, he's never gonna agree no matter what I do. "Yes," I reiterate. "He'll do it."

If I play it right. You don't beg Ixion Vanir for anything, let alone a favor. He does it, or doesn't do it, based on what kind of fucked-up mood he's in when you ask for said favor.

Nothing lost is gained, my ass.

Ix can still take a lot away from me. And even though he hasn't done that—yet—that doesn't mean he won't.

And I gotta ask myself the same question Chella did. *What does he have that I think I need?*

So. Much.

23

CHAPTER TWO

IXION

An overly loud buzzer snaps me out of the most peaceful sleep I've had in years, but the clanking of the jail-cell door brings me back to reality. Real fast.

"Ixion Vanir," the sheriff calls. Like there's anyone else in this fucking jail. "That's some name you got there. And some lawyer as well."

I sit up, rubbing my eyes, wishing I didn't get so drunk last night.

"Took him two days, but he did it."

Make that two nights ago. Since I've apparently been unconscious for a while.

I stand up, wobble because I might still be a little drunk, and shoot the sheriff with my finger. "He's the best."

"Don't I know it, cowboy. I owe him a favor, which is why you're getting out today. I don't know what makes you so special aside from that ridiculous name you've got. But he's managed to persuade me to erase the fact you took a baseball bat to Drake Metcaff's pick-up. I guess you owe him now too."

"Wait," I say, blinking the blur away and opening my eyes wider so I can, like, participate in what's happening and catch up with the conversation. "Who we talkin' about again?"

"Who else," the sheriff says. "Jordan Wells."

Fuck.

Fucker.

Mother*fucker.*

That piece-of-shit asshole has the *nerve* to bail *me* out of jail? Some balls, right there. "I don't owe him," I say, managing a few steps towards the open cell door. "He owes me. And this unexpected favor isn't enough to change that."

The sheriff just says, "Whatever you say."

He's about as tall as me. About twice as old as me. And if I know Jordan, and I do—even though I haven't talked to the dude in a pretty long time now—this here sheriff is more like me than he'll ever admit. Anyone who owes Jordan a favor like this is not an upstanding citizen.

"Welp," the sheriff says. "He's outside, cowboy. You can pick up your gun on the way out."

We go through the motions of unbooking me for crimes I have now never committed and the sheriff hands me a plastic bag with my leather jacket, my gun (still loaded), my phone (which says I have like ninety-one missed messages) and my wallet.

"Have a nice day, son," he calls as I shrug the jacket on and hit the door.

"Back atcha, gramps."

Outside it's a balmy thirty-seven degrees with a wind chill that makes it feel more like seventeen. But this is Northern Wyoming and it's January, so I can't complain.

Jordan Wells is sitting inside the only car in the parking lot, which is actually the sheriff's SUV, talking on the phone. He nods at me, then points to the passenger side, motioning me to get in. I spy a helicopter out in the nearby field, and the rotors begin to spin up for takeoff.

Perfect. Because I just remembered I don't have my fucking car and I don't live in this two-horse town. I live thirty miles north in a one-horse town. So the ride home is a nice perk that makes Jordan's visit a little more pleasant.

I get in the truck, slam the door, and warm my already cold hands in the blast of heat coming from the dash.

"Yup," Jordan says into the phone. "Got him. I'll be back in town tonight so… dinner and we'll discuss?" He listens as the person on the other end talks, then says, "Mmm-hmm. Right. Perfect. See you then."

He looks down at the phone, sighs, and then trains that infamous stoic glare right on me.

"What?" I ask.

"Why are you such a fuckup?"

I shrug. "Just my natural talent, I guess. And no one called your ass begging for help, so this is all you, man."

"Well it cost me a favor I didn't want to cash in, asshole. I need this fucking sheriff to play and now he doesn't have to. Because you"—he points his fucking finger at me—"decided to get drunk and destroy a man's brand new truck. You owe me, Ix. Seventy-five thousand fucking dollars plus a favor."

"Fuck that," I say, reaching into my jacket for my pack of smokes. "I don't need you to save me. I can pay my own debts, thank you."

Jordan eyes me. It's a look that hides so much. But I can read his mind. He's wondering… was that a jab at the past? Was it an innocent remark? What was it?

He grabs the pack of smokes from my hand, opens the driver's side window, and tosses them out. "You quit," he says. "So remember that when you get to Denver."

"Fuck Denver too," I say, running my fingers through my hair. "I'm not going to Denver. I'll go back in that fucking jail and take my chances before I go back to Denver."

"Well, unfortunately, Ix, that's not an option. I need you in Denver for a job."

"Fucking job. What job?"

"I'll tell ya when you get there." He shuts the truck off, pockets the keys, and opens his door, letting in a blast of Arctic air. "Call me when you get home and I'll give you directions."

"What?" I ask. But he's already slammed the door and is walking off towards his helicopter. I get out and jog to catch up. "You're not leaving me here, dude. I don't have a fucking car."

Jordan spins around, angrier than I've ever seen him. "I'm sure you'll figure something out. Because I'm not doing shit for you until you pay me back. So get your act together, Ix. This bad-boy attitude is way old."

He spins on his heel, adjusts his coat, and walks to the waiting helicopter.

I stand there, pissed off and still a little drunk, watching as it lifts up and disappears into the darkening sky.

"Asshole," I say, the sound of spinning rotors fading.

When I turn back to the sheriff's station, I'm alone again. Just me, and the wind, and the cold.

I shove my hands into my pockets and head for the road to hitch my way back home.

Jordan Wells can fuck off.

"So here's the deal," I tell the girl on the phone as I run my fingers through my now-wet hair. That shower felt good. Like the best shower in my entire life. I'm currently sitting on my bed in my one-room house on the edge of Washaki Ten, Wyoming, sucking on a smoke, and doing my best to placate the angry woman on the other end of the phone because I don't have a clue what she's talking about. "I'm fucking sorry, OK? I just need to come by your place and get my car. And my keys," I add. Because she's got those too.

"Fuck you, Ix. Just fuck you. I told you not to get involved."

I sigh and pinch the space between my eyes, then stop. Because that's a Jordan gesture if ever there was one and I haven't done that in years. Dude's back in my life for five minutes and I'm already picking up his mannerisms. "Look, I'm sorry about the other night and... whatever happened."

"You're such a dick."

I don't even remember what happened. This girl just called me up yelling like I ruined her life or something. But how much of a life can one man ruin in one night? And you'd think I'd have some sort of recollection of that, right?

I didn't really have ninety-one missed messages. It was only forty-seven. And most of those were from Jordan. Dude must've been looking for me about that job he's got lined up and that's how he figured out I was in jail.

The other fifteen or so were from this girl. My caller ID says her name is Rachel. Sounds a little mean, if you ask me. And not in a hot way, either. So I called her back and she's been yelling at me for—I look at the clock on the side table next to my bed—eight and a half minutes. And the only reason I'm *still* talking to her is because one of those almost incoherent sentences in her long rant mentioned my car and the fact that she was gonna throw my keys in the river.

"I just need the car, Rachel."

"I'm not Rachel," she snaps. "That's my sister, you asshole. You broke my phone, remember?"

Oh.

"The caller ID…" But I trail off. Because if the caller ID said Rachel, I've obviously been talking to her, right? Yeah, losing battle, this one. "Fuck it. Either give me your address so I can come get my car or leave it somewhere and text me the location, or whatever. Because—"

She hangs up.

I consider how much I really need that car back and decide she can have it. I don't care. I got a bike sitting six feet in front of me. And yeah, it's gonna be a helluva cold ride to wherever I decide to go next. But ya know what? I'm tired of this place anyway. Losing the car is a lucky break. Now I don't have to worry about the logistics of getting my bike outta *this* crap-ass town and into a *new* crap-ass town.

My phone rings in my hand and I have a moment of hope it's Rachel's sister coming to her senses about my car and maybe I won't have to ride the bike in sub-freezing weather…

But no such luck. It's Jordan.

"What?" I say, answering it.

"You're coming to Denver," he says. Like it's a command. Like I actually take commands.

"You think so?"

"It's a good job, Ixion. And it'll give you… direction for once." He's a lot calmer than he was yesterday. But that's Jordan for you. He's all act, ya know. Everything's a game to him. If he's pissed it's for a reason. If he's calm, also for a reason. There's not a true emotion in that heart of his. Not one. Just an act.

"Fuck you," I say, blowing out the smoke from my cig.

"Are you smoking? You better not show up smoking."

"Don't worry 'bout that," I say. "I'm not showing up at all. I don't need your charity, Jordan. I can pay my own bills. In fact, I'll cut ya a check for the seventy-five grand and send it—"

"I don't need the money back," he says. "I need *you*."

I barely contain a laugh. "Why?"

"I can't talk on the phone."

I almost choke on my smoke. "You never fucking change, do you?"

"That's not why. Be at my office tomorrow at noon. Talk then."

The line cuts and I just stare at the dead screen for a few seconds.

Asshole.

I decide tomorrow is a long way off and I'm not gonna ride my damn bike to Denver anyway, so hardly matters. I suck down the rest of my smoke in darkness, put it out, then rip the towel off my waist and get in bed naked.

Sleep is probably the only part of my day that makes sense anymore.

It eludes me.

Sleep, I mean.

Because I'm thinking about Jordan all goddamned night. I haven't seen him in a very long time. Don't even know how many years. Maybe seven? Eight? Somewhere around there. And that last night we were together runs through my head like a fucking movie on repeat.

If I never talked to the guy again I'd be fine. Shit, I haven't even thought about him. Like at all. Just… moving on, right? Doing my thing. Being me.

But him showing up like that? The cryptic nature of his motives, and the fact that we've got that history together, well, it fucks with my head more than I'd like to admit.

And that's why, at five AM, I push the bike out into the blowing cold wearing almost every article of clothing I own, and get on the highway heading south.

It takes me seven fucking hours to get to Denver. There's no snow or ice, and the sun is out for most of the ride, so that's a lucky break. But sun hardly matters when it's twenty-three degrees and you're on a bike going eighty on the fucking freeway.

I go because I can't not go.

The memories, the questions, the way it all ended.

You know how there's some people who drift in and out of your life and you like them and all, but you don't have a reason to look them up and talk? Or go see them?

And then there are some people you had a really hard time letting go. But eventually you do let go, and then one day there they are again, and it's like… it's like no moments passed at all since the last time you spoke. Like they've always just been there, even though they weren't. They were.

That's what kept me awake all night.

I could've just stayed up in Wyoming doing my thing and being me. But it didn't take much self-reflection to come to the conclusion that I'm doing a whole lot of nothing. Not to mention being me isn't as much fun as it once was.

If it ever was.

Maybe I should be somebody else?

By the time I walk into Jordan's swank office in downtown, I'm pissed off that I talked myself into doing this, tired as fuck, and so cold I might never get warm again.

"What the fuck are you wearing?" Jordan says, eyeing my leathers.

"What every goddamned biker wears," I snap. He's wearing a goddamned suit that looks like it costs as much as that car I left back at Rachel's sister's house.

"You rode your bike down here?"

"Long. Story." I close my eyes to signal that I'm not in the mood to tell said story, and he takes the hint. Because he knows me just as well as I know him. "Why the hell am I here?"

He stares at me. Looks me up and down. A whole scenario flashes in my mind in the time it takes him to reach down to pick something up off his desk, where he says, *I found her.* Or, *She found me.* Or, *You wanna go to dinner with us? Because we've got reservations at the Grant.* And he means her and him, as in the whole thing about us that made us an us in the first place.

But of course, he doesn't say anything like that. He says, "Here's the job," waving a large yellow envelope, handing it to me. "Everything's in there. Just..." He sighs and pinches the space between his eyes—stupid fucking

Jordan gesture—like I'm the one on his last nerve, and not the other way around. "Just do it, OK? And be super fucking discreet. This is all anonymous. You do not show your face. You do not make any sort of contact. It's strictly surveillance. Got it?"

I rip the envelope open and take a peek. Two keys, two bound stacks of hundred-dollar bills, which should be twenty thousand dollars, and some paperwork. "Is it legal?" I ask, taking out the stack of papers.

It's a dossier—female. Mid-twenties. Dark hair and gray eyes—for one Evangeline Rolaine.

"Of course it's legal. Why does everybody always ask me that? I'm a goddamned lawyer, everything I do is *legal.*"

"Yeah." I laugh, reading the woman's short bio on the top page. "You're a goddamned lawyer, all right. Why does this name sound familiar?"

Jordan eyes me, waiting to see if I'll take that first comment any further, and decides I won't—and he's right. Because after the morning I've had, I can't think of a single reason I need to rehash the past too. "She was famous once upon a time."

"Child prodigy," I say slowly, reading her bio at the same time. "Yeah, I remember this chick. She was all over the TV when she was a kid."

"Right. And then she wasn't. It's your job to watch her. That's it. Just watch her. You got it?"

"Watch her do what?" I ask, flipping through the pictures.

"Just… everything. Nothing specific."

"*Why* am I watching her? Someone after her or something?"

"You don't need to know why. You just need to take that money, buy the fucking equipment, go to that address, put up the fucking cameras, and then when she gets there, you watch her."

"Where's the home base?" I ask, looking at the blueprint of the house, trying to wrap my head around why he's asking me to do this shit.

"In the basement. There's a lock on the door and a separate entrance that leads to a gate. You do not ride that fucking bike to this job, you got me? She'll hear you and the whole fucking point of this is that she never hears you. OK?"

"So I'm spying on her and she doesn't know it?" My laugh is loud. Because... "That's some creepy shit, dude."

Jordan sucks in a breath of air. It's cautious, that inhale. It's long too. And it's filled with all the things that we left unsaid between us after college. "She knows," Jordan finally says. Carefully. Like he's picking his way through a minefield. "Just... just fucking do what I tell you. You've got a week to get set up and then a few weeks of surveillance, tops. Then I'll pay you."

"I don't need the money, asshole. You know that's not why I'm here."

I hear the unasked question. He hears it too. *Then why are you here?*

But he knows why.

"I'll pay you anyway," Jordan says, ignoring what wasn't said. And then his tone softens. "You just need to slow down, man. I mean it. You can't live like this much longer. It's gonna catch up with you."

"I don't have a car," I say, changing the subject back to business as I stuff the paperwork back into the envelope. "Hence the fucking leathers and the winter ride."

He looks at me. Not the way he has been, or the way he used to, but something different. "Why are you such a fuckup?" he finally says. But that's not the question he's asking. What he's really asking is, *What happened to you?*

I shrug. "Just natural talent, I guess."

He goes to his desk drawer, finds a set of keys, and throws them to me. I catch them one-handed. "Take mine. Leave your bike here. I'll ride it home and keep it for you."

"Home, huh?" I ask, looking down at the handwriting on the front of the envelope. "Where's home these days?"

"Same place."

I look up at him. "Really?"

He nods, then shrugs. "I like it there, what can I say?"

"Yeah," I whisper. "I used to like it there too."

His eyes lock with mine. "I'm sorry, OK?"

I shrug. "This car might make up for it," I say, tossing the keys of his BMW up and down in my palm.

"Don't crash my fucking car," he starts.

"Crash?" I snort, cutting him off, playing down the moment where we said absolutely nothing and everything all at the same time. I don't know what I'm doing here, but the feelings in this room make me want to get the fuck out and stay the fuck *put* at the same time. "I'm not gonna crash shit. Where is it?"

"Over in the 16th and Lawrence parking garage. Level one. Space sixteen. Just click the alarm and you'll find it."

I have a million things to say before I leave and none of them sound right.

So I say nothing.

He sighs. Heavily. "Look, man, I know—"

36

But I cut him off. "Don't get weird on me, asshole. I'll do the job. I'll even take your stupid money. But then you owe me again, got it?"

He puts his hands up. Surrendering to my terms. "Fine. I owe you. *Again.*"

We hold each other's gaze for longer than we should. It's a knowing gaze. Filled with ugly things in a shared past. And regrets. And all the things we should've said and never did.

I turn away first, heading for the door.

And we won't say them now, either. I'm gonna make sure of it.

"Hey, Ix," Jordan calls after me.

"What?" I say, my hand on the door handle, staring down at it, refusing to look back. Ready to get the fuck out of here.

"It's nice to see you again. Thanks for coming."

I swallow, then nod. "Yeah. No problem."

After I grab the car I head over to the electronics warehouse and buy the equipment, spending all of Jordan's money. The house I'm supposed to rig up is huge. Proper fucking mansion is what it is. Cheeseman Park Historic District, which is pretty swank. Seven bedrooms, two media rooms, two offices, three living rooms, two kitchens, a game room, a library, and a ballroom that is now a formal living area, according to the blueprints.

Ten thousand square feet of space to cover. So much space I had to chip in an extra five grand to Jordan's twenty because I wanted the newest control panel and a two-thousand-dollar leather chair.

If I gotta watch this chick for whatever weird, fucked-up reason, I'm gonna do it right and I'm gonna be goddamned comfortable too.

It only takes me a few days to rig everything up, so I kick it in the house to wait out the rest of the time before this Evangeline chick comes by, enjoying the media room. It's fucking sweet with a ninety-eight-inch, 4K ultra screen.

And the game room. Because it's got a mini-arcade from the 80's in there. Pac-Man and Tetris. Frogger and Galaga. Reminds me of the nickel arcade Jordan and I used to hang out at when we'd ditch in middle school. God, how I used to love playing Galaga when we were kids. He's even got Dig Dug and Centipede.

There's a house-wide intercom, so at first I figured I'd just leave that on all the time and I wouldn't have to wire the place for sound. But I tried it out and it sucks. Like, that thing is from the seventies or something. Back when house intercoms were the epitome of high-tech. This one's all crackly and static-y. Practically worthless unless you don't mind your voice sounding like someone using an AM radio that doesn't quite pick up the station you're listening to.

So the microphones go up.

The day before she's supposed to show up I go through all the rooms, trying to guess which one she'll choose to sleep in. Usually, when I'm not drunk and high and in the mood to bash brand-new trucks up with a baseball bat, I can predict things like this.

I have a natural intuition. Which is why I do what I do, I guess.

38

But Evangeline Rolaine is kind of a mystery to me. I've read up on her over the past few days. Spent her whole childhood performing like a trained monkey then poof. Disappeared.

Will she like the feminine bedroom? Does she like white mosquito netting hanging from the ceiling? Does she see herself as a princess? Because that room is kinda princess-y. Something your eight-year-old baby sister would have.

Or maybe she'll like the teen boy bedroom? I can't imagine she'd pick this one because it's nothing but shades of red and gray with a bunch of framed sports memorabilia on the walls, but who knows? Maybe Evangeline is a sports fanatic?

There's a nursery too. But unless she's gonna curl up in one of those gliding rocker chairs, she won't pick that one. Because it only has a crib.

Maybe she'll take the master? I would. It's got a California king bed that even accommodates my tall frame. I've slept in it three times already just to check it out. I'm thorough like that. Plus that room is classy. Not too personal, like the kids' rooms. Or gaudy, like the guest rooms. They look like they were decorated to impress... well, you know. Guests.

Maybe she'll sleep in one of the offices? They both have couches. Or the media room? Does she like to fall asleep in front of a TV? Hell, you could even sleep on the kitchen island, it's so big. If, that is, you don't mind a ten-foot-long slab of soapstone as your bed.

I decide to make a little bet with myself just to prove I've still got game. That I haven't been fucking off wasting my family money all these years. That my mind is focused on the task. That I'm not still having that imaginary conversation with Jordan back in his office where he tells me he found her, and that's why he found me, and then we all go to dinner at the Grant like nothing ever happened.

The one where she forgives me and says, *God, I missed you, Ix.* And then time melds together, like we were never apart. And we fall into old habits—just the good ones though. And we laugh again. And it's good. The way it used to be.

But of course... if he really did tell me he found her, and he really did tell me that's why he came looking—I'd be back on the road so fast.

Because there's only one reason for him to do that.

So he could have her again.

It's got nothing to do with me, other than I'm the one he needs, not the one he wants.

I sigh, close my eyes and shake my head, pulling myself out of the past and refocusing on the present. And then I open them and say, "I choose the library. And not because Evangeline Rolaine might like books."

CHAPTER THREE

EVANGELINE

It's never going to snow again.

The thought pops into my head unwanted and takes me by surprise. Ever since I started seeing Lucinda last year things have been getting progressively better for me.

Actually, they got *significantly* better.

After just six months of seeing her I went outside without a hat and sunglasses. I was wearing a sundress. Bare shoulders, bare legs. I went down to the 16th Street Mall and walked through all the crowds without bolting home or hiding in a bathroom until dark.

After that I walked the Mall every day for weeks. I went to the library every Sunday and checked out books. I even went to my favorite Chinese restaurant and sat there, alone, and ate an entire meal. Twice.

I. Was. Normal.

Lucinda has been a godsend. And even though I was reluctant after she explained her therapy methods, I gave her a shot. Then another. And another. Until I was going to see her three times a week.

She explained her practice to me the first time we met, which included highlighting (anonymously, of course) a lot of former cases involving sexual issues.

I don't have a sex problem. Not even a small one because I don't have sex. Haven't in many years. It's hard to find people to have sex with when you're a recluse.

Yes, I've come to terms with that descriptor of myself. Estranged is another word I've learned to embrace. Well, maybe not embrace. I don't want to be estranged from anyone. Not even my asshole parents. I don't want to be a recluse, either.

It's just… I am those things. What more can I say about it?

But Lucinda said she's not a sex therapist, she simply uses sex to conquer fears and psychological disorders.

My treatment plan does not involve sex. She made that very clear. I have an unusual phobia. The fear of being watched is pathological in my case and it's called scopophobia.

Lucinda is fairly certain it comes from repressed performance anxiety when I was a child. So I didn't get a hook-up as part of my cure. Which is too bad. I could use a hook-up, if I'm being honest.

Things got better the longer I saw Lucinda. I became braver. Bolder. More in control, more assertive (well, a tiny bit more). I mean, I did go outside, and read books, and have small essential conversations with people like waitresses at the Chinese restaurant.

The problem is… I think all that talking, and embracing, and self-reflection, and courage led me to believe I was recovering.

Which was a mistake because I'm not.

I'm right back where I started that day I first called her. Afraid, riddled with anxiety, and unable to go outside.

My phone buzzes on the couch, but I let it go to voicemail so I can continue looking out the window wishing for snow. Rain. Hell, hurricane-force winds. I'll take anything at this point. I'm dying up here. *Dying.* I need to get out but I can't go out until the people go in.

Every once in a while I go out at night, but it takes me days to work up to it. And I don't understand. I don't get it. Things were going so well... weren't they?

They were.

And then I looked at my bank account and realized I'd spent almost a hundred thousand dollars on therapy with Lucinda last year. And then I paid my property taxes because I was behind. Two years. (I'm not the most organized person.) So that was another eighty-two thousand dollars because the penthouse is now valued at eight million, not three.

I should sell this place. Move to Mississippi, or Louisiana, or Texas. Somewhere down south where the real estate is cheap and so are the taxes. I could live like that for a long time. Little shack in a bayou, maybe? Something you'd need a boat to get to. Hidden in all those weirdly twisted cypress trees with Spanish moss hanging off every limb like a curtain. Maybe? Couldn't I?

Could totally do that. *Should* totally do that.

A hard knock at my door makes me whirl around, startled. Who the hell got up here?

"Evangeline!"

"Fuck." I breathe the word out, giving it life as a whisper as my manic episode recedes.

More hard knocking. "I know you're in there. Open. The. Door."

What should I do? Should I run? Jump out the window? Hide in the bathroom?

"I'm not kidding," Lucinda shouts. "I'll stay here all damn day if I have to. Open the door right now and tell me what's going on."

"I'm sick," I yell at the door. "And contagious. A really bad virus—"

"Open the door *right now*, Evangeline. I'm not going away."

"I'm moving to the bayou! I'm leaving tomorrow!"

I hear her laugh. Which makes me smile. Because I'm being fucking ridiculous and I *know* this. I just can't help myself.

"OK," Lucinda says. "Fine. You're moving to the bayou. Let me in and I'll help you pack."

God, why did I ever call the number on that card? Why?

"Come on," Lucinda says. "Open up and I promise not to ask you any questions. Cross my heart. I won't, OK?"

I think about her offer. Because I've been up here for weeks now. I'm desperate for someone to talk to and Lucinda is my only candidate.

"Evangeline…"

"Fine," I huff. I pull my hoodie hood over my head, put my sunglasses on, walk to the door, and open it up. "What?"

Lucinda's smug smile at winning this standoff falters as she registers the meaning behind my outfit. Up until I quit seeing her three weeks ago, I'd stopped wearing the sunglasses for our visits.

She sighs, pushes past me so I can't shut the door in her face, and then goes over to the window and doesn't turn around. "You're regressing," she says.

I actually have the gall to form the word no.

But enough sense not to say it.

Because she's right. I'm back where I started last year. I'm worse, in fact. So much worse.

"It's the show, isn't it?"

Oh, God. Just hearing the word 'show' makes me want to vomit. "I can't do it," I say, breathless from my now rapidly beating heart. "I cannot fucking do it."

Lucinda turns around but keeps her eyes lowered, not looking at my face.

I cannot stand it when people look at me. I fucking hate it. And three months ago when I was doing well, and I let people look at me, and I went outside, I thought I was cured.

But then… when I noticed how little money I had left in my bank account… I called my old manger and told him I wanted to do a performance and what would it take to make a comeback?

"Cancel it," she says.

"It sold out in ten minutes," I say. "It's two and a half weeks away!"

"So? Cancel it."

"Ten thousand people, Lucinda!"

"Cancel it."

"I can't," I shout. "I can't fucking cancel it. I need the money. And the people… God, the people will hate me."

Lucinda raises her head and meets my gaze. I fumble with my sunglasses, paranoid that she might get a glimpse of my eyes, then almost have a panic attack when I realize I'm not wearing gloves and she can see my hands. I tuck them into my hoodie pockets and swallow hard, praying I don't have a heart attack, because it feels like I'm gonna have a heart attack. Then hoping I do, because if I die, all this anxiety will just… go away.

"I have one last option for you."

I laugh as I turn my back to her. She can still see me, but it's better when I can't see her seeing me. "I can't be fixed," I say. "It doesn't matter what your option is, I cannot be fixed. I'm gonna disappoint all those people who bought tickets and I'm gonna go bankrupt and end up living in a shack in the bayou with only a canoe to my name."

"That's ridiculous," Lucinda says. "If you sell this house you'll make at least seven million dollars. Just sell the house."

I shake my head. "No. It's mine. It's all I've got left. If I sell the house then… then everything about me has failed."

"Then do the show. Make more money. And go back to being the girl you are underneath all those clothes."

"It's not that simple."

Lucinda grunts. "No shit, it's not simple. Do you think I'm an idiot? Do you think I don't know what you're going through?"

"You don't," I say. But I'm whimpering like a sad puppy right now and that makes everything worse. Then I get angry and turn to her. "Do you think I want to be this way? Do you think I want to feel exposed and afraid all the time? Do you think I don't miss playing my violin? Do you think I like living vicariously through the substandard vinyl recordings of other child prodigies? I mean, what the fuck, Lucinda? I'm not doing any of this on purpose. I just…" I deflate and sink onto the couch, folding like a woman who's lost everything. Because I have. "I had it all at one time, but now it's gone. Even my music. It's gone."

Lucinda is quiet as she walks over to the couch, sits down next to me—so close our legs are touching—and takes my hand out of my pocket to stroke it as she talks. "I have one last-ditch option for you, Evangeline. If you truly want all those things the way you say you do—"

"I do!" I yell. "Why don't you believe me?"

"Then listen to me. Just take deep breaths and listen to me. I know a man," she says. "He deals with... special cases for me and I think you qualify. Not because your phobia is so out of the ordinary, because it isn't. Lots of people have the same fear as you. Not as severely, I admit. But it's very common. What isn't common is needing to conquer it in two and a half weeks. So... because you need results and you need them quick, I want you to consider this next option. And just hear me out before you say no, OK?"

I nod—"Fine"—and do as I'm told. Just sit quietly and listen as she tells me more about her partner. About her plan. About the house, and the cameras, and the stranger who'll be watching me. She says she's set it all up and I can move in on Friday.

And when she's done she waits.

"That doesn't even make sense," I say.

"It's called flooding, Evangeline. It's a tried-and-true technique. A respected technique. Another term for it is exposure therapy, whereby a patient with certain phobic conditions is continuously exposed to their irrational fears over a period of time, forcing them to confront them and make changes." She says all of that in a single breath, like she needs to talk fast, get her idea out into the real world where it can't be dismissed. Must be taken seriously. Considered.

So I don't dismiss her idea. I take it seriously and consider it. Picture what she just said, trying to imagine it and what it might mean. "How long will it take?"

I feel Lucinda's shrug. "It varies by person. By your commitment to see it through, of course. We can't hold you prisoner, that's illegal. So this has to be one hundred percent consensual."

I wave a hand at her. "Right. But if I did all that, if I committed to it, then how long?"

"A few weeks?"

"I don't have a few weeks. I have two and a half. And if I move in to this house on Friday, that's two weeks, almost to the day. Can it work in two weeks?"

I hold my breath waiting for her answer.

"I don't know," she admits. "I can't say, Evangeline. It's really all up to you. I'm not a part of this treatment. You have to take responsibility and see it through. But if you do that, the chances of a quick success are extremely high."

"Define quick and high," I say, letting myself feel a little whisper of hope building.

"A week?" she says, not very confidently. "It's fairly fast because of the in-your-face nature of the treatment. You can't run away. You can't ask for help. You just have to learn to deal."

The word *week* echoes in my head. "I could perform my show?" I murmur.

"Possibly," Lucinda says. "If it works."

I lower my sunglasses, take them off and hold them in the hand she's not still stroking, and look at her. "*Will* it work?"

"It's up to you," she says, lowering her gaze so she's not meeting mine. "None of your fears are rational,

48

Evangeline. People look at you. People look at everyone. They can't hurt you by looking."

She's wrong. They do hurt me. A gaze—a direct stare into my eyes—it's painful for me. Not like a bee sting or stubbing your toe. But like… agonizing anxiety that cripples me. Makes me irrational. And how can I possibly stand up on stage with my heart beating so fast I make myself pass out from hyperventilating?

"The cameras will help you. Twenty-four hours a day someone will be watching you."

"Who?" I ask, too quickly. A chill runs up my spine at the thought, but I can't decide if the tingling is pain, or cold, or what.

"You don't need to know who. It's anonymous. Who the watcher is isn't important. The fact that someone *will* be watching, and you *know* they're watching, that's what's important."

"My watcher," I say. "They'll see me all the time?"

"Yes. All the time while you're in treatment."

"They'll follow me if I leave the house?"

"Yes, if you're in treatment. If you leave the program, all surveillance will stop immediately."

I swallow hard. "So I can opt out at any time?"

"Of course. I already told you, this is all consensual."

I sit there for many minutes, dreaming of the life I might have if this works. A week? Is it possible I could cure myself in a week? After all this time, after all that money spent, and all those visits to Lucinda, not to mention all the miserable years I've spent up here in this apartment, hiding from the world, now I learn I can cure myself in seven days? With cameras?

"This is real?" I ask.

She squeezes my hand. "I swear, it's real, Evangeline. I think it can help you. You just need to commit to it. Surrender to the plan and see it through. I can't make promises because the outcome all depends on you, not me. Not the watcher, but you. So you have to decide… can you do this?"

Lucinda, to her credit, waits as I think it all through.

I picture the performance. The applause. Playing music again. "I'll need a violin," I whisper. "To get ready."

"Yes." Lucinda laughs. "You will. And you do realize that you were never going to go through with this show, right?"

"What?" I gasp. "Yes, of course I was. Why would I plan a performance and not follow through?"

"Because you were looking for a way out, Evangeline. And the performance was your excuse. How do you think you'll play the violin in front of a sold-out crowd in two and a half weeks if you haven't picked one up in over ten years?"

I think about that for a little bit. Is she right? Was this all an act of self-sabotage? Was getting better just a trigger to get worse? "I'm a prodigy," I say. "I never learned the violin. I just… always knew it."

"You were a *child* prodigy, Evangeline. Now you're just another adult who needs to work hard at things. You decided thirteen years ago to withdraw from society. You neglected your imagination and stopped expressing yourself. You found solace in the predictable and boring. In hiding away and pretending that attention was painful."

"It is!" I insist. "You have no idea what you're talking about!"

"Evangeline, I'm a fucking doctor, OK? I have a Ph.D. I'm board-certified in psychoanalysis."

"You're a fucking sex therapist!"

"No," she says, her calm demeanor wavering slightly. "I use sex as part of my therapy. There's a big difference. I don't treat people with sex problems. I guide patients and sex is one tool I use to help them recover. In your case, we will not be using sex as therapy. I told you that a long time ago. We will use a completely anonymous watcher with cameras. That's it. So forget about the sex."

We sit there quietly for a little bit. I put my sunglasses back on and withdraw my hand from hers. "Friday?" I ask.

"Yes."

"You had this planned?"

"Yes. It's all been set up for you."

"You knew I was failing?"

She smiles, takes both my hands in her to give them a squeeze, and says, "I saw it coming from the first time I met you. Moving past hurtful things that trigger a response as debilitating as yours isn't easy, Evangeline. Yes, I always knew you'd fail. But I also knew you had what it takes to get better. I'm treating you because I believe in you. You're not my typical case. You know that."

"I know," I say softly. "You've done a lot for me. And I appreciate it."

She stands up and looks down at me. I don't want to look her in the face, but I force myself. Because she's right. I'm the only one who can cure me now. I am my own last resort.

I swallow down the self-loathing all this self-assessment brings up, raise my chin, and square my shoulders. "OK. Let's do it."

CHAPTER FOUR

I sit up straight and stare at the largest of the monitors I've got set up in the basement control room. Someone is at the front gate. A woman.

I push away from the panel of screens, jog to the door and yank it open, then sprint across the obscenely large basement to the stairs. I take them three at a time, see my shoes over near the kitchen, slide across the hardwood floors in my socks, grabbing them by the shoelaces as I slip past, and then duck around the corner of one wall, just as the front door opens and the alarm sings in protest.

The woman—tall, long, dark hair, wearing a long winter coat, and carrying a brown paper grocery bag— pushes all the right numbers of the alarm keypad to make it stop screaming, and walks towards the kitchen.

This is not Evangeline Rolaine. I know that for sure. Because this woman is pregnant. Very pregnant. "Excuse me," I say, coming out from behind the wall. "What the fuck are you doing here?"

She doesn't jump at my voice or anything stupid like that. Just smiles and sets her bag down on the dark soapstone countertop. "You must be Ixion," she says.

"It's just Ix," I say, annoyed. "And you are?"

"Oh." She laughs. "Sorry." She extends her hand for a handshake. I take it as she says, "You don't remember me, do you? I remember you though. Who could forget that name, right?" She's still smiling. And I still have no fucking clue who she is. "Jordan reminded me, so I cheated, I guess. But our parents were friends. Marcella Walcott. Ring any bells?"

I squint my eyes at her. I have no clue.

"Well, it's Baldwin now." She wiggles the fingers on her left hand to flash her diamonds at me.

"Baldwin?" I say.

"Smith. You know him, right?"

"Not really," I say. "But your name…" I think back.

"My father is the senator?" she adds, trying to be helpful.

I point at her. "Oh, fuck yeah. I know you."

She makes a gesture with her hands that says, *Of course you do.* "Lucinda had an emergency, so she asked me to bring groceries over before her patient checks in tomorrow. So." She turns back to her grocery bag. "That's what I'm doing."

"Got it," I say.

"So you and Jordan have been friends all this time?" She looks over her shoulder as she loads vegetables into the fridge.

"Sorta," I say, fascinated by her. And a little weirded out that two childhood friends have reappeared in my life lately. "We go way back, as I'm sure you're aware. But we don't talk much now."

"Ah," she says, closing the fridge with her hip and walking over to the subzero freezer on the opposite wall. "So he conned you into doing this job, huh?" She laughs a little. Like she knows him pretty well and this is just… one of those cute things we can count on Jordan doing.

"Are you and Jordan friends?" I ask.

"Sorta," she says. And then she winks at me. "He went to the Club a lot when I first met the guys."

Mmmmm-hmmm. Interesting. The Club denotes a place called Turning Point. Been around for decades. Jordan wanted to be part of that place in the worst way back in college. But they have an age requirement, and then he went to UCLA for law school, and I was there, and we did… with… yeah. Fuckin' club. Sex is what they do there. "So that place is still rollin', huh?"

"No," she says. "Bric sold it about a year ago and I understand that someone is turning it into a hotel."

"Ah." I point to her belly. "And that's Baldwin's baby?"

"Of course," she says.

"Uh-huh," I say. I have a lot of details I could fill in just based on what she's told me already. None of them come from her and all of them come from that statement about meeting Jordan at Turning Point Club.

I wonder if she fucked him?

"Well," Marcella says, folding up her paper bag and stuffing it in the universal place people stuff folded paper bags—that thin slot of empty space between the fridge and the wall—"that's it for me. My job is done. Good luck with yours. Oh, and if you find yourself downtown, I own a tea shop next to where the Club used to be. Stop by and we'll be friends again." She smiles broadly. "Or something."

I just… kinda laugh at that and watch her walk out. Weird.

I lock the house back up, re-arm the alarm, and go back downstairs to a buzzing phone on the desk top. "Yeah," I say. Its caller ID says it's Jordan.

"I told you not to be seen," he says.

"Well, you didn't tell me that some strange chick was gonna show up out of the blue."

"It's none of your business what happens outside your little control room, Ix. I thought I made that clear."

"Look, I just didn't know she was coming. A little heads up next time, right?"

"Stay away from this Evangeline girl, Ixion."

"Why the fuck wouldn't I?"

"I know you, remember. You fuck girls just to see if you can."

I actually fuckin' guffaw. "You are no one to judge me."

"Do not fuck with this girl, Ixion. Understand me?"

"Dude, Evangeline Rolaine is the definition of boring. Don't worry."

"Good," he says. "She's so not your type."

"No shit. She's kinda..." Well, I was gonna just say ugly as kind of a default answer, but I've got her picture up on the wall where I always keep a picture of my targets. And she's not ugly. So I can't even lie about it.

"She's kinda what?" Jordan asks.

"Uptight," I say. "You know I hate girls like that. Fuckin' high-society bitches with their fancy debutante dresses and fake giggling."

"Yeah, from the information I've gathered on you up in Wyoming, you like the mean ones. The wasted ones. The easy ones."

I shrug. "So? Someone's gotta like 'em. Might as well be me."

"Stay in the control room. If you see a problem, call me immediately. Do not go upstairs. Hell, do not leave that room under any circumstances unless she leaves the house and you need to follow her. And if that happens, you call me then too, got it?"

"Got it," I say. "You're just like her. Uptight and shit. You got a thing for this girl, Wells?"

"No." He laughs. "I just provide a service. Nothing more."

"Uh-huh. Sure. Well, you don't have to worry about me. I'm not the least bit interested in Evangeline Rolaine. And I can't wait for this shit to be over so I can be on my way. Gonna hit up Oregon next."

"Yeah? Why there? Why not stay here?"

"Why should I stay here?"

"You've got roots here," he says.

"Not anymore," I say back.

"That's harsh," he says.

"I'm just a realist, that's all."

"Sure," he says. "Whatever. I'll call tomorrow afternoon to check in. Stay in that fucking room."

I hang up on him. He's told me that like five times already. He can fuck off. I have no intention of interacting with the boring ex-child prodigy. But if I did intend to, I would.

Because Jordan Wells does not get to make rules for me.

Not after he broke them all and ruined my life.

In fact... this girl might be good for something after all. I don't need the money, but I could use another game.

How about it, Miss Rolaine?

Would you like to play a game?

CHAPTER FIVE

JORDAN

I tap Chella's contact on my phone. She picks up immediately. "Hello," she sings. She's always in a good mood, like perpetually happy. Even though I love Chella best, sometimes her eternal optimism grates my nerves. I prefer the Rochelles of this world. The Nadias. If Ix likes the mean ones, the wasted ones, and the easy ones, then I like the broken ones. The falling-apart ones. The lost-in-the-dark ones.

"What did he do?" I ask her.

"Nothing really. You know, you're a strange guy, Jordan."

"How so?" I ask.

"Why do you do this shit? Why can't you just settle down?"

"Like Bric? And Smith? And Quin?"

"And Lucinda. She's out as well. But you? You keep playing. Don't you get tired of these games?"

"It's not a game, it's a business."

"Right. Smith has told me all about your new business. So is that what you're doing with Ixion Vanir? Giving him a business experience?"

"He's just an employee," I say.

"Really?" she asks.

"Really."

"So no hard feelings between the two of you?"

"What's that mean?"

"I know about you. I looked you up before I went grocery-shopping for the house this morning."

"So?"

"So I didn't find anything."

I laugh. "What's your point?"

"On *you*, at least. But I did find something interesting about Ixion."

"He's an interesting guy."

"Yes," she says. "I think you're right. He is. And he's connected to you. And you're quite interesting, in a missing-information kind of way."

"Anything else, Chella? I'm due in court."

"Just one more thing," she says.

"What's that?"

"Who are you trying to fix?"

"What?"

"Is it him? Or is it you?"

"I have no—"

"You're so much like Bric."

"Fuck you," I say, forgetting who I'm talking to for a moment.

"But you're different in a lot of ways too. Bric just played for fun. You take this all very seriously, don't you? It's almost personal, isn't it?"

I huff out a breath of air. "Goodbye, Chella. Thanks for your help."

"No problem," she sings back.

The call ends and I look at the screen as I stare out the window of my corner office in my father's law practice.

I'm nothing like Elias Bricman.

CHAPTER SIX

EVANGELINE

"Why can't you at least come with me?" I'm whining. I realize this. And even though Lucinda is patient, my neediness is wearing her down. I can almost feel her close her eyes and ask the Lord for patience. And I'm pretty sure she's an atheist, so... yeah.

"I told you," she explains. "You must not associate this house with me. It must become your own."

I huff out some air. "Well, that's fuckin' stupid."

"Well, your phobia is fuckin' stupid."

We both sit on the phone. Silent moments tick off. I think we're holding our collective breath. I think she just closed her eyes again. This time asking the Lord she doesn't believe in to take that back.

"I'm sorry," she finally says.

"Whatever," I say. "It *is* stupid."

"It's not stupid," she counters. "Your feelings are legitimate and I'm totally one hundred percent committed to your—"

"Forget it," I say, sorta pissed, but... sorta not. "I'm mad that you're making me go alone, but I'm certainly grown-up enough to not make you feel bad because the truth slipped out."

"That's mentally... mature of you, Evangeline."

We both huff out small laughs. So I beg again, "Just walk me to the gate."

"No," she says. "I'm not going near that house. Ever. When you feel like it's time to leave, you leave. And you call me. And we'll meet. That's how this has to go."

I say nothing. She's not gonna give in on this.

"You still there?"

"Yes," I say. "I'm picturing everything, that's all."

"What are you picturing?"

"I'm not sure yet."

"Well, keep the preconceived notions to a minimum, Evangeline. Just... go there with an open mind."

"It is a man?" I ask. "My watcher?"

"I'm not going to say."

"And there's cameras in the bedroom."

"Of course. Everywhere but the powder room on the main floor. I've already told you that."

"Is the watcher the guy you work with?"

"No," she says. "I will say that. It's not him. That's not professional."

"Who is that guy?"

"It doesn't matter."

"Do I know him?"

"No," she says through a sigh. "Forget about him. He's just the person who sets things up. That's it. He's not part of my treatment plans."

But I'm so intrigued. It's like... there's this whole underground world humming along just below my feet. And everyone up top has no clue at all. Like a secret, forbidden city hidden away in plain sight. Who is this guy? And how does one get offered the job as Evangeline Rolaine's watcher? I mean, really, how does that happen?

"How do you find these people?" I finally ask. "The watchers?"

"This is the only watcher we've had to find. And it's someone we both trust. So you can trust him or her as well."

"Is it an old woman?" I ask.

"*Evangeline.*"

"What? I think that's legitimate. I mean, I think old people watching me is creepy. How can I get better if I'm consumed with creepiness?"

"The watcher is not old."

"How old?"

She sighs again. "Thirty... thirty-one, maybe? I'm not sure. Right around there."

"It's a guy, isn't it? Is he hot? If he's hot, that might be... kinda hot."

"This conversation is over now," she sings. "Get to the house by noon and settle in. If you decide to stop the treatment, you call me the minute you step out the door. Got it?"

I sigh too. "Fine."

She waits for more. But when I don't give her anything, she says, "I think this is gonna work."

"I hope so," I say back. "I really hope so."

"I've left you a gift in the house."

"What is it?" I ask, unexpectedly excited.

"I'm not going to tell you." She laughs. "It's just a housewarming gift. To make you feel at home."

I sigh again. "Thank you, Lucinda. I really do appreciate how hard you've worked this past year to help me. And for thinking outside the box as far as this plan goes."

"It's... it's a risk. We've talked about this. I wouldn't set this up if I didn't think it would help, so I think the chance for total recovery outweighs the risks."

"I think so too. I've been thinking about my dress, ya know? The one I'll wear for my comeback performance. And I've never done that before."

"Well, if you need to go shopping for that dress after treatment, I would love to be your second opinion."

I smile, picturing Lucinda and I as friends. She's older than me by almost twenty years. But I like her. And she's honest. That comment about my stupid phobia just proves it. "Deal," I say.

"OK, so you know the rules."

"One week's worth of clothes. If I have to stay longer and I run out I can do laundry or go shopping."

"In person," Lucinda stresses. "Not online."

I swallow hard, but I'm not going shopping. In one week I'll be cured. I'm so sure of it, I force myself not to think about needing to stay longer. "Got it."

"And you have groceries stocked in the fridge for a few days. But if you need anything else—"

"No deliveries," I finish.

"Right." She pauses, then says, "Take chances, Evangeline. That's my best advice. When you think about leaving, pause and tell yourself, 'Just one more night.'"

"OK," I say. But this time it's low, and soft, and barely audible.

"You're going to do this," Lucinda says. "You're going to beat it."

I nod my head, then say, "I will. I must."

I imagine her smiling on the other end of the phone. She thinks I'm brave. She believes in me. Not just my talent—that's easy to believe in once you see me play. But my spirit. "Call the number for the car service when you're ready to go and I'll see you soon."

She hangs up.

I put my phone down and look at my suitcase. It's packed with normal things. Things I wear around the house. Jeans. Yoga pants. Sweatshirts. T-shirts. I have my toiletries and my hair dryer.

It feels a little bit like the old me. Back when I was a kid and we'd travel all over the world. My passport was so full by the time I turned sixteen and needed a new one, it was nothing but a mess of indecipherable ink.

I don't have a current passport these days. The last one expired a few months ago. And that makes me sad for a few moments. That I was so worldly and sophisticated once upon a time. And now I'm small and lonely.

"That's why you're doing this, Evangeline." I give myself a pep talk. "And if you do it right and stick it out, in two weeks you'll be that girl again. Only better. Because you won't have your parents backstage waiting for their next opportunity."

When the driver pulls up outside my building I roll my two suitcases outside, doing my best to blend in with the people. Trying not to stand out or be conspicuous in any way. Covered up in head to toe with outerwear. Gloves, long winter coat, scarf over my face, large, round sunglasses covering my eyes. It's very cold and snow is falling like glittering dust. But it's not enough to cover me and my heart starts beating wildly in my chest.

JA HUSS

The driver must've been told not to make eye contact, because he's wearing sunglasses too, and bows his head as he wordlessly takes my luggage and puts it in the trunk of the long, black town car.

I get in the backseat without waiting for him to open my door, and quickly shut myself up inside.

There's a blackout screen between the front and back, and that, at least, is comforting. There's almost nothing worse than a nosey driver glancing into his rearview trying to get a glimpse of me.

Twenty minutes later, after fighting afternoon traffic in downtown, we pass through a small restaurant and shopping district and arrive at a stately manor in what would probably be a very nice tree-lined street in the summer time.

There's a tall, wrought-iron and brick wall surrounding the entire property. It's got something akin to a small guardhouse off to the left, where a driver might interact with security if he were going to pull into the driveway, but my driver stops on the street and doesn't attempt to pull in.

There's no one in there anyway. Not anyone to help because it's only me and my watcher until I decide to leave.

I wonder if he or she is spying on the car?

The driver gets out, but I wait until he's got my luggage lined up on the sidewalk and he's back in the front seat before I let myself out and close the door behind me.

He drives off, leaving me there alone. Standing in front of the gate, looking up at the imposing mansion, tiny silver snowflakes falling on my cheeks like slippery wet kisses.

66

I gather myself, eager to get inside before any of the neighbors see me, and pull my luggage through the thin layer of snow that's collecting on the ground.

There's a code to open the gate, which I use and pass through. And it closes back up automatically when I'm halfway up the front walk.

It's an interesting Italianate-style mansion, stucco exterior painted a smooth moss-green. There are two ornamental wrought-iron balconies in front of the tall, second-story rounded windows, and another directly above the main door.

The house is probably almost a hundred years old. But everything seems well-kept and modernized on the outside. The grounds are manicured, even in the winter, and the long hedges of holly planted up against the perimeter wall have sharp edges defining their shape that say in no uncertain terms someone loves this place.

Even though the house is large and imposing, I am eager to get inside before I can notice anyone noticing me. If I can't see the watchers, they're not there, right?

It's how I sell myself on going out at all these days. Dark or not. Bundled up or not. I need the illusion of being one hundred percent alone. Even though I realize it's not possible to control the actions of others and there could've been fifteen people peeking through their front curtains as I got dropped off.

As long as I don't see them, I'm fine.

Which is why I think this whole camera thing has a chance at working. My one saving grace is the exact thing being exploited here.

I key in the code to the front door and the automatic locks disengage. My hand is shaking as I push the front door open, pull my suitcases inside, and close it behind me.

I let out a long breath of anxiety-filled air and look around. My heart is thumping in my chest so loud, I swear I can hear it echo off the tall foyer ceiling.

In the center of the ceiling is a shimmering chandelier that reflects sunlight coming through the arched window over the door in just the right way so that tiny dew-drop shapes dance across the upper walls like a light show.

It's mesmerizing. And beautiful.

But that's when I see it.

A flame-shaped black lightbulb in a chandelier filled with white ones.

A camera, made to look like a lightbulb. With a small blinking red light piercing through the shiny opaque lens.

"Hello," I say, surprising myself with my own voice. My brain catches up with the implications of what I just did and my heart beats erratically at my audacity. Sweat beads on my brow and heat consumes my body as I realize—actually *understand* for the first time—that someone I don't know will be watching my every move until I say stop.

I can't do this. I cannot.

Breathe. I hear Lucinda's calming voice in my head.

But I'm already gasping. I turn, ready to flee back into the safe world I've made for myself, and realize there's no car out there to take me home. Leaving would be worse than staying.

Breathe.

The powder room. My one sanctuary in this house. The only place where there's no cameras.

I open the closest door and find an office. The next is a coat closet. The next is another closet. I rush into the main living area, stunned by how big this place is. By the size of the windows and the knowledge that some stranger is watching me right now as I lose my shit. This has my head spinning and the only sound in my ears is the loud, *thump-thump-thump-thump* of my own terrified heartbeat.

I whirl around, desperate to find the powder room, because that's my only escape. I'm stuck here until dark. Because the thought of going outside in the light and finding help... and that's hours and hours away and there's no possible way I can stay here and let this watcher watch me. Especially now, when I'm freaking out.

There's a hallway, and many, many rooms. But I see the bathroom. I run for it, practically throw myself inside, and slam the door shut. I don't even turn on the light. Just press my back against the wall, slide down until I'm sitting on my butt, and wrap my arms around my legs.

This was the dumbest idea ever. What the fuck was I thinking? Where the hell do I get off wanting more out of life? When people are starving all over the world, and children are homeless on the streets, and there's like... millions of women who fear for their lives in their own homes? And I'm not talking about my stupid fear. But their very real fear. And people dying, and sick, and hurting, and I'm just... just afraid of what amounts to *faces pointed in my general direction.*

This makes me selfish, and ungrateful, and stupid.

So very, very stupid for coming here and wanting... *more.*

CHAPTER SEVEN

IXION

Her panic attack—because that's what it is—alarms me. For a few seconds I'm glued to the screen, unable to stop watching. But then I'm running for the door, an overwhelming urge to reassure overtaking all the rules Jordan gave me.

I stop myself just in time. My finger is hovering over the first number on the keypad lock. I'm ready to leave the secret room and go find her. Help her.

Breathe.

So I do. I inhale deeply, let the swirling, conflicting emotions settle with my racing heart, and think this through as I let it out.

She's here for a reason.

She hates people looking at her and that fear has made her life a living hell. Turned her large world into one that's now so small, she barely has room to breathe.

I can't relate to it. Honestly just can't.

As a child, my world started small and only got bigger with each passing day. At first that's because of the family I was born into. We went everywhere together.

But even after I was kicked out of the family with only my trust fund to rely on—I know, poor me—my world expanded, it never shrank.

I go everywhere alone now. Never staying too long in one place. I get a job, not unlike this one, and I go do it. Then I leave, or stay, or leave.

The road, I decide, is my home now. The vast never-ending road that leads to nowhere and everywhere all at once.

Now I'm at the point where there's no end to my boundaries. I own things, but aside from that bike over at Jordan's house, they're all things I'm willing to walk away from when my world needs a little more expanding.

Like the car back up in Wyoming, for instance. It's a nice car. About six years old. But it's not a great car. It's not my dream car. It's just... a fucking... thing. A replaceable thing. So walking away when I felt the need to cut my losses was just normal for me because the amount of effort it would take to get that car back just wasn't worth it.

That would involve a conversation. An explanation too. Not to mention some self-reflection, since I don't actually remember what the fuck happened that night.

And fuck that. Not many people in this world get a conversation out of me, let alone an explanation. And I am in no mood to do any sort of self-reflection at the moment.

But I can put myself into Evangeline's mindset and wonder how debilitating it would be if I couldn't bear to leave the fucking house. How would it feel if I wasn't able to walk out on people? How would I ever get any peace if I couldn't leave it all behind?

Like it or not, she's stuck here now. I cannot imagine she will muster up the courage to walk back out that door and find her way home after this little psycho display. I just can't. Because that means her world gets bigger instead of smaller. Even if it's just for a few hours. It means she has to go out into it, deal with it, submit to it.

I back away from the door, run my fingers through my hair, and then walk over to my chair and sit. Force myself to wait her out.

I stalked her a little the past few days. But only online. Which is a damn shame. Because I also hunted down all the video I could find on her childhood performances and was mesmerized by her talent. And she's pretty to look at. Not the kind of woman I normally feel attracted to—too prim. Too uptight. Too fearful.

But she's young, slender, and from what I just saw of her as she entered the house, she might have nice tits.

OK, that's all kinda shallow. But I *did* think about her talent first, so I'm not gonna beat myself up for being a normal thirty-one-year-old man.

Especially when I'm never gonna get the chance to talk to this woman. Jordan's contract specifically stated that I will not talk to her. Ever. Even when this is all over. So it's pointless to think about her body, or her face, or her tits, or her fuckin' talent, for God's sake. She doesn't even play anymore.

So I'm not. Thinking about any of that. I'm just thinking about her mind. And how sad she is, and how lonely she must be.

I had a small moment of hope when she entered the house, looked up and found the camera that looked like a black lightbulb, and greeted me with a "Hello." Maybe three seconds of hope that this might not be a totally fucked-up assignment. That she's more normal than she appears, or maybe it's all an act.

But then her absolute panic over what amounts to a one-sided greeting, nothing even close to a fucking conversation, wiped all that hope away.

It's not an act.

She's crazy.

However, I do relate to her lack of enthusiasm for talking to people. I could care less if I talk to anyone. But it's not fear stopping me. It's just...I'm kind of an asshole and I prefer my own company.

That makes me smile, but then I remember she's got herself locked in the bathroom.

I fish out my phone and call Jordan. Because I'm just not sure what to do. Am I her fucking therapy? Does this little display of mental illness qualify as an emergency? Does she need a doctor? Will she try to kill herself?

And most importantly, what are my legal obligations in this little job? If she does hurt herself, will I be responsible? Implicated in some sort of... crime?

I have enough of those on my record, I really don't want to add another over a girl I don't even know.

"Yeah," Jordan says, picking up the call.

"Dude, what's the deal with this woman?"

"She's there then?"

"Yeah, she's here... but she kinda freaked out and now's she locked in the bathroom you told me didn't need cameras."

"Define freaked out."

"Full-on fucking panic attack, man. I'm not kidding. She came in, looked around a little, spotted the camera in the foyer chandelier, and then said 'Hello' to me."

"So what's the problem?"

"The problem is she fucking went crazy after that. Racing around the house looking for the bathroom, I guess. Now she's locked in there doing what-the-fuck-ever and I'm just not sure what I'm supposed to do."

"I'll call you back," Jordan says. "And whatever you do, do not leave that room. Got me?"

"Yeah," I say.

But he's already ended the call.

I sigh and lean back in my chair, wondering if I made a mistake in taking this job. I don't need the money, so why bother?

But I know why I bother.

People think money is all you need in life. And yeah, it's nice to have money. It's even better to have so much you never have to think about it. Or anything, if you so choose. Which is how I deal with it most of the time.

But every once in a while I'll meet someone, or hear something, and then...

Don't fucking go there, Ixion.

So I'm lucky, I guess. I have more money than I can ever spend. Sick reality, I get it. Puts me squarely into a subset of the human population called grotesquely rich. But I don't squander it. Unless you call walking away from a six-year-old Jeep Grand Cherokee squandering. Which some might.

But I'll make up for that. Send that chick the title or something. Let her keep it. Sell it, whatever.

I'm just... trying my best to stay unattached and make the most of the life I have. That's just about my only aspiration. Live this fucking life like it's the only one you get. Spend it all because you can't take it with you. And never stop moving. The past might catch up if you stop moving.

My motto is faltering today, because against my better judgment, I find this Evangeline woman *interesting*.

What happened to her? Why did she just disappear like that? Did she do something? Did someone make her disappear? Was she forced out?

Normally I keep this caring shit to a minimum. It comes at a price, but I can't help myself. It's just intriguing. I want to know the answers to all those questions. Not to mention how she got mixed up with Jordan. It makes no sense at all. Because Jordan doesn't gravitate to the kind of women I do, and I have a feeling Evangeline Rolaine is more my type than his.

"So was Augustine."

My comment surprises me. Where the fuck did that come from? I have not so much as thought her name in seven years, let alone spoken it out loud.

Why did it have to end that way?

Stop fucking thinking about her. Now!

I know why.

My phone buzzes, so I answer it, happy to end the internal struggle I've been avoiding for seven years. "Yeah."

"OK, I talked to her doctor and she says leave her alone. She has strict instructions to leave the house if she wants out of the treatment. So if she's still in the house, she's still in treatment."

"So if she leaves, I call you?"

"Yes," Jordan says. "If she leaves, call me and let me know what she's doing. Then you follow her. Discreetly. If she leaves and calls her doctor. I'll call you and then the treatment is over and you can just... fucking come over here and get your money, I guess. Job's over. Got it?"

He says 'got it' like this is some super-simple shit to process. It's not. So, "No, man. I *don't* got it. Just what the fuck have you gotten me into?"

"Your job is simple, OK? You watch her. That's it."

"And if something bad happens? I'm just supposed to ignore it?"

"Yes."

"What if she tries to kill herself?"

"She won't."

"How the fuck do you know that? She's mentally unstable, Jordan. I can't just let her hurt herself. I can't—"

"You're *not*," he says. "She's under the care of a very well-respected psychiatrist. This treatment was planned for a long time. We know what we're doing."

"We?" I ask. "We? You're not a fucking doctor."

"Correct," Jordan says. "I'm just the partner who arranges her treatments."

I open my mouth to say something. Like, *What kinda fuckin' game are you playing now?* Or, *Who the fuck would trust your twisted mind with people who need mental guidance?* Because both of those questions are valid.

But the call drops. Like... three this-convo-is-over beeps hit me like a goddamned slap in the face.

A flash of movement on the monitor makes me look up.

Evangeline Rolaine has opened the bathroom door.

CHAPTER EIGHT

EVANGELINE

The powder room is small, and cramped, and the mirror is way too big for my comfort. My image staring back at me is the last thing I need to see.

But in the dark… this place is almost perfect. I can't see the mirror. And the walls are close. The heat is on, so it's cozy and warm. The rug is soft.

Jesus Christ.

What the fuck is wrong with me? I'm extolling the virtues of being locked in a five-by-five room.

I am one sick woman.

But I'm out of here. I might be sick, but this is sick too. Cameras? Everywhere? Some stranger watching me? What the fuck was I thinking?

Thank God I still have my phone on me.

I fumble with the phone, trying to press the little icon for contacts, but my hands are shaking so bad I hit just about every app surrounding it. Messages, then photos, then camera.

"God. Fucking. Dammit!" I don't even care if my watcher heard that. Finally my trembling finger hits the right one. The contacts come up—I only have about a dozen, so Lucinda's is in the middle of those. I force myself to hit her name and not the Chinese restaurant I order takeout from, or my building concierge, and get it on the first try. This small success should not be enough to make me happy, but it does.

"Don't tell me you're out already?" Lucinda asks.

"I don't think I can do this," I say, breathless from the panic attack.

"Did something happen?" Her voice is so calm, and normally I love that about her, but right now I just find it irritating.

"I'm in a strange house filled with cameras. I think everything about that qualifies."

"OK," she says. "But you were ready for this. You made a decision. And you packed your suitcases. And you got into the car and got out of it again. And you went inside. Which was only about twenty minutes ago, Evangeline. So what happened?"

It's almost imperceptible. But I can hear it in her voice.

She's annoyed with me.

And for some reason that makes me smile. I'm not playing games with her. I've been pretty straightforward, in fact. No, I haven't told her everything. There are some stories that should never be told. But I've been sincere.

Now I don't feel like being sincere. Because this whole thing is fucked up.

"I don't think I can deal with the cameras," I say. "Can't the watcher take some of them down?"

"Evangeline," Lucinda says, an even more annoyed edge to her words. "It's called *flooding* for a reason. You need to be inundated with the stimulus that causes your fear in order to get over it."

"I understand that. But I need some time—"

"You don't *have* time. You've got a performance in two weeks and you haven't even picked up a violin in over a decade. If I were you, I'd be a lot more worried about that than some silly cameras."

"Well, you're not me," I snap. "I'm the only me there is. So you wouldn't understand why this is important. And I don't want to hear how many stupid degrees you have. You're not me!"

"I'm going to hang up now," she says. "And if you call again, it better be to quit."

I open my mouth to say something, but I get three short beeps letting me know the call has ended.

"Bitch!" I yell to the ceiling. And then I throw the phone down on the floor and the screen shatters into a million little spiderwebs.

"Fuck," I mutter, reaching over to pick it up. "Fuck." It's still working, miraculously, but it's useless. Because even though I try to hit that little phone icon like seventy billion times, the screen is cracked so bad, the touch won't register.

I guess I just have to quit then. I can't stay here without a phone. What time is it? One in the afternoon? Maybe?

I think this through rationally. If I wait until dark I can probably... I don't know. Walk home? Jesus, how far away am I from my building? It took about twenty minutes to get here. So miles away.

But if the reward at the end of the night was being back at home, locked up tight in my own apartment, I could do it.

I could call the concierge at my building at a... fuck. There are no phone booths these days. But if I could find a phone in the house... yes. There has to be a phone in this house. What kind of mansion has no landline, right? Surely there's one tucked away in an office or something. I could call the building, ask the concierge to have a car come pick me up.

I'll need the address. I don't even have the address. I think I could manage a trip outside to get the street and house number though.

Yes.

That's exactly what I'll do. Wait until dark, go outside, get the address, come back in, find a phone, call the concierge, have him send a car, and go the fuck home.

There's a few holes in that plan. Like, what if there's no phone here? If that happens, and I wait until dark, then I really will have to walk. And I don't even know this city. I haven't been more than a few blocks from my apartment since I moved in. I could get lost. And end up having to ask a stranger for directions. I might be so lost, I don't get home before dawn. Then I'll be outside in the light, lost, and probably losing my mind.

I should check the house for a phone first. Then call the concierge immediately, tell him what I need and that car can come as soon as it gets dark.

Perfect.

I stand up and straighten myself out—I'm still wearing my winter coat, so my whole body is covered in sweat because this bathroom is small and the heat is blasting out of the vents. I take it off and say, "You can do this."

So I reach for the doorknob and pull it open, confident I will enact this plan and be home soon. This whole nightmare behind me.

It's quiet when I peek out. And empty. And not well lit because it's cloudy outside. I creep forward along the hallway, back towards the front door, glancing all around me just trying to get my bearings, and find myself in a wide living area.

I search for a phone and in doing so, look up and gasp at the beauty on the ceiling. They're coffered, but not in the typical box pattern. It's rectangles and quarter-circles with an intricate hand-painted design that goes perfectly with the Italianate exterior.

Quite striking.

The room is long. Like a ballroom where people throw parties. There are several sitting areas, a floor-to-ceiling fireplace with woodwork as elaborate as the coffered ceiling, and gorgeous side tables with lamps. Several windows are tall arches with fancy trim. But others are rectangles and have long, overflowing sheer curtains that sweep along the inlaid hardwood floor.

I stand there admiring the entire presentation, picturing parties. Maybe even a string quartet over there in that corner by the arched windows. And the two credenzas on either side of the fireplace filled with food. Triple-tiered trays of sweets, and platters of finger food. And punch bowls. The kind that have ice cream floating in them, perhaps.

"Jesus Christ," I mutter. "Focus, Evangeline. That's the dream of a child and you're not a stupid child."

I look up again, but this time my eyes skim past the decorated ceiling and land on the cameras. Whoever put these up didn't bother to hide them. They're mounted on the walls. There's one on the mantel and two pointed at each of the double French doors that open into other rooms. One of which is pointed right at me.

"I hope you got a good look," I growl, moving along the hallway. "Because I'm out of here tonight."

There was no phone in that room, but up ahead is a kitchen. If people are gonna have a landline these days, they'd put it in the kitchen.

And for some reason, that makes me think of how it must've been before phones were portable and could fit in your pocket. In old movies there was one phone in a house and it was either in some special phone niche in a hallway or in the kitchen.

So yes. The kitchen.

I move forward into it and stop, once again taken aback at the beauty of this place.

It's white, and gray, and light blue. Which sounds a little bit boring, but it isn't. There's a huge farm sink. Huge one. And I know they're trendy today (I watch a shitload of HGTV), but as I get closer and notice the small chips in the enamel, I realize it is, in fact, made of cast iron underneath that white enamel. I get the feeling this sink is as old as the house itself.

It's a modern kitchen in all other ways. Many shades of blue glass tiles on the backsplash. White marble countertops, black soapstone on the island, and stainless-steel appliances. The stove has a million burners on it with those fancy red knobs that let everyone know you overpaid for that thing and probably don't know how to use it. Painted cabinets. Not traditional white as one might expect, but a dark gray color that warms the place up and makes it feel... homey.

I scan the room for a phone as I make my way around the large center island, but once again come up empty.

Hmmm.

The office, I decide. I stumbled into an office in my panic to find the powder room. That's where I head next.

The hallway continues, like all the rooms branch off this corridor. It's not completely closed in, which bothers me. If this were my place I'd wall up all these French doorways that lead back to the kitchen and living room. Open-concept isn't for everyone, after all.

It's not my place, I gently remind myself. *You're only going to be here a few more hours. So stop playing fixer-upper, ya dingbat.*

A smile creeps over my face at my internal monologue. It is a beautiful house though. Like, if I were to ever sell the penthouse I could see myself living in a house like this. It's got a wall and a gate. And I bet the backyard is also surrounded by those thick, high hedges that give you a sense of privacy in the city.

The next set of double doors are closed. So I pull them open at the same time and find myself staring at a library.

Shelves and shelves and more shelves of books. Two soft, butter-yellow velvet couches face each other in the middle of the gigantic room. And there's a light gray upholstered ottoman that spans almost the entire space between them with glossy magazines sitting in a neat pile on top of a tray.

I get lost in this room for just a moment. Allow myself to appreciate how beautiful it is. Wonder what it would be like to sit on those velvety cushions and read a book on a wintery afternoon—just like this one—free of all the worry, and panic, and fear.

But that all stops the second I see what's propped up in the far corner near a bright window.

And I think I forget how to breathe.

CHAPTER NINE

IXION

She creeps out of the powder room like a frightened mouse. Or a small child making her way through a haunted house, knowing someone is going to jump out at her, just not when.

I never liked haunted houses. I don't see the point in knowingly scaring the fuck out of yourself, acting like a dumbass the entire time you're in there, and then patting yourself on the back when you come out because... because what? You made it through fake shit, screaming like it's real, and didn't die when it was over?

Please. There's enough real scary shit in the world to go around ten times, no one needs to make it up. Society is really on a downward spiral, if you ask me. Making it through a haunted house is the kind of stuff we're calling courage these days.

Movement on the large screen in the middle of my semi-circular control panel brings my attention back to Evangeline.

She's inching her way down the hall. Going so fucking slow, I just want to turn on the microphones and scream at her to hurry the fuck up. I mean, how slow can a person walk? How timid can one woman be?

87

A momentary flash of shame washes through me, because I know damn well how timid women can be. And why.

She glances up at one of the hallway cameras just as I think that thought. Eyes still covered by her ridiculous dark sunglasses. Cheeks blotchy red. Sweat pooled on her upper lip.

I place my hands on the console table and lean in to see her better.

Jesus Christ. She's almost hyperventilating. Her chest is rising and falling so fast, she must be making herself dizzy.

She lowers her gaze and continues to inch down the hallway until she's standing in the open double doors of the main ballroom, which has been turned into sort of a grand receiving area.

My family home has one of each. The ballroom is empty most of the time. Just a sad, open room with extravagant wood floors and tall rectangle windows with sheer curtains, much like these, that pool down onto the floor and always made me think of how much dust they must collect.

And our receiving area looks more like a men's club than a living area. Large wing-back chairs upholstered in soft leather and seams held together by large brass nailheads.

This house is smaller than ours. And really, who needs a ballroom? So Jordan—or whoever the fuck owns this place—has turned it into a formal living area. A place to talk with guests and be served afternoon tea, and just generally be ostentatious.

She scans the room, looking for something, but then gets distracted by the ceiling.

I don't blame her for that. It is a nice ceiling. But a few moments later she snaps out of her awe when she finds the cameras.

She mumbles something which I can't understand and will have to replay later, and then moves on towards the kitchen.

Same shit in there. She looks around. Perhaps impressed, perhaps not. I mean, she *is* Evangeline Rolaine, right? I think this is a pretty cool mansion, but does it impress me? Are you fucking kidding? This might as well be the children's playhouse compared to what I grew up in.

She was quite the little worldly globetrotter as a child. She played for Saudi princes and the Queen of England. I bet she's seen her share of swank.

But she touches things in there. The red knobs of the stove. The smooth, cold countertops. The dark gray cabinet doors. Perhaps picturing herself living here. Or maybe comparing this place with hers, the way I'm doing with my own family dwelling.

She looks around, again, like she's searching for something, then backs out into the hallway, like she's reluctant to leave.

I wonder if she cooks?

It's been a long time since I had a home-cooked meal. I literally cannot remember the last time I didn't grab food from a restaurant.

Her steps are quicker now. Still tentative, but less so than before she entered the kitchen.

And that's when she stops.

My smile is automatic. Because this *will* be the room she falls in love with.

She reaches for the double doors, pulls them both open at the same time, and then...

Stunned silence as she takes it all in and then... and then she sees what I've been wanting her to see since I first discovered it myself.

I grin wide. Because I was right. This room will...

She walks in, hand over her chest, that terrible fast breathing making her sound like a panting dog, and stops next to a yellow velvet couch, reaching for it, like she might fall over.

"Can it..." but that's all I catch as she begins to mumble out a constant stream of words.

She rushes towards the violin in the corner. It's a beautiful violin. Soft, subtle shades of red. Ebony-black knobs. The strings look silver in the dim light filtering through the long, sheer curtains.

She gets about a foot away and stops, her head shaking back and forth. No, that shake says. No. And then she backs away from the instrument. She trips over the rug, bumps into the arm of a couch, and falls to the floor.

No. That's not what happens. She *crumples* to the floor.

I lean in again, trying to see more than the camera allows. "What the fuck are you doing?" I ask the screen.

It only takes me a second to realize she's crying. This chick is seriously disturbed. Flat-out fucking crazy. I sit down in my chair to watch—because that's my job—and grab a pen and piece of paper sitting off to the side for notes.

Jordan didn't ask for notes, but it's just part of my process. I'm not normally so... uninvolved in the surveillance process. I typically work with husbands—or wives—who think their wives—or husbands—are cheating on them. Occasionally I work for parents concerned about a teenager. Or some rural sheriff's department that doesn't have the right resources. Which was how I ended up in Wyoming last month and just… never left. And even the side jobs get notes. It's the least I can do for those women.

"Why do you do it?" Jordan asked me that a couple years ago. He called me on Christmas. Why? I have no idea. We hadn't talked in years. No one died. Nothing to report. Just a fucking out-of-the-blue phone call. "You've got more money than God. You could buy any house you want. Hell, dozens of them. Get a fucking yacht, private jet. And if there's such a thing yet, a spot on the next space shuttle to the moon, or Mars, or wherever the fuck people book tickets for in space."

My answer… "There's no space shuttle anymore."

To which Jordan responded with a grunt.

And that was the end of that.

He hung up and never called back.

No, he just showed up to bail me out of jail couple weeks ago.

Because he needed you, that nasty voice in my head says.

I rationalize that internal suspicion. Cameras and shit… I'm just kinda good at it. I don't have to think about it. I know where to put them, how to set up a control room, how to keep busy as you watch so you don't get bored. I have regular cameras too. With those long zoom lenses. Sometimes I just sit in a car, or a van, or a fucking U-Haul and take pictures.

And I like compiling data. My clients don't ask for it, but I give them all a little report at the end. Assign motive to certain actions, put pictures in chronological order so they make sense, and bind it all up with brass brads and a plastic cover sheet with their case number on it. (Plus a coupon for ten percent off their next order. It's got little dotted lines and a miniature pair of scissors around the words, letting them know they should cut it out and present it to me. They never do that. But I try.)

My phone buzzes on the console table next to me. I glance down at the screen, which says Number Unavailable, and answer out of sheer curiosity alone.

"Yeah," I say.

"Ix," the woman says on the other end of the line.

"Who's this?" I ask back.

"Chella." She laughs. "Remember? Saw you the other day and—"

"How'd you get my number?"

"Jordan. But that's not why I'm calling. I'm having this thing next month."

"Thing?" I ask.

"Yeah, I told you I own that tea room next to the place that used to be the Club?"

"Right."

"Well, I'm having a thing and you're coming. We should catch up."

"Nah," I say, my eyes darting back to Evangeline on the screen. She still hasn't moved.

"Good," she says. Like I just said yes instead of no. "It's Saturday, February fourteenth at three o'clock."

"Isn't that Valentine's Day?"

"Right! Bring your lady friend, OK? She's so interesting and I'd really like to meet her."

"Chella, I'm fucking *working*. I can't go to your thing. And she's not my lady friend, she's my fucking... client." Which isn't really true. Jordan is my client. But I don't have another word for her.

"I'd love to hear her play. Can she bring her violin?"

"She doesn't like people watching her. She won't even go outside, OK? There's no way in hell she's gonna show up at your tea party."

"Perfect," Chella says. "See you then."

I just stare at the phone once the call ends. That chick is fucking weird.

I'm not going to her *thing*. Even if I wasn't working, I wouldn't go. Chella, and Jordan, and this city, and... fucking childhood bullshit. I mean, I haven't seen Chella Walcott—Baldwin, whatever—since she was like nine years old. And now she's suddenly calling me up like we're old friends?

We weren't old friends. She disappeared to... wherever the fuck her crazy parents took her, and I got left with Jordan. And...

Fuck!

Why the hell did I take this job?

Because Jordan bailed me out of jail, I rationalize.

But that's not even true. I didn't need bail money. I didn't call him for help. And if I'm being totally honest here, I would've stayed in that cell until my court appearance, then pled guilty, and happily served my time.

It would've been like a vacation to me.

Because you've got nothing better to do, Ixion. That's why.

Yes. That right there is the truth.

I have absolutely nothing better to do than sit in this stupid basement and watch some psycho fall apart because people might look at her.

Of all the stupid things I've heard in this life, this is right up there with *I deeply apologize for my inappropriate actions and I'm seeking treatment for my sex addiction.*

I stare at the screen. Willing her to get up and do something so I can stop thinking about my life and go back to feeling sorry for someone else.

The minutes tick off. She stays there, all crumpled up on the rug, playing with a string, or a piece of lint, or whatever the fuck she's rolling between her fingers. And she's chanting something. Like a poem, or a song, or something like that. I can't really hear it, the microphones in that room aren't the best. And I try to find a good angle to see her lips to try to read them as she mumbles. But it's no use. Her long hair is mostly covering her face.

I'm a bird... in a song... and the wind...

Fuck, I don't know what she's saying. It's a nursery rhyme, maybe?

Eventually she stops playing with the lint ball, and her lips stop moving, so the chant is over, and then one side of her stupid sunglasses falls away from her face and I see that she's sleeping.

Guess I won that bet, right?

Too bad there wasn't money riding on it.

Like I need the money.

Like the bet was with someone other than myself.

Like... I *really* need to get out more.

Sometime over the next several hours, she rolls over and grabs for a blanket draped over the arm of a couch, and tries to cover herself.

It's one of those blankets that aren't good for anything. They're usually too thin, and too short, and too decorative to have any useful purpose whatsoever.

My mother used to have those things on all our couches when I was a kid. It annoyed me, even back when I was short, that they never covered enough to get me warm.

And then I start wondering if she's cold.

Of course she's cold. She's sleeping in a giant mansion that can't ever be warm enough because that's the way of mansions. And she's on the floor. And that blanket doesn't even qualify as a blanket, so I press the button for the microphone in that room and I lean in, ready to tell her to get the fuck up and go sleep in a real bed because, you know, there's like twenty-seven different things to sleep on in this place and none of them involve *the floor* and… I stop just in time.

Because I'm under strict orders not to talk to her. And if I do talk to her, she'll know I'm a man, and she'll freak the fuck out, and then she'll walk out of here and call her therapist or whatever, and then… fucking jig is up, right?

Ixion and Jordan do what they do best. Fuck people up.

I don't know where that just came from, so…

I glance over at the notebook, then notice I'm still fucking holding the pen in my right hand, and…

I'll just write her a note. And quietly make my way up to the library, and place it next to her, and then kick her or something, so she wakes up and finds it.

Good plan, Ix.

So I turn the page in the notebook and think about how to put this.

You're being dumb. Go to bed.

Probably not the best way to handle it. So I flip the page and try again.

Turn up the heat.

But there's like six or seven thermostats in this house. That might just confuse her.

You haven't seen the master bedroom yet. It's very nice. Go sleep there.

That conjures up a lot of innuendo…

95

You're cold. Go upstairs. Find the master bedroom. Get in the bed, cover up, and go to sleep.

There we go. That's the winner.

I fold it in half, write her name on the front, get up, leave the control room, make my way upstairs, and walk down the hallway to the library.

It's weird to see her in person after watching her all day. Her body is contorted into some semblance of a fetal position and the blanket is diagonal across her upper body—because that's the only way it's big enough to cover anything, and whoever the fuck came up with decorative blankets needs to spend the night in this cold-ass mansion on the floor trying to use one—and she's... shivering.

I enter the room as quietly as I can, wishing I wasn't wearing boots, acutely aware that the hardwood floors are ancient and most of the boards are creaking.

But I manage, because that's how I roll, place the folded piece of paper right next to her softly breathing mouth, and back out the way I came.

CHAPTER TEN

EVANGELINE

I dream of birds and summer days.
I string together words in books that earn me praise.
But the words are notes and the books are songs,
and the birds and summer days are gone.
The winter wind is strong and sounds
like the missing music I lost and found.

I wake up, confused. Still hearing birds. Still thinking it's summer. But I am chilled to the bone, and shaking in my core, and the winter wind is blowing outside with force. And then I remember where I am. What I'm doing. And why the fuck are there birds in this house?

My sunglasses are all askew on my face, so when I open my eyes in the darkness, I can see a little more than I'd be able to had they been affixed properly.

The library, I remind myself.

I glance at the corner where the violin is propped up on the stand. The sun has set and there's just a faint glow of light coming through the window. Outlining it, as if I needed it outlined.

The song of birds is coming from a speaker somewhere. I look up and find all the cameras, then quickly straighten out my sunglasses to hide my eyes. But that just sucks all the remaining light out of the room, blinding me.

Pushing up from the floor, I get dizzy. So I stay on all fours and hang my head for a few moments, staring down at the pattern on the rug. It's an ancient rug. Like a real, ancient Persian fucking rug. I can feel the bare threads under my fingertips. The softness of the wool it's woven of.

And that's when I see the note.

Evangeline, it says, written in neat print and all caps. And there's a little squiggly line underneath the letters that looks like a fancy, elongated cursive lowercase e, but it isn't an e. It's... just a fancy little squiggly line.

I look up at the nearest camera again and say, "What's this?"

I'm not expecting an answer, and it never comes, so I just sit up better so my legs are underneath me. I straighten out my sweater. The second the thin blanket falls down from my shoulders, I shiver with cold.

But the cold can wait.

My watcher has sent me a message.

Is this part of the treatment?

I don't think so. And I don't care. When was the last time someone sent me a *letter*?

I can't even recall. I was a child, probably. It was a fan. Or one of the many perverts who used to stalk me online and after performances.

Read it! my mind screams. *Open it and read it!*

My fingers are so nearly numb, they fumble with the folded sheet of thick paper. It's nice paper, I realize, as I manage to open it up.

You're cold. Go upstairs. Find the master bedroom. Get in the bed, cover up, and go to sleep.

One fact and five commands.

Just as that thought leaves my head the birds stop singing.

I think about that for a little while, unexpectedly reflective about the loss of music. My heart is racing, but not too bad. Which surprises me.

You're cold.

I'm chilled so bad, all I really want is to be at home taking a hot bath in my giant, private tub. But that's not gonna happen. Not while I'm here, at least. There are cameras up there. In all the rooms, even the bathrooms. That much I know.

Go upstairs. Find the master bedroom. Get in the bed, cover up, and go to sleep.

It's the answer I'm looking for.

Simple. Direct. Obtainable.

I push up from the floor, still clutching the note in my hand, and exhale.

It's dark now. I could leave. Find a phone somewhere. Call the concierge and go home.

But it all sounds like so much effort.

I look at the note again and sigh.

That all sounds so easy.

So I do what I'm told.

I leave the library, closing the double doors behind me so I don't have to see that stupid violin again should I wander down this way tomorrow, and walk down the dark hallway until I come back to the grand foyer.

I stand there, looking up, the wide staircase beckoning me like an old friend. I go to it, heeding the call, and place my hand on the smoothly polished wood of the banister. Still looking up as I climb, wondering if my watcher is waiting for me up there.

And unexpected heat rises from my lower stomach. A stirring between my legs as I picture him. Maybe it's a her? No, the printing was very masculine.

What if he is old? And Lucinda was lying?

What if he's not?

It doesn't matter because when I get to the top of the stairs, he's not there.

I look left and right. Nothing but closed doors in both directions. There's another staircase at the end of the hall to my left. Is he in the attic? Did he mean for me to go up to the third floor?

Find the master bedroom was his next command.

So I do that. I open the first door and find a bathroom, then notice a little red blinking light in a plug and wonder how hidden his cameras are. If it wasn't dark I probably wouldn't notice that red light. I'd think that was just a useful adapter for my phone.

I close the door and go to the next. A bedroom, but small and decorated for a small princess, so not the master. And then another, a nursery. And another, a teen room. And another bathroom. Then more bedrooms, but none are what I've been assigned to find.

So I turn back, pass the grand staircase again, and head towards the second set of stairs. I pass several doors, but they are closets, and one is a bathroom. And another bedroom, still too small to be a master in this size house.

I stand at the bottom of the second staircase and look up into darkness.

Is he up there?

Is he waiting for me?

What's that noise?

I crane my neck forward, head tilted, desperate to hear more.

Birds…

I climb without thinking. This is where I'm supposed to go. And even though I have this tiny, niggling thought that this whole fucking setup is dangerous and stupid, I don't care.

I just want to hear the song again.

At the top there's a small landing. The darkness is complete. So much so, I have to inch forward and feel for the doors I know must be there.

I find a knob, then a second, and realize they are double doors, just like the ones downstairs.

I turn both knobs and push them inward and find a softly lit bedroom.

The master.

There's only one small light, and it barely counts as a light and it's shaped like a quarter moon. More like one of those decorative things you place in a baby's nursery to give off the glow of comfort.

But it's just enough for me to see everything.

The bed has been turned down. The comforter is either white, or pale yellow or cream. Can't really tell. But it looks soft and inviting

Did he do this for me? Turn the bed down?

Or was that Lucinda? Was she in here? Did the watcher know she came and got the room ready, so he told me to come upstairs?

Did Lucinda tell him to write that note?

I deflate at that thought. It's an unexpected sigh of sadness to even think about it.

I don't want her to be responsible for this turn of events. I want it to be him. His easy commands. His firm expectations. And not her just playing mother with me.

I don't need another mother. One was more than enough, thank you.

There's a camera in the corner, facing the bed. In fact, I count six total. Each of the four corners, one on the fireplace mantel at the foot of the bed, and one directly above the bed in the form of a reflective black bulb among white ones nestled in the intricate chandelier.

Get in bed, cover up, and go to sleep.

I walk towards it, curious about the room and the dark doorway that must lead to the en suite bathroom, but wanting to follow directions, I push that curiosity aside and kick off my shoes.

The rug underneath my feet is soft sheepskin. My toes wriggle, eager to feel it on my bare skin, so I pull off my socks and give them that luxury.

I feel like I suddenly have a lot to say. A million questions. What song is this? What kind of bird? It sounds familiar. Like something in a dream.

Which is probably why you were dreaming poetry, Evangeline.

Right. Because that's all I do these days—dream.

I kneel on the bed, feeling it give with my weight, and then crawl in, fully clothed minus socks.

The sheets are cold, but they warm quickly. I pull the heavy comforter over me and bury my face in the pillow.

Something leaves me in this moment.

Something not worth keeping, I think. It's dread, maybe. Or anxiety. Or fear. Maybe it's fear?

Or, I think, maybe it's something returning and not leaving. Maybe it's curiosity.

When was the last time I was curious about a person? Or anything?

And the recordings of child prodigies don't count. Because I know why I was doing that now. That was the very first thing Lucinda and I worked out.

I wanted to feel safe in their failures so I didn't judge myself too harshly.

Almost all of them had trouble as adults. Most of them stopped playing just like me. They made me feel like a statistic. I wanted to feel like a statistic.

When I finally said all that out loud Lucinda smiled at me and said, "How does it feel to be reduced to a number?"

That was the first time I really thought about why I had this fear of being watched.

"Not good," I said back.

I felt very used, honestly. Like I was nothing but a fulfilled expectation.

I'd worked that out as a teenager too. I remember feeling used, voicing that feeling to my parents. And I remember their reaction. And what my father said next. How I agreed, and did what he asked. Let him use me again. And then...and then, when it came right down to it, I didn't. I refused. I took a step away. A step forward. I fixed things. Made them better.

But then why did everything get worse?

Fuck. Let it go!

Anyway, when I called up my old agent and told her to schedule the performance, Lucinda said, "How does it feel to want something?"

"Exciting," I said. "And scary. Mostly scary."

And now I know why. Because it was a lie.

She was right. I was never going to go through with it. That's why I was getting worse instead of better. I needed an excuse to back out.

But then every time I thought about backing out I just wanted to vomit.

The birds are suddenly gone, the room quiet.

And then the light on the bedside table, the soft one lighting up a porcelain moon that absolutely belongs in a child's bedroom, dims and then darkens. Like it was on a timer.

Maybe my whole life is on a timer and now it's over?

I close my eyes and force myself to stop thinking, listen to the winter wind outside the windows of this stranger's bedroom, and pretend I hear a whisper in its blowing gale.

The wind says, "Good night."

CHAPTER ELEVEN

IXION

To call myself mesmerized at how the evening plays out would be an understatement. Once I decided on the substance of the note and placed it next to her sleeping body in the library, I went up to the third floor and pulled back the bed covers. I found the little moon nightlight in the nursery and set the timer for ninety minutes, which was as long as it would set to.

I got a little lost in the family who no longer lives here. Who were they? Where did they go? Who owns the house and how the hell are the two of us in here playing this sick little game without them knowing? Objecting?

I made a note to ask Jordan about it the next time we talked, knowing I'd never get that answer. For all I know, this is his house. Maybe he has a family? Maybe he sent them all off on vacation until this little experiment was over? How the hell would I know? I haven't really talked to him in years. Why the hell do I care?

I convince myself I don't. Care.

But then I went back down to my basement control room, searched the internet for recordings of songbirds, pumped one through the library speakers at a soft volume, and made myself comfortable while I waited her out.

Her little poem or whatever it was gave me that idea. She was mumbling something about birdsongs. And shivering so hard when she woke up I had an urge to leave and turn up the heat. Not that I had any better idea of which areas all the specific thermostats control, because I didn't. This room was warm from the hum of technology. I could've used some AC down here, to be honest.

But now that the spell is over and she's either asleep or very good at faking it, I am realizing just how fucking strange all this is.

This woman and I are alone in this house for... well, until she fucking calls it quits, I suppose. And I've already broken just about every rule I was given.

I left the basement.

I made contact with her.

Shit, more than contact. I gave her directions. Orders, maybe.

And she followed them.

Is she so lost that a stranger's commands are better than making up her own mind?

"Huh," I say out loud. "I guess it's not that unusual."

Which makes me wonder what she'll do tomorrow. She could leave. Walk out that door and call her therapist. Tell her everything I did. I might've even have fucked her up worse than she is. Because let's face it, this chick has issues.

Then there was that fucking rhyme she was chanting. What was that? I'm so damn curious I do a search on the internet.

Birds and wind poem. Birds and wind nursery rhyme. Birds and wind songs.

Nothing.

And then there's the violin. It seemed to… make her wilt. I didn't expect that. She's an accomplished violinist, so one would naturally assume she loves the instrument and would find it comforting. Except it seemed to have the opposite effect.

"Fuck it," I mumble to myself. "She's a nutjob."

I got her to stay a night. Big deal. I don't even know how much I'm getting paid. I don't even care. I don't even know why I'm here.

I do a search for *her* now, convinced I missed something the last time I searched.

Evangeline Rolaine comes right up on Wikipedia. It's long enough. Childhood. Parents. First performance at age four. Then a complete list of them in chronological order.

But it's the section on child prodigies—the internal link that phrase points to, in fact—that consumes me well past midnight.

I get lost in it. The weirdness of them. The claim by alternative types that these kids are just reliving past lives. The fact that almost all of them dealt with some sort of mental breakdown in their teens and twenties.

Evangeline is twenty-eight now. So yeah. Fits.

Then I get consumed by an image search. Pictures of her as a small girl. Then growing up. All of which showcase her prominently with her violin.

There is no trace of a smile after age eight.

I contrast her upbringing with my own. She wasn't born to a rich family, but she was so young when their fortune changed, she might as well've been.

And all that money came from her.

Like those child actors that score a big role and the whole family suddenly goes from dirt-poor Alabama to swanky rich and famous Beverly Hills… it's a little unnatural.

Not the money. But the illusion that *you are important*.

Shit like that is a mind fuck because no one's important to anyone unless there's some sort of relationship involved. And the relationship her parents were forging with elite insiders was one of mutual gain.

Take the gain away and the relationship goes with it.

This plays out in every economic status—people just see it less when they're not in the top one percent.

For example, you get a new used car so you don't have to take the bus to work like most of your other co-workers. Bam. You find new friends based on your ability to give them a ride. Something they want and need. Yes. People use you like this. Almost all of them, in fact. People are assholes like that. They like you for what you have, not who you are.

I can imagine the scenarios her parents went through as they climbed the social ladder. She needed an agent, and after her first performance at age four, I'm sure they came crawling out of the woodwork. There was probably a little battle as her parents negotiated what they needed versus what they had. More appearances and money went up against a little girl with God-given talent.

Once the agent was secured they needed more access to even more influential people to keep what they just got. The cycle continued. The family rose on the shoulders of little Evangeline. The money poured in as her talent grew. Her face was everywhere, her talent undeniable, her youth intoxicating until the vultures who only wanted her for what she could give them became flocks circling overhead waiting for her to die. It was only a matter of time before what they saw down below was exhausted and they took their final meal.

And... she broke.

She was too young to know why. She was too innocent to understand how. She was too trusting to rebel until...

She wasn't.

The court records for her emancipation are fascinating. Since she was petitioning for adult status, they were never sealed. It's a simple public records search that gives me more insight into her psyche than should be allowed. I feel a little dirty just reading them.

But I can't stop.

After that she sold her violin.

Ah...this is the defining moment in her life, I realize. Her amazing career rose to a crescendo and that breakdown in the library was the encore. A moment when something lost might've been found again, and wasn't.

I do a search for the Stradivarius she sold at auction twelve years ago, but the buyer was anonymous.

It was a ridiculous dream of hers. An inevitable downfall. Because whoever bought that violin would not sell it without global fanfare. She'd have known if it was sold. It would've been in magazines and on the news as one of those general interest stories.

She had to know the violin in the library wasn't her Stradivarius when she walked in there.

Still... she hoped, didn't she?

And felt the loss all over again last night.

I sigh for her. So close... and yet not close at all.

Gazing up at the monitor, I ask the sleeping girl, "Do you want it back, Evangeline?"

Not the violin. It's gone. She's never getting that back. Certain things are just not for sale and that violin is one of them. Even money like mine can't buy that back. Not that I would. (What a freak fucking thought.) She wants herself back.

I feel sorry for her. I see her vulnerability splayed out before me like a banner in the wind. I relate to it a little, I guess.

The loss, maybe. She lost herself much the way I lost myself all those years ago.

And the sadness. Though I'm not a sad guy. More indifferent than sad. But I can relate to her. The way she was used. The way she gave up what she loved to find her own way in the world. The courage it must've taken to drag herself over to this house and let a stranger watch her.

Why?

I press Jordan's contact on my phone. He picks up on the first ring. "Yup," he says.

"Why?" I ask.

"Why what?"

"Why is she here?"

"Why do you care?"

"I just do."

There's a prolonged silence after that. I let it hang there.

"She's got issues, man. And she wants to get past them, that's all."

"But why *now*?"

Jordan sighs, long and loud. "Don't ask questions, Ix. I don't really have answers anyway, but even if I did, I don't think you need to know."

He ends the call after that. Leaves me hanging like the silence I left him in a few moments before.

I set my phone down and watch her. It's my job, right? So I watch her. The way her leg sneaks out from under the covers when she gets hot. The way it slips back under when she's chilled. The way her body occasionally thrashes, like she can't get comfortable. The way she keeps her eyes closed, either asleep and doing all this unconsciously or just squeezing them shut to keep the world away.

I have the pen and notebook in my hand almost unconsciously. The pen writes of its own accord. Sharp-edged letters printed out in my own hand run across the page like a horse racing for the finish line.

I read it over and over again, then tear the page off, fold it once, and print her name on the front, just like I did earlier.

I have no second thoughts as I get up, punch in the code to unlock the door, and exit my room.

I think of no one but her as I walk across the basement, ignoring the flashing lights of Pac-Man and the digital song of Centipede, and climb the stairs to the main floor.

As I walk down the hallway towards the grand foyer, my attention never falters. I don't see the chandeliers or the intricate ceiling of the once-ballroom. I take the stairs two at a time, my hand sliding along the smooth banister, and never once compare it to the banister of my childhood.

On the second floor I don't look right, towards the bedrooms of forgotten children. I see only the open stairs that lead up to the master on the left. My feet know where to go. Know to step lightly as I climb once again, hand on the railing, head tilted up, eyes focused on the double doors ahead.

I don't even stop when I get to them. Don't hesitate at all.

They must open for me, like all this was meant to be. Because I'm in her room. Watching her, not on the flat screens of my control room, but here, in person.

If I care if I wake her, it doesn't show. Because my boots are allowed to thud across the hardwood until they land on the soft rug in front of the bed and go silent. There's a moment when I imagine myself leaning down to brush the hair out of her face so I can see the contours of her cheekbone. But that passes.

I leave the note on the bedside table and retreat, confident that this is the right way forward.

I'm helping her, I decide, making my way down to the second floor.

She needs this, just like she needed that last note. She's here for a reason. She wants to get better. She's strong, and willful, and none of that has helped her so far.

But I can help her.

I know it.

I see what she needs and I'm gonna give it to her. And she'll accept it because she's practically my prisoner. She'll accept it because she won't be able to stop herself. And when the day comes when she does walk out of this house, healed, and focused, and put back together...

It will be because I didn't follow directions.

Sleep comes easy when I get back to my room. I strip down to skin, get under the covers, and dream of all the ways I can help her.

All the things I can make her do.

All the holes I can fill inside her.

JORDAN

"What's the deal with you two, anyway?"

I'm sitting with Chella at the courthouse coffee shop, grabbing a coffee because she just happened to be here at eight-thirty AM and I had no good excuse to blow her off since I don't need to be in court for another thirty minutes.

I take a sip of my coffee, all casual and shit, and reply, "What's the deal with you and your mom?"

Chella's reaction and recovery happen almost simultaneously, but she manages to keep that smile on her face. "She's dead. You know that."

"Yeah, and you know that whatever the deal is with Ix and me, it's none of your business."

She doesn't miss a beat. "I asked Smith about you."

"Smith doesn't even know me."

"Bric does."

"Bric knows me now. But what you're asking is who was I back then? And Bric didn't know me then either. Don't bother with Quin. He's got no clue."

"So you're proud of this secret past you're keeping from me?"

"It's not a fucking secret, Chella. It's just none of your business. Don't you have to be at work or something?"

"You had sex with him, didn't you?"

I sigh. Roll my eyes.

"Oh, my God," she says, lowering her voice. "Wow. He's fucking hot, Jordan. I salute you."

"Shut up. It wasn't even like that. It was like… the stuff I did with Bric. Or Quin. Club stuff."

"OK," Chella says. "So who was the girl?"

"Why do you care?"

Chella shrugs. "I just… I just think he looks sad, don't you? I mean, I've seen it before. Sadness and I are well acquainted and he definitely looks sad. Is that why you're helping him?"

"I'm not helping him. I'm not doing anything. He's just a fucking guy who can run some fucking cameras."

"And keep his mouth shut."

I glare at her.

"What? It's obvious that whatever you're doing with Lucinda is on the down low, right?" The ding of Chella's phone saves me from answering. "That's Smith," she says, checking her text. "He's done with his little permit thing."

I scoff. "So you really were here for business."

"I told you I was, Mr. Wells," she says, standing up. "Come to my tea party next month. It's on Valentine's Day. Ixion's coming."

"He is not."

"I invited him. So he's coming." Chella is the only woman I know who seems to think she controls the universe. Like she has it on a leash. Like her request is a done deal.

And it's kinda true. Chella is pure. Sweet, considerate, loyal, and honest. I'm sure she has vices, but I've never seen them. So it's like… everyone goes out of their way to make her happy. If she invites you to something, you go.

Because it makes her happy. If she asks for something, you give it to her. Just to make her happy.

Chella deserves happiness and the whole world knows this.

She leans down to kiss me on the cheek, and in doing so, whispers, "I just worry about you, Jordan. You're adrift. Don't float too far away from us."

I stare at her as she straightens up. Exhale. Loudly.

"So Valentine's Day?" she says, hiking her purse strap onto her shoulder.

"No," I say, holding fast.

"Three o'clock. Don't be late. Ixion can be your date."

She leaves before I can say anything to that last remark.

But in her wake she leaves something behind too. An air thick with the memories of past regrets. And yes, sadness.

It's not like we planned it. Not at all. What happened... just happened. It was almost a natural progression of things. An inevitable conclusion.

"Shall we go up to my place?"

Her question lingers in my head like the terror you feel waking up from a too-real nightmare. Her voice is clear, like she's standing here next to me, her intent obvious. The promise of something coming evident.

I should've said no.

None of this would've happened if I had just said no.

But Augustine had me from the first time Ixion introduced her. "My Augustine," he joked.

His.

His Augustine.

And where is she now?

115

God, that's the problem, isn't it?

And I'm sick. Fucking stuck on a girl who walked out seven years ago. And she didn't just walk out. She stormed out. Like a raging fucking wind. Upending lives in the process. Friendships severed. Love lost.

And then that was it.

I didn't plan what happened. And I didn't ask Ix for the favor.

Which is the part that makes me feel so shitty. I didn't need to ask. He gave, just like Chella. He knew what I wanted, what needed to happen, and he gave it to me like a gift. With no expectations of receiving something in return. And I was selfish, because I accepted his gift and gave nothing back in return.

I should've said no. At least I wouldn't have lost both of them. Augustine was already on her way out. Ixion was never leaving.

At least, not until I fucked everything up. We'd still be friends today if I had just owned up to what I did. If I hadn't let him take the fall for me instead. If I hadn't ruined his life, and his family, and his future.

Ixion picks up on the third ring, just before it goes to voicemail. "What?" he asks, irritated. Like he's a mind-reader and he knows what I was just thinking about.

"You know, I meant it when I said I was sorry."

"When did you say you were sorry?"

"Don't be a dick."

"No, I'm really asking."

"Couple weeks ago, asshole. When you were in my office."

"Oh, that?" Ix laughs. "That's your idea of an apology?"

"Why are you here?"

116

"You called me here, remember?"

"But why did you come?"

"You know why," he says.

"Because—"

"What the fuck do you want from me *now*, Jordan? Huh? What more do I need to give you that I haven't already?"

"I'm sorry," I say. "You know—"

"I don't know shit. I don't know you, I don't know her, and I don't care, either."

"Liar," I say. "Liar."

"Is this girl a gift or something?"

"What?" His question is so inappropriate, so unexpected, I am at a loss for words.

"This job, Jordan. Is this some kind of *gift?*"

"No," I say. "No, it's just a fucking job."

"And you couldn't find another guy to sit in this stupid room and watch her? It just had to be me, right? Is that what you're telling yourself?"

"It's just a job," I say again.

"Is that why I'm here on the anniversary?"

"What?"

"The night you—"

"Stop it," I say. "That's not why. I didn't choose this timing. I'm just a guy who fulfills a need. That's all."

"Yeah. Sounds familiar."

"Ix." I sigh.

"Coincidence, then. That seven years ago tomorrow is the day you fucked up and ruined my life."

"I didn't—" I pinch the space between my eyes, a headache throbbing into existence. "Why are you here?" I ask again.

He takes a breath. Like he's about to talk. But the moments drag on in silence.

"Ix?" I say.

"For you, asshole. Why the fuck do you *think* I'm here?"

And then he hangs up on me.

CHAPTER THIRTEEN

EVANGELINE

I awake confused, sweaty, heart racing, panic ready to overtake me… until I remember how I got here.

Not here the house, but here the bed.

I turn over, looking for cameras. Find them all. Count them up. One, two, three, four, five, six. And for some odd reason it calms me. Just knowing he's there. Just a little. Just enough to fight back the full-fledged attack that would surely be coming if I hadn't been led up to this bedroom last night by his note.

God, Evangeline, you're gonna feel really stupid if that he is a she.

It's not. I can feel him. His gaze on me, his mind a mess of thoughts just like mine.

It's his job. He's not infatuated with you. You're just desperate for attention. You're just craving an emotional attachment, so you're inventing a relationship that isn't real.

It's something Lucinda might say to me. Though she never has. I've had no contact with people other than her in the past year. Not in any significant way.

I roll my eyes at my own ridiculous assumptions. I'm not infatuated with him either. I just find it comforting that I'm alone, but not. It's like a halfway point. Somewhere safe but challenging at the same time.

I have a sudden urge to talk to him. Say something mundane like, *Good morning.* Or, *How did you sleep?*

Does he sleep?

He must.

That has my heart fluttering. What if I wake up in the middle of the night with an urge to leave so powerful I just walk out of the house? And he misses it because he's asleep?

Which is downright stupid. I had that urge last night and the problem that prevented me from leaving hasn't changed. I broke my phone in a fit of panic. There's no landline in here. No way to contact anyone. I have no idea where I'm at in the city. I'm unsure of where the nearest public phone might be, and I have no clear plan to get myself home.

All those things weren't enough to walk out last night and they won't be enough tonight, either. Even if I do wake up in a panic.

I'll just go to the downstairs powder room if that kind of reaction happens. Just hide away in there until he figures it out and delivers a note with directions on what to do next.

That's when I see the note on the bedside table.

Not the one from last night. Because that was in my palm when I fell asleep and now it's somewhere in this massive bed.

A new note.

Which means he was *in here.*

An unfamiliar flood of heat between my legs sends a quiver through my body.

He was in here. My stranger. With me. Watching.

My heart rate kicks up a notch, but not because of panic.

I hold my breath as I scramble over to the edge of the bed and snatch the note in my hand.

Evangeline.

It's the same crisp, symmetrical print from last night. I trace a finger over my black-inked name. And that little lower-case e squiggle thing is there too. His mark.

Inside it says, *You're rested, but now you're hungry. Go downstairs to the kitchen. Make yourself a filling breakfast. Then take a shower and get dressed. I'll tell you what I want after that.*

I look over at the nearest camera and say, "Do I know you?"

There's no answer. And I didn't expect one, but talking to the camera feels like... a conversation. And I don't have many of those. The last one was with Lucinda yesterday on the phone. But I haven't talked to anyone except Lucinda in a very long time. Not even Dan from Mott's.

He called me once and left a message. It was about six or seven months ago now. Explaining that he had a lead on the very last recording of Evangeline Rolaine.

Which was ridiculous because I am her, and I have that stupid recording, and I know damn well no one else has one except me. But I called him back anyway just to see what he had to say.

The "lead" fell through. Surprise, surprise.

So that was the last time I talked to someone other than Lucinda in any meaningful way.

Until yesterday when I said hello to my stranger. And now I've asked him a question too.

I get up, use the bathroom, put my socks back on because this house is freezing, and then make my way downstairs to the kitchen. I'm secretly hoping for another note when I get there, but find none, and a sad longing washes over me.

Which is crazy. I don't even know this person. This watcher, this stranger. And there's no possible way to be attracted to someone from two stupid handwritten notes.

And yet... irrational as it is, that's how I feel. *Attracted.*
You're rested, but now you're hungry.

I am, I realize. I didn't eat yesterday. Not at all. I was too wound up to eat breakfast and the afternoon was a hazy nightmare filled with panic attacks and anger.

But I'm starving now. So I open the fridge, not sure what to expect, but find it stocked, just the way Lucinda said.

It's weird, all of a sudden. To feel... taken care of in this small way. The groceries. The notes. All of it hits me as a collection of very touching gestures.

There's not a lot of variety of food. Lucinda wants me to run out sooner rather than later, so I know she did this on purpose. There's fruit, a slab of bacon, half a dozen eggs, some lunchmeat that looks to be turkey or chicken, a tomato, a head of lettuce, and butter.

In the pantry I find nothing but a single loaf of white bread.

Yeah, this is not gonna last more than a few days. I suppose she didn't want to spend too much money on groceries when I could bail out on day one.

And almost did, I remind myself.

But I'm still here. Thanks to the stranger.

I make bacon, eggs, and toast with butter and scarf it down so fast, I regret not making more.

But I'm eager to see what's next from my stranger. So I go upstairs and take a shower. I don't see a camera in the shower, but he's clever, right? There could be one. So I pretend there is one. I wash myself seductively, soaping up my breasts and rubbing bubbles between my legs until I have to close my eyes.

And then I feel stupid because I'm like ninety-nine percent sure there's no camera in here, even though I wouldn't mind if there was.

When I get out, I realize my suitcases are still downstairs.

There's a brief moment when I consider walking down to get them...*naked*.

What would he do?

Would he like that?

The heat between my legs and the quiver in my stomach are back.

I'm kinda horny. I might like to masturbate and take care of that.

Instead, I wrap the towel tightly around my body and snap back to my senses. I've just been so alone for so long, these small flickers of attention are enough to make me irrational.

He's probably old, I tell myself. And not my type.

Do I even have a type?

I laugh out loud at that as I make my way over to the double doors, but stop short when I pull them open.

Because my suitcases are already there. At the top of the stairs. Right outside my bedroom door. And there's a note attached to them.

Evangeline, it says on the outside.

Take off that towel. Find the black panties and bra, the white sweater and the gray pants, and put them on. Then put on your coat and shoes and take a walk outside in the yard.

Don't forget... I'm watching you.

123

X

Is that x as in x? Or an x as in hugs and kisses? Like *xxoo*?

I look up and find every single camera. Look straight into each one.

Your move, Evangeline, that silence seems to say.

So this is a game, is it?

I should be mad. Pissed off even. That Lucinda told me to come here as a place of safety. Somewhere I could be watched anonymously. Get used to the idea of eyeballs on me twenty-four seven. Get past it, over it, move on with my life and never have to think about my watcher again.

This is not about sex, Evangeline.

Sure, Lucinda. Sure it's not.

But I'm not pissed off at all. I'm not the least bit unhappy about the fact that this is, after all, about sex. It has to be. In fact... I'm thoroughly intrigued. A little turned on. Maybe ready to play his game. Maybe even ready to strategize my own game.

CHAPTER FOURTEEN

IXION

She stares up at me. The camera me. Challenging.

She's been through so many emotions since she got here it shouldn't surprise me how far she swings. But it does. Because challenging glares imply power and if there's one thing Evangeline Rolaine isn't, it's powerful.

"Are you watching me?" she asks the cameras.

"Yeah," I say through a smile. "I'm watching."

"Because I'm about to put on a show." She looks away, her cheeks red with... what? Shame? Embarrassment?

I don't think I care at the moment.

Her chest rises and falls dramatically. Like she just took a deep breath of courage. And then she turns her back to the camera I'm watching through, peeks over her shoulder, and lets the towel fall down her body.

Her shape is hourglass curvy. Her legs are long and her wet hair trickles water down her spine and right over her plump, tight ass.

She's still peeking over her shoulder when she sighs, closing her eyes. Her arms are moving and I search each camera angle trying to see what she's doing. Her position in the room is ironically perfect. Because I don't have a view of her front.

I think she's playing with her tits. She might even have fingers between her legs.

The urge to speak to her through the microphone is almost overwhelming. I want to tell her to turn so I can see. I want to tell her to do other things too.

Dirty things.

Stick your fingers in your pussy, then stick them in your mouth. Suck them like you would my cock.

These thoughts make me hard and my hand wanders down to my growing dick.

She begins to pant heavily. Her eyes still closed, her arms still moving. Conveying the impression that she's masturbating.

This… is *not* what I expected out of the terrified prodigy recluse.

I lean back in my chair, unbutton my jeans, pull my cock out, and join a game that can't lead to anything but self-destruction.

I like those games though. It's been a long time since I've played a proper one.

She stills for a moment, opening her eyes to stare over her shoulder at the camera.

"Keep going," I whisper, wishing she could hear me. Wanting her to hear me. "I'm just getting started."

But she doesn't. It's like she heard me, because she shakes her head, stills her hands, and then steps forward towards her suitcases.

I *can* see her body now, but suddenly it's not enough. I need more. Her nakedness can't make up for the show that just ended. My balls are as hard as my cock. They need relief.

But Evangeline, again, like she knows this, is abruptly task-oriented as she pulls her suitcases into the room, closes the door, and drags them over to the closet.

I spend the next thirty minutes frustrated as hell, watching her take garments out, hang them up, all in the nude.

I mean, what the fuck? She hates people looking at her, but she's OK with hanging up clothes naked?

She's taunting me, I decide. Playing a little game with me.

"Bitch," I whisper. "You're playing with the wrong guy today."

For a woman who's locked herself inside for twelve years, afraid of the most innocent of glances, she has taken to this new role of manipulative exhibitionist uncannily quick.

I hear her giggle a few times. Like she's thinking about me sitting in this room, watching her, all frustrated at her lack of cooperation.

What the fuck? Is she like… *crazy*? I mean, obviously she's crazy. She thinks eye contact is something to panic about. But is she… sick? Perverted?

I tuck my dick away and breathe through the frustration. Watch her finish hanging up her clothes, then find the outfit I chose for her.

She lays it out on the bed and looks up at the camera. "You won, I guess."

Did I? I scoff out a laugh in my little basement room.

"Because I'm still here, right?"

Yeah.

"And I just hung up my clothes like I'm staying. So congratulations, stranger. You win. I'm gonna see this through, I guess."

My unexpected smile is so wide, if anyone saw me, they'd call *me* the lunatic. All these years she's hidden herself away. And all it took to make her face her fear was a little *kink*?

Maybe she's not psycho? Maybe she's just sexually repressed? Maybe all she needs is a good fuck?

For a second I consider going upstairs and fucking her right now. Showing myself. Jordan can shove his rules up his ass. Fuck his rules. Fuck her doctor's orders too.

But that last one makes me stop.

She's under the care of a doctor right now. I would be a monumental douche if I took advantage of her... *condition.*

She gets dressed, her game seemingly over now, because she does it quickly and efficiently. She dries her hair, puts on a little bit of makeup, and then makes her way downstairs to find her coat in the powder room, right where she left it.

She returns into view bundled up, gloved hands holding her phone, which she thrusts at the nearest camera in the hallway, and says, "Could you get me another one of these?"

I lean in to get a better look and see the telltale spiderwebs of a cracked screen.

"I promise not to call Lucinda if you do," she says, almost too sweetly.

"Who's Lucinda?" I ask out loud. "Her doctor?"

"I just like to have it, ya know?" she continues, sighing loudly. "There's no landline in here." It's like she knows I'm wavering on this request, because she keeps going. "I'll stay. I promise. I'll do what you say."

God, that makes me hard again.

"I promise."

She stares up at the camera a little longer, then she sets the phone down on a table in the hallway, puts her sunglasses on, and walks away.

I follow her, changing camera views, as she makes her way to the ballroom where there's a set of double doors leading out into the back garden.

I realize there's no cameras out there. I didn't put any in. Just... never occurred to me. And Jordan never specifically asked for them. So now she has two places she can hide from me.

Is she hiding from me?

Did she, a woman who came into the house powerless yesterday, just take control?

No. That's not how this goes down, Miss Rolaine.

I'm the one in control here.

CHAPTER FIFTEEN

EVANGELINE

I'm tingling with the pent-up sexual frustration possessing me so thoroughly, it hums through my body like electricity.

The property walls in the front of the house continue into the back, the thick, evergreen holly hedges high enough to make it feel cozy and confined. It's a place all my own, I realize. Outside. Nothing like the terrace at my apartment. That's not really private. At least it doesn't feel private. This... this feels a million worlds away from that.

I begin picturing this yard in the summer when the trees are filled with leaves and the garden beds are blooming with flowers.

Someone loves this place.

Who?

Is it Lucinda's house? It's got a lot of bedrooms. And they're all set up for a family. Two girls and a boy, I realize, picturing the children's rooms on the second floor. And they must have a lot of friends or relatives to feel the need for so many guest rooms.

What would that be like?

The lives of other people fascinate me. Have always fascinated me, ever since I was a small child. I had my life. It was the only one I knew. But I saw the way others lived and it made me so curious. How they interacted and shared things. Stupid things like inside jokes. A shared history. Little—or big—experiences that bound them together into a unit.

Granted, the families I interacted with growing up weren't typical in any way. They were celebrities. Royalty. High-powered political officials and blue-blood old money.

Their lives were nothing like mine.

So almost all of what I witnessed wasn't anything close to a normal family. And it put a lot of ideas in my head.

My father's words. Which was why I was not allowed to play with other children.

Maybe if I had played with children things would been different?

The first time I heard the word 'vacation' I was seven. Vacation. It baffled me that people didn't get up and work every single day. I asked my mother about it and she grabbed me by the shoulders, spun me around, and marched me over to my father and said, "*Your* child wants to know what a vacation is."

Whenever I did something that made my mother unhappy, she always called me Your Child. Your Child Rolaine. The first time I ever stepped into a school classroom I was ten. It was in the Philippines because we'd been living there for several months and the local authorities started coming around, asking questions. My father said they were looking for bribes, but I didn't know what that meant back then and have no idea if it was true. But I went to school so my father didn't have to pay hush money, as he called it, and when I was told to write my name on the top of a worksheet, I put *Your Child Rolaine*.

My father looked at me after my mother told him I wanted to know what vacation was. The same look he always gave me, one I assumed was fatherly well into my teens, but wasn't. And he said, "A vacation is something we can't afford."

I remember being confused because I didn't know what the word "afford" meant. So whenever people asked me things like, "Why don't you have a home?" Or, "Why don't you go to school?" I would reply, "Because we can't afford one." Even after I knew what "afford" meant, I still said that. It really pissed my mother off. Because of course we could afford one. Whatever "one" was, we could afford it. That's why the word "vacation" didn't exist in my family vocabulary.

I have no siblings. No cousins or aunts and uncles. I had grandparents once, on my mother's side, but they both died when I was very young and I hardly remember them.

So it didn't matter that the families I saw weren't typical. They were more than what I had. They were something elusive and distant from my own life.

Something to wish for in a coveting way.

Wandering the garden on the intricately laid stone pathway, I look for cameras. The trees are all bare, which should make them easy to spot, but I find none and feel disappointed.

Can't he see me out here?

A wave of panic washes over me. Irrational, I realize, since the panic I'm feeling is akin to that which overtakes me when strangers *are* watching, not when they're *not*.

But he's not just any stranger.

He's *my* stranger.

I smile at that, hoping he can see my smile, wanting him to understand what it means. Just how long I've gone between smiles before this day.

How did this happen? Not seemingly overnight. But *literally* overnight.

Yesterday when I came here I was terrified of his incessant invisible gaze.

Today I'm craving it.

What does that say about me, I wonder?

Lucinda would analyze it. Overanalyze it, probably. It would be some clinical explanation about lack of true affection growing up. Feeling used and having no power to change that, so I crave attention, but punish myself at the same time, so my mind mentally breaks down with the paradox.

But maybe I'm just in need of a good, hard fuck with a stranger?

The first boyfriend I ever had was in Phoenix. We'd just come back to the States and we were living with a family near Camelback Mountain for a summer. Huge fucking mansion on several acres. We stayed in the guest house. They had a son a couple years older than me. He was leaving for college in the fall and I was just starting to have… issues. I was there to play at a few parties they were throwing over the summer. My career was winding down. I had tits after all. The child prodigy thing was over. I think they were important people, but I paid no attention to who they were or what they did.

His name was Austin. He fucked me in every room of that mansion. Like… every room.

God, my clit is throbbing just picturing how he took me from chaste to insatiable in the span of a few weeks. His cock never got soft. Or so it seemed.

134

That was a long time ago. And there's been no one since.

I didn't love him. Nothing of the sort. I just liked what he did to me.

I come upon a tree swing in the corner of the yard. Ropes hang down from a thick limb jutting out of a massive tree that must be quite impressive in the summer. The swing is long enough to fit a family. This family. The older boy, and the middle girl, and the infant girl in the mother's lap. The father in the center, surrounded by the people who make up his life, his arm around his wife on one side and his middle daughter on the other, letting them know they're cherished.

I picture this perfect family for a moment. Imagine all the times they've sat out here on this swing and just... swung together.

I sit in the middle and feel the loss. The understanding of what I don't have sinks all my easy thoughts in an instant, the empty space on either side of me glaring proof that I'm very much alone in this world.

It's not a husband I want. Not really. A husband isn't enough for me.

Nothing's enough for you, Evangeline.

That might be true.

It's the sense of belonging I crave.

I just want to fit in somewhere. The way the older boy fits into the space on this family swing. The way the infant daughter fits into the lap of her mother. The way the mother and middle daughter fit into the embrace of the father.

I glance at the perfect house that holds the perfect family in this unobtainable embrace. The tall, slender, arched windows that might actually be original from the look of the threads of lead separating the glass panes into smaller rectangles. The aged, but still beautiful, smudged look of the moss-green stucco that looks more like an Italian plaster wall than the typical exterior stucco you see these days.

And this garden. It's so perfect, I ache just thinking about the mother and her daughter as they wander through, pruning dead petals in the summer and...

They must be somewhere else, I decide. For the winter. This house is half what it can be in the winter, surely. They are somewhere warm. The south of France. Or the Fiji Islands. Or maybe somewhere more exotic like the Maldives. Regardless, they are on a beach right now.

I sigh as my feet push off from the stone pebbles beneath them and the ropes creak with the effort of swinging.

I can't even imagine going to a beach. Not during the day. Not unless it was some uninhabited island, far from the spying eyes of watchers.

The cold wind hits me suddenly and I wonder how long I'm supposed to sit out here reflecting on all the things my life is lacking.

Does he even care? Is he even watching?

The sun is mostly shaded with cloud cover. Just a pale yellow blob filtering through gray, high overhead. It must be noon already. I've been out here for hours. Lost in the lives of the perfect family and feeling more morose and melancholy by the second.

This is stupid, I decide, getting up off the swing. I'm going back inside. Nothing about this exercise is helping me. There's no point to it. Just another excuse for Evangeline to throw her own personal pity party.

My feet crunch into the still air as I walk along the stone pathway towards the house.

I should leave. This is crazy. Playing stupid games with a stranger. Imagining him watching me walking around my room, naked. What the fuck was I thinking?

I'm sick. Depraved. And this craziness is perverting my thoughts and making me wish...

I see it as soon as I enter the ballroom. On a console table, propped up against a lamp, is a notebook. Written on the cover, in the same boxy print as the other letters he's left, is a title.

It doesn't say my name. It says, *Jordan's Game: Total Exposure.*

I pick it up, open the front cover, and read the now-familiar handwriting.

CHAPTER SIXTEEN

IXION

I grew up in a house bigger than this one. Twice the size, if you can imagine that. It was me, my mom, my dad, and my sister.

At least... that's how it started.

I was a precocious child. A name like mine is a lot to live up to, but I did my best. Might've fallen a little short. But all in all, my parents were happy with their rambunctious male progeny.

I don't know how I first became interested in cameras. Taking stupid pictures on vacation like most budding photographers, I suppose. Palm trees and sunsets. Maybe seals on the rocks off the coast of Monterey. Or the white-capped peaks while we were snowboarding in the Alps.

But I do remember the first time I realized the power of video.

I left my camera in my parents' bedroom one morning before school. Forgot to turn it off—which is the important part. So it kept recording until it ran out of battery.

When I got home from school I found it. I was twelve. That's when I discovered my father didn't love my mother.

It was a conversation about nothing, really. But it said so much. Their argumentative back-and-forth wasn't playful or sarcastic. It was dull and without flavor. It was bland and tired. It was just words between two people who had other things on their minds and better ways to waste their time.

But when my father said, "I'm taking Jillian to the summer house this year. So you can do what you want as well," my whole life changed.

I played that one sentence over and over like a million times, trying to make sure I heard it correctly.

I didn't know who Jillian was, but taking a woman who is not my mother to our summer house wasn't normal marriage behavior.

Jordan was my best friend back then. He's a mind fuck kinda guy. So when I showed him the video he got this wild gleam in his eye that I mistook for mischief.

"Let's play a game," he said.

It's a lot like the game you're playing right now, Evangeline.

No.

I take that back.

It's the very same game.

Total Exposure, it's called.

He's gonna help you. Whatever your doctor has sold you, it's a lie. This is Jordan, through and through. Every bit of this is him. I know him better than anyone. I know him better than myself. He wants something from you. And if you give it to him, you'll get what you came for, whatever that is. And he'll take what he wants and leave you behind, because that's what he does.

That probably confuses you, doesn't it? Because if you had something to give people, you probably wouldn't be playing his game right now.

Allow me to explain.

He craves something he can only get through others. He wants your secrets. He wants your soul. He feeds off the lives of others. Like a fucking vampire... or hey, let's just call him what he is.

A parasite.

And if you stay here in this house with me, you're gonna give him every bit of you. You can shake your head all you want, but it's the truth. He always wins.

I know this better than anyone because he played his first game with me and my family.

I had access to money. We both did. So we bought cameras. Lots and lots of cameras. Little secret cameras you hide in stuffed animals. Or the ones that plug into outlets and look like phone charger adapters. Or just the cheap kind people buy for vacation in case they get stolen.

We hid them all over. We got hundreds of hours of video. We caught my father in the act on my mother's custom couch in the living room.

I didn't know why Jordan wanted all this footage or what he planned on doing with it. That part still baffles me a little. Because he never said anything about showing it to my mother. And I really don't think he did that. Why? My mother knew. It was an... arrangement, after all.

It's like that part didn't matter to Jordan. What he wanted... the only thing he wanted... was the exposure.

To see people for what they really are. To flay open their souls and uncover the sins underneath.

It makes him hard. His cock throbs for hidden things. He comes on the face of your privacy.

That's his price and everyone pays it.

Looking back, I have to say, I got nothing out of that game. Not a single win. Yeah, I knew the truth. That's what Jordan kept telling me. "You're getting to the bottom of things. Solving the mystery of your family."

But since when is that a victory? Don't all families have secrets? Shouldn't most of those stay in that dark closet where we put them?

I lost a part of myself getting to the bottom of things. And the sad part is... I don't care anymore. I'm like him now. I want it. I crave it. He knows this. He paired us up for a reason and your doctor, good intentions notwithstanding, has nothing to do with what's happening right now.

I want to own those things inside you. All those sick, bloody fears that make you afraid to leave your house. I want your memories. I want your stories. I want your secrets.

If you stay here with me and we play his game together, we're gonna take them, Evangeline. We're gonna take everything you've got bottled up in that messed-up head and shake it out of you. And if you think that little tease of a show you put on for me this morning can compete with the mind fuck we'll be subjecting you to... think again.

His game is my game.

His rules are my rules.

I am Jordan's sick obsession.

So stay and play if your prize is so precious.

We'll deliver what you need, we always do.

I'll go one step further and give you me in return.

Take me. I'm yours.

But know going in… you're mine right back. And you will never be the same.

If your answer is yes, then start writing. I want to know why you're here and I want the truth.

And yes. I'll know if it's a lie.

That story had better be good or I'll walk out. Leave you here. And you'll be right back where you started. Alone. Afraid. The loser.

So write for me, Evangeline. Leave it on the kitchen counter, go outside, wait thirty minutes, and then come back inside for your next command.

X

CHAPTER SEVENTEEN

EVANGELINE

Stunned silence is my reaction to what he just wrote. In fact, I have to read it several times over to make sure I'm getting this right.

But I am, in fact, getting this right.

He's an asshole.

No. He's a psychopath.

I look up at the nearest camera and shake my head. "Total exposure," I whisper. "Well, you're not getting that. I'm getting exactly what I need from you and there's no way in hell I'm gonna tell you anything. I don't even know you. And what kind of name is X anyway?" I huff out some air. "X." I toss the notebook on the counter. It goes sliding across the smooth stone surface, stopping just short of falling off the edge.

I turn away, walk into another hallway and follow it to the ballroom. There's a nice view of the tree with the swing. I sit on the couch facing the window and imagine him in here, watching me out there.

"Are you sure that's how you want this to go?"

The voice is gruff and crackly, coming through an intercom positioned on the wall that looks like it's decades old. Masculine behind the static. Hard-edged and deep underneath the distortion.

"Not knowing might kill you," the voice continues. At least that's what I think he said. One or two words are half missing from the bad connection.

"I don't think so," I say back to the empty room. "I think... I think I'm gonna walk out of here today and go home. Because I'm pretty sure my doctor never authorized this sick game you're playing."

"How sure are you?"

"One hundred percent," I say.

She didn't, right? I ask myself. *Lucinda didn't set me up with this... this fucking psychopath. Did she?*

"You can call her and find out," he offers.

"I broke my phone. As you well know because I asked you to get me another one."

"There's shops a few blocks down. Go out and get one yourself." The crackle in the speaker makes his words skip. So what I hear is, "Go... and... yourself."

But I get his meaning. His *threat*. Because that's what that was. "Maybe I will. Maybe I'll just walk out, get a phone, and never bother her or you again?"

"Maybe you'll die alone."

"Fuck you," I say. "You don't even know me."

"Not yet."

"Not ever. I don't know who this Jordan guy is, but I do know neither of you are getting anything from me other than the peephole you're being paid to look through."

He grunts a laugh. Which is very clear. And I have to admit—reluctantly—that I like his laugh.

"That peek doesn't include *talking*," I add. "You're not supposed to talk to me. Not supposed to contact me in any way. You're supposed to shut up and watch. So why don't you go back to doing that and let me worry about my future."

"You talked first, Evangeline."

A shiver runs up my spine when he says my name. Even if it is missing the first syllable because of the intercom.

"You wanted to play earlier. When you were naked in the room. You did that for me and only me. To give me pleasure. Were you masturbating? Or just pretending?"

My face flushes hot with embarrassment. But I rally. "What do you think?"

"Coward," he sneers. "I think you're afraid of everything. I think—"

"Well, I think you're an asshole."

"So leave."

"No."

"Then do what you're told."

"I'll do what I want."

"Why are you here?"

"That's the question you want answered so badly, is it? Why am I here? Because I'm tired, that's why."

"Of what?"

"Waiting."

He pauses for a second, thinking that through, then says, "Was it worth it?"

"Was what worth it?"

"The thrill you got upstairs. That's the real reason you're here. So I hope that little tingle was worth it, because if you don't play with me that's all you'll get. Probably for a long time, because you'll run back to wherever it is you keep yourself and spend the rest of your life in hiding."

"What is your problem? You're mad because I was masturbating and you had to watch? Then I stopped and let me guess, you didn't get off? Poor baby. Not my fault you took this stupid job."

He's silent for a little bit. Long enough for me to wonder if he misjudged me. If Lucinda told him to play with me like this, then my temper wouldn't surprise him. She's seen it enough over the past year to know that's just part of me now. Like the color of my eyes.

"Why are you *really* here?" he finally asks again.

I huff out a half laugh. "Why are *you* here?"

"You tell me, I'll tell you."

Now it's my turn to think. Maybe I should play? For a little bit, at least. Maybe I can get some answers out of him? A better picture of what he looks like. I'm not leaving, not tonight, anyway. So it would be nice to picture him as he watches. "How old are you?"

"Why?" This time his response is almost a laugh, and even though it's combined with the static, it almost sounds real.

Yes. I like his laugh. "Because you want to picture me?" he asks. The intercom cooperates a little more now. Like he adjusted it. There's still static, and his voice is still very much distorted, but I hear most of his words instead of disjointed pauses.

"Yes. You can see me but I can't see you."

"I'm here to watch you. You're here to be watched."

"Is that your turn-on?" I ask.

Another laugh. "In a way. But not the way you think."

"Then how?"

"Write me your story," he says. "And if it's a good one I'll give you one back. How's that sound?"

"Just play your game?" I ask. "Lucinda did not sanction this. I could make you stop, ya know."

"Then do that. If you want to be a quitter. You're good at quitting, right? I expected as much. Believe me, I didn't get my hopes up over *you*."

Well, that's a curious way to respond. Asshole. Psychopath. I think through my options as he remains silent, then say, "I'll write a story for you."

"Not just any story, I want to know why you're here."

"And if I give you that, then you give me what I want."

"What's that, then? What do you want?" I don't know if it's the fucking intercom or what, but his tone has gone dark, his voice deep. Maybe that's called seductive? Maybe it's called sinister? I'm not sure I can tell the difference.

I hesitate, thinking about how to put this without coming off as desperate.

"Evangeline?" he asks. "What do you want in return?"

"I want to go home," I whisper. "Walk out of here feeling safe, and free, and not have to think about"—I swallow hard—"gloves, or hoods, or sunglasses. That's what I want."

"It's not a very big ask," he says, that darkness I heard just a moment ago gone now. "You just have to do the work, that's all."

"Yeah," I say. "But that doesn't include telling you my personal story. It's mine, OK? I have very little left of my old life. That story is pretty much it."

"I offered myself up in return," he says. And even though the intercom is skipping words again, making him sound like unreal and artificial, it's the way he says it that

149

has me intrigued. "Don't you want to know what happened next?"

"Happened when?"

"After Jordan and I grew up. Do you think there's no story there? I mean"—he laughs—"come on. I'm here, watching you. Cameras all over this fucking house on Jordan's orders. There's a very fucked-up story behind all that. Aren't you a little bit curious, Evangeline? How filming women like you became our job?"

"Yes." I say it automatically, heat pooling between my legs. What did they do? And what are they doing with me now?

"Want to know who we watched?" he asks.

"Yes," I whisper.

"What they did for us on camera? Do you like to picture that, Evangeline? Do you like to watch people?" The intercom is nearly all static. So much that I can barely make out his words.

"Better than the alternative," I say softly, my focus on the empty swing out in the yard.

"OK," he says. "Get the notebook, write your story, then leave it on the counter and go outside so I can read it. If you satisfy me, I'll satisfy you."

That last part comes out crystal-clear. Like it's the only part of this conversation that matters.

"Why can't I see you?"

"Because I make the rules."

The crackling of the intercom speaker cuts off, the conversation over.

Dear Stranger. That's how I begin my entry in the notebook.

I am here because...

God. I really don't feel like telling personal things to someone I don't know. Hell, I hate telling people I know things too. Not that I know a lot of people.

You're procrastinating, Evangeline.

Yes, I am.

I am here because...

I let out a long breath and write...

I am here because I gave up a while back and... and I don't want to give up anymore. This fear, which, as you so callously pointed out, will cause me to die alone, started back when I was about ten years old. My public debut started at the age of four. I was one of those special children. Prodigy. Gifted. Old soul. Call it whatever you want, that was me back then. I don't play the violin. I am the violin. It's part of me, like an arm or a hand.

But everything has a price. My gift is no exception. I was watched constantly. Not the way one usually watches a child. It's different. And most people don't understand it. But I don't care. This fear I have comes from all the attention I was subjected to when I was young. It got to a point...

I stop and take a deep breath. I'm back in the ballroom, sitting on the couch facing the window, staring out at that stupid empty swing.

It got to a point where I couldn't have people around me. It started with my staff. Managers and agents and lawyers. I refused to see them. I imagined all the things they thought about me in my head and... and I didn't like it. Eventually, it spread to everyone, including my parents, and then one night I was in the studio recording a Christmas CD so my parents could afford to pay some of the monumental bills they racked up in my name, and I said, "I can't do it anymore."

I put my violin away and walked out in the middle of a song. They never did release that CD. The production company took my parents to court and they had to pay back the advance. Well, I had to pay it back. They were penniless and I was emancipated by the time that was settled.

And that was it. I never performed again.

But your question was, why am I here? Assuming you know that I've booked a comeback performance and that date is fast approaching, there's another reason. I'm out of money. I need to make some fast if I want to maintain my lifestyle. And since playing the violin is the only skill I have, that's my only option.

And now you owe me. So make sure your story is a good one, Mr. Stranger. Because if it's not, I'll be the one walking out on you.

CHAPTER EIGHTEEN

IXION

I watched her write. She stopped and started so many times, sighing with such frustration and angst that I assumed the story would have both those qualities to it.

It doesn't.

Aside from the revelation that she's booked a comeback performance and needs money—I wasn't aware, thank you very much, Miss Rolaine—there's absolutely nothing of note in that story.

But she's trying. So I'll try back.

Dear Evangeline,

I like your name. It's pretty and quite unusual. And I have an affinity for names like that, since I myself possess an unusual one as well.

But your story sucked.

Yes, this is me being gentle.

You tell me facts. No one cares about facts. Stories are good because of the emotion inside of them. And while you displayed a lot of external emotion as you wrote it, none of it came out on the page.

Try again.

"Fuck you! Fuck you! Fuck you!"

She screams it over and over again as she stomps around the house, spewing her anger at each and every camera.

"Now that is some display," I say.

She whirls around to find the intercom on the wall behind her in the grand foyer. "Fuck you!"

"Come on now, Evangeline," I say. "You can do better than that."

"You owe me!" she seethes. "It's your turn. And if you don't give me something back, then fuck you!"

Her voice is distorted on the intercom, but I've got the microphones turned on too, so I'm actually listening through the headphones as I speak through the intercom.

I process that little bit of good fortune. She's not getting my real voice but I get to see and hear her in perfect clarity. I get a lot more satisfaction out of that than I should. This intercom sucks, but now that I know she's into talking, I'm gonna deny her as much as possible.

After I get her where I want her.

God, if this woman really was meant to be a gift from Jordan to make up for the fucked-up shit he did in the past... well, I might have to forgive him.

Because this isn't me. This is all him. This is Jordan's deal. The games, the women, being a player. But it's always intrigued me. Not enough to join in. Fuck that. I'm just not into it. I do what I do for very different reasons than Jordan Wells.

But this is my job, right?

It's a stretch, Ix, my inner voice says. Kind of a long one. But... he did put me here. With her. And she does have this very unusual problem.

"Quitting, huh?" I ask. "Typical."

"Your game is stupid. I bet you never did anything with those cameras, did you? You and your boring friend, Jordan. You're probably a bunch of fat, worthless, bearded guys who live in their parents' basements and get off on animated porn!"

"Well." I laugh into the intercom. "Now that's more like it. Put that in your story."

"You can shove that story up your ass," she screams. "I bet this Jordan guy isn't even real. You're making all this up. Fucking liar!"

Wow. She is one angry woman when she gets going. "Would you like to meet him?" I ask.

She stops, mid-rant, finger pointing up at me via the camera, and lets out a long breath. "Who?"

"Jordan," I say. "Would you like to see him? You don't believe he's real. He's kinda hot. And this opinion is coming from another man. So, you know. Don't discount that."

"How?" she breathes.

"Trick him, of course."

She smiles, but lowers her head so I only just barely catch it. "Trick him how?"

I shrug, even though she can't see it. Because I hadn't really planned this out. "Let me figure it out and I'll get back to you. But until then, keep writing, Evangeline. I want something real from you."

"When?" she demands. "When can I see him?"

"Soon."

"Today."

155

"Not today. He's smart. He'll know. But if we do this right, believe me, we can get some really good shit out of that guy."

She has to piece that last sentence together. The intercom is fucking up my delivery. But a few seconds of thought have her huffing out a small laugh. "Do you hate him? For what he did to your family?"

I'm speechless. But only for a moment. "He didn't do anything to my *family*."

"No?" Evangeline asks. "I disagree. I think that's your story, Mr. Stranger. That's what you're hiding. He fucked your family up, didn't he?"

"Do you want to see him or not?" I ask.

"Yes."

I smile. Because she's tipping her hand right now. And I'm figuring her out far faster than she can fight it. "Then write your story and go upstairs. It's late. I'll have something for you up there to get you through the night."

"Where are you?" she asks, looking at all the cameras in the ballroom in quick succession.

"Close," I say.

She shivers. I see it. I want to feel that sensation the next time she does it. But... *Control, Ixion. That's what's needed right now.*

"Will you be waiting for me upstairs?"

"No," I whisper. "Not in person. But I'll be watching."

CHAPTER NINETEEN

EVANGELINE

What the fuck does he want from me? Some kind of emotional breakdown? I scoff. Literally scoff. Because that's never gonna happen. I might be afraid of some stupid things in this world, but I am not a coward. How dare he call me that?

He has no clue who he's dealing with. I have played for queens and kings. I have played for rock stars and opera singers. I have played for presidents and ruling heads of criminal organizations.

I am no coward.

I grab the notebook and pen from the kitchen and then settle on the window-facing couch back in the ballroom and think.

He wants a personal story about why I'm here.

Fine. Let's see what he thinks about this.

Have you ever felt like a number?
Just a number on a line, at a time
when no one else is there to see you stumble?
Anonymous child with preposterous guile
and an innocence that wants to take you under?

I scribble the words down. Furiously fast. Trying to get them out and get this over with.

Well, I have.
That was me.
Dressed up pretty.
Rolling waves of ribbon lace
and lights above me on the stage.

And then the nothing.
The great big nothing
as you walk away and try your best
to burn the joy you'll never know
like a brand on your mind
echoing like a cheer
to the fear
of being everything you will ever be
at the age of eight.

I am just a number.
That's why I'm here.

Take that, stranger. Mr. X. Whoever you are. You want something from me? You want words that have meaning? There they are.

I get up, clutching the notebook with both hands, leaving the pen behind like a murder weapon, and take it to the kitchen.

Stare at it.

Change my mind sixteen or eighty-three times.

Then feel the heat of anger well up inside me and turn my back on it.

On all of it.

I go upstairs—and not because he told me to, either. I go because this day is over now and I'm tired. So fucking exhausted, climbing up to the master bedroom on the third floor almost wipes me out.

I left the house today, I remind myself as I make it to the top and stand in front of the closed double doors. It was only the backyard, but I left. And yesterday I was hedging my bets on even staying here at all.

I count that as a win as I reach for the doorknobs and push the door in.

The nightlight is on next to the bed. Moon glow dances across the ceiling in fuzzy approximations of stars.

I let out a breath, feeling a sense of calm and relief that I haven't felt in… I have no idea. Decades, I think.

And it strikes me as so strange—that being up here in some other couple's bedroom, being virtually stalked by a stranger who has very unorthodox ideas of what his job is here, is calming.

How is that possible? How does it even make sense?

That's when I see the note on the pillow.

I walk over and pick it up. The paper is different this time. Thicker. Special. But the handwriting is the same sharp printing, and my name is the same, and the little e decoration underneath.

I look up at the nearest camera. "Why are you doing this?"

When he doesn't answer, I look around for an intercom and find it behind one of the double doors.

I press the button to speak—"Are you there?"—and startle when I hear my question echo through other rooms.

Nothing but silence in return.

So I look down at the note in my hand and wonder what's next. Should I even open it?

It's a stupid question. I almost rip it apart trying to open it.

Congratulations, it says. *Just a few more commands to follow and then you can close your eyes and dream about tomorrow.*

Look up at the camera. Take your clothes off.

Slowly. Never breaking eye contact.

Get in bed naked. There's a blindfold under the pillow. Put it on. Lie still.

If you do that I'll come say good night.

But you have to promise not to peek, Evangeline. You have to stay in the dark and let me do whatever I want.

I let out another breath, but this time nothing about me is calm. My heart is galloping inside my chest. My head is pounding with excitement as blood rushes to my brain. And my stomach flutters with some foreign feeling I might never have felt before.

Reaching for the nearest wall, I bow my head and breathe through the spell this stranger has cast.

What to do?

I'm practically panting, imagining what following this order will do to my life.

Will everything unravel?

Or is this… experience just what I need to put myself back together?

It makes no sense. I realize that. It's nothing but a request for sex.

Right?

But isn't that what people do these days? Anonymous sex?

It's right up my alley, so to speak. I mean… I'm the one who won't know anything, but as I have determined after one very expensive therapy, I'm seeking the anonymous. Or was. Anyway. I want to be seen now. But what's one more night, right?

I take a deep breath and turn around, looking straight up at the camera. "I want to see this Jordan guy. I think you made him up. It's some kind of trick."

Silence from the intercom and the camera doesn't even have the decency to blink a red light at me to let me know he's paying attention.

"I said," I say, louder this time, "I want to meet him. Not at your leisure, but tomorrow. I need to know more about this treatment plan. What he's doing. Whether or not this was all approved by Lucinda. Or if this is just your sick, twisted idea of mind games."

My answer is silence.

I exhale and walk back over to the bed, the note still clutched in my hand. Balled up and scrunched.

I read it again. And again, and again, and again until I've got it memorized. I throw it across the room and it slides under a dresser. Disappears.

His commands cycle through my thoughts, over and over again as I wrestle with the decision that must be made.

Yes. I do what he says.

No. I don't.

Yes, I stay in the game.

No. I forfeit.

Do I want to win? I don't even know what that means. "I just want to play my show," I whisper. Mostly to myself, but he probably heard me. "I just want to walk out of the house like a normal human being. I want to feel the sun on my face and laugh at people's dumb jokes. And not be afraid. And... live. That's all. Why does it seem so far away? Why does it all seem so hard?"

The telltale crackle of the intercom makes me look up, hopeful. But then... nothing. He doesn't reply. Just leaves me to figure it out on my own.

I try to rationalize what's happening. It's treatment. All this, to the best of my knowledge, has been prescribed by my doctor. A woman who has reminded me over and over and over that she's some know-it-all professional in the field of weird psychological phobias.

It's a lie. Not her, or her credentials. The rationalization that's going on here. I cannot even imagine that she knows what's happening inside this house. And the really disturbing thing is... I'm rationalizing not calling her with the fact that I broke my phone.

I mean come on, Evangeline! You are sick! Because a normal person would walk out the door and keep going until she got home, whatever that took, and call up her therapist and demand to know just what the fuck is going on!

Sure. I have this fear of being watched. But it's night now. I've already come up with an escape plan. All I'd have to do is implement it. Just leave, walk until I find a phone at a local bar or an all-night grocery store, call my building concierge, and end this madness immediately.

That might even cure me, for fuck's sake. I mean... really. It's a big, huge, monumental step that requires a whole lot of participation.

The intercom crackles again. Another tease, because that's all it does.

He's reminding me that he's here. As if I'd forget that little detail.

Why can't I make a decision?

Because I want to say yes even though I know I should say no.

One. Look up at the camera.

I do. I look at all of them. Holding each in my gaze for several seconds before going to the next.

Two. Take off your clothes. Slowly. Never breaking eye contact.

My hand goes to the hem of the cashmere white sweater. The sweater he told me to put on this morning. I hesitate, my heart racing with a staccato beat that makes me long for the past. For the sad nights alone where no one expected anything of me.

With much reluctance, I admit I'm still here because of the possibility of sex with a complete stranger who gets to watch me. Like a voyeur. And he's probably jacking off right now. His hand is slowly pumping his cock, his eyes on me—only me—as I sort through the kind of person I am.

And then I just do it. I just do it. Because I'm her. That person who stays in this kind of situation because she's turned on by it. Because she's sick in more ways than one. And she doesn't even care.

Why live anymore? Why live if you're just gonna deny yourself everything? *Everything.* The music, the people, the pleasures.

There is no point to life if that's all there is.

Both hands reach for my hem and the sweater comes up. I have my eyes trained on the camera directly in front of me. I only break contact for a moment when the sweater goes over my head, but my eyes return as I toss it to the floor.

I exhale as I stand up, my fingers reaching for the button on my gray slacks, and a moment later, down they fall. Pooling in a puddle of fabric at my feet. I kick off my shoes and step out. Stand there for his inspection. Looking at the faceless, blank lens like I might find answers in there.

The intercom crackles, as if to say, *Keep going.*

So I do. And I do it all slowly, just like he asked. Fingertips on the strap of my bra as I slide it over my shoulder. Then the other side, until the straps are loose on my upper arms and my breasts are heavy in the black lace, begging to be released.

I want to close my eyes now. Pretend I'm in the darkness and not illuminated by the glow of the child's moon light on the bedside table. I reach behind for the clasp and then they are free. The lace drops to the floor on top of my pants, next to my sweater. My nipples are peaking rigid in the coolness, my heart thumping now. Not sharp staccato, but the hard banging of a percussionist hitting a bass drum.

I swallow hard as my fingertips find the edge of lace on my black panties and ease them over my hips.

The spot between my legs—the one that's been neglected for so long—throbs. So much faster than my heart. A deep-seated longing that wants what it wants so badly, I've gone far, far past the point of no return.

I bend down, step out, never taking my gaze off his black stare from the lens, and let him look.

"Like this?" I ask, my body so ready for more, I feel a climax coming even though no one is touching me. Even though I'm not even touching myself.

It's the watching that turns me on.

My own personal voyeur.

His own personal entertainment.

We're both pretty sick.

I breathe deeply. Panting to keep my body from doing the unthinkable. I cannot come like this. I cannot, I cannot...

The intercom crackles once more, reminding me there's more to do if I want my reward.

So I turn towards the bed, placing my hands and knees on the soft, down comforter, and crawl to the headboard. One hand searches under the pillow, finds a slip of silk, and pulls it out.

A man's necktie. Black.

My blindfold.

I place it over my eyes, tying it tightly in the back, and feel an immediate relief.

I can't see anything now.

I can pretend now.

The song of birds pipes through some speaker. Not the intercom, because there's no crackle. The music is soft, and sweet, and reminds me of warm sunny days as I lie back on the bed, my legs straight. My arms at my side. And I wait.

Because he's coming now and this is the signal that I've given him permission to do whatever he wants.

Only moments later I hear footsteps coming up the stairs just outside the open doors.

I take several shallow breaths, trying to calm myself down, but it doesn't work. My heart is playing its own song now. A combination of quick and hard. A symphony of dark and light. Here and there. Quick, then slow, then quick, quick, quick as he enters the room and lets out a breath that I imagine is... satisfaction.

"What—"

"Shhhh," he corrects me.

The mattress dips with his weight. His leg, or hip, or back touches my bare leg, sending an uncontrollable shiver up my whole body. My nipples, already peaked and ready, find another level of arousal when his fingertips brush lightly across one.

I respond with a pool of hot wetness between my legs and I know it's impossible, but I feel that feeling again. The one where I think I might come. Like I'm so close and if—

"Shhhh," he says again, his gentle caress turning into a firm squeeze of my breast to pull me back from the edge.

I'm cold, but I don't care. So cold I begin to shiver. But he continues with the tease, his fingertips brushing back and forth across my nipple, almost flicking it, but not quite. Not hard, so soft. Too soft. So that the feeling begins to build again and I have to gulp air.

He takes one of my hands, his body turning on the bed so he can continue what he's doing to my breast with his other hand, and he places it between his legs. Pressing my hand up against his jeans so I can feel his hard cock. He makes me rub him. Slowly, the way he's caressing me. Back and forth as his dick grows with my insatiable desire.

His breathing is heavy now too. And I want to scream at him. Tell him to do more. Touch me everywhere. Be fast. Fuck me hard and—

"Shhhh," he says, but this time it's got an edge to it. Like he's driving himself as wild as he's driving me.

He presses my hand into his cock and I can't stand it anymore. I squeeze him through the soft fabric of his jeans. He moans and I swear, I will just come all on my own if he—

His fingertips stop the tease at my nipple and trace a light, soft trail down to my ribs. I suck in air and scissor my legs, pressing the folds of my pussy together, searching for the sweet spot that will put me out of my misery. But his other hand is there, hard, as he pushes down on my thigh, telling me in no uncertain terms that I need to be still.

Lie still, was his last command.

And I want to obey right now. Because if he gets up and walks out—

His hand presses on my inner thigh, spreading me open.

God, yes. This is what I want. *Put your mouth there*, I want to scream. *Put your fingers inside me. Lick me until I explode.*

He leans down, his hot breath skimming across the skin of my stomach, and he kisses my belly.

Breathing is difficult for both of us now.

My chest is heaving. Up and down as I take air in and out.

I squeeze his cock as my other hand slips over my thigh and right between my legs. It bumps into his hand and I grab for it, greedily, and place him where he needs to be.

His fingers slide inside, instantly becoming slick and wet. I make him pump, in and out, and then he slips another one inside me. Then another, stretching my pussy open as he presses his face into my stomach, licking his way down until his mouth clamps around my clit and sucks.

I let go of his hand and grab his hair, pushing him into me. My hips buck up and down with the rhythm of his movements like I'm fucking him.

His hips respond too as I clutch his cock hard, massaging him through his jeans.

167

And then, before either of us can stop it, we grunt, and moan, and pant through the release. I come all over his fingers. He comes in his pants, the hot wet evidence leaking through the fabric as I continue to hold on to him.

I sigh, breathing hard, my legs closing on his hand and head involuntarily as the relief washes through my body in shuddering waves.

He rolls to the side, his whole body on the bed with me, but in some unknown position that I have to imagine in my mind.

I turn my body automatically into his. He kisses me on the soft spot right above my clit, then moves up my body, his legs straddling mine, his arms on either side of my head as he climbs on top of me.

God, I want him. All of him. I'm ready to go again. And his dick is still hard enough for me to feel the bulge as he rubs his hips back and forth across mine.

He lowers his head, kissing my neck, then my ear, then my cheek, and my nose, and finally my lips.

"Tomorrow," he says, barely a whisper. "I'm gonna let you see Jordan. But only if you do as I say."

"Can I ask him—"

"No," he says, cutting me off. "You can watch *him*, Evangeline. The way I watch *you*. But that's it. For now."

He gets up, leaving my spent body trembling but still wanting more. And a moment later I know I'm alone again, because I'm cold.

CHAPTER TWENTY

IXION

I make my way down three stories of stairs, ignoring the call of Galaga and Pac-Man, enter the code to get into the control room, push through, and close it behind me, not slamming, of course.

Mustn't fuck things up that bad.

I flop down in the chair in front of the screen and immediately my fingers are on the keyboard, pulling up the footage of what just happened on the far left screen, while simultaneously zooming in on the center screen and adjusting the night vision setting so I can see her lying in bed.

She still hasn't moved.

It didn't take me long to get down here, but a couple minutes at least.

Why is she still lying there?

I zoom in further, until the resolution can't resolve and her face is a mess of pixels that make no sense.

Is she crying? I won't be able to go through with it if she's crying.

She still has the makeshift blindfold on, so I can't really tell. I scan her cheeks for almost a minute, just waiting for something to happen.

But she stays still.

Do I need to tell her she can move?

I'm just about to reach for the intercom when she sits up and pulls the tie down her face, so it's around her neck. I zoom out so she's in perfect focus again, and we stare at each other.

Her looking at me through the black lens of the camera mounted on the fireplace mantel at the foot of her bed. Me looking at her through the filter of green night vision.

"Who are you?" I ask.

"I know who you are," she says back. Even though I didn't say that into the intercom.

It sends a chill along the nape of my neck that I can't seem to shake.

She swings her feet over the side of the bed, her naked body highlighted in bright green instead of the creamy white she is in real life. She stands, baring her sexy physique to the voyeur on the other end of the lens, and whispers something so low, I can't make it out.

And she reaches over to the moon nightlight, finds the manual switch on the cord, and turns out the lights.

I watch her—I can still see her in the night vision, and it's my job to watch her, anyway—as she pulls the covers back on the bed, gets in, and hides.

I lean back in my chair and let out a long breath.

It's a dangerous game I'm playing. There are a lot of things at stake. But I just don't seem to care. Jordan is the perfect addition to the chessboard. A play for checkmate if ever there was one.

I spend the next thirty minutes rewinding the footage of what we just did up in her bedroom.

I obsess over every breath she takes. Tormented by her small whimpers and moans as I eat her pussy. Haunted by her need. Consumed with the idea of what will come next.

It's only after I start to get hard again that I realize I'm still wearing come-stained jeans.

That shakes me out of it, but only long enough to wander over to the pile of clothes I stacked in the corner the second day I was here and pull on some cut-off sweats.

I take off my shirt, sit back in my chair, and rewind. Again, and again, and again. My hand inside my sweats, on my cock, pumping up and down as I think about how all this is gonna end.

Not caring.

There's so many more plays to make before we get to the end, it's not even *time* to care.

I come into my hand, gushing more than should be possible after emptying myself earlier, then get up, wipe myself off with the t-shirt I just took off, and settle back into my chair to watch her.

She wants to watch too.

I'm feeling generous, I guess. Because I'm gonna give her that gift.

When he asks me why, I'll tell him I didn't plan it. It's the truth. I didn't come here and accept this job to fuck with Jordan. It was just an opportunity, I'll say. Just another move in the game.

Besides, Evangeline's into it. She obviously gets off on being watched and there was no way to miss the breathless excitement when I offered her Jordan up as a potential target. And the way I see it, what better way to cure her, right? Let her switch places for once. Be the watcher instead of the watched.

171

When I'm sure she's asleep and there's nothing more to be seen tonight, I reach for my phone, find Jordan's contact, and press his number.

"Yeah," he says, after the first ring.

"What do you think of this girl?" I ask.

"In what way?" he asks. He sounds distracted—or maybe annoyed—and I can hear him shuffling papers around, like he's still at the office or maybe working from home.

"Do you think she's pretty?"

"I've only seen pictures of her, and none of them were very telling. So"—I can practically hear him shrug—"fuck if I know. Fuck if I care, either. And neither should you. I'm not paying you to care if she's pretty."

"You know, you're pretty cocky for a guy who holds no cards."

"You're here, aren't you?"

Yeah, I think to myself. *I'm here all right.*

"What happened?" he asks.

"What do you mean?"

"Obviously you're calling, asking what I think of this girl, for a reason. So what happened?"

"Nothing," I say, thankful that didn't come out defensive. "She's just... wound up tight, ya know."

"Bottled the fuck up," Jordan says. "Which is why we're here. Push her to face her fear. I'm surprised she stayed, actually."

"Why?"

"Because Lucinda told me she's been locked away in her apartment for like ten years."

"Lucinda," I say. "That's the doctor. Evangeline's mentioned her."

Now it's not a shrug I detect. It's a stiffening. "Tell me you did not talk to her, Ixion. I will be so fucking pissed off—"

"Relax," I say, my eyes darting to the screen in front of me just in time to see her turn over in bed and stick her foot out from under the covers. She must be hot. "She was talking to the cameras."

"Crazy bitch," he says. And not in a joking way, either.

"Why the hell are you so antagonistic about her? Is there something I'm missing?"

"Like I said," Jordan explains. "She's weird. And she's not really my client. I'm just doing a favor for Lucinda."

"Your client?" I ask. "What's that mean? You do this kind of thing often?"

He laughs. "Need-to-know basis, Ixion. Just do your job."

"Are the others all being watched?" I ask. And then I quickly add, "Just asking in case you need me again."

"No one but Evangeline Rolaine has this stupid phobia. Most of them are just your run-of-the-mill sexually repressed thirty-somethings."

"Hmm," I say. "So why me, Jordan? Why, after all these years, do you suddenly care?"

He's silent for a few moments. Then he clears his throat and says, "You know I never meant—"

"Yeah." I cut him off. "Sure. I know."

"Don't be a dick. I got you out of jail. She never pressed charges."

No. She never did that. She did something much worse. "We're not even," I say back. "Not even close. And I never asked you for that favor."

"I didn't mean to hurt her," Jordan whispers back.

173

"What about me?"

"Dude..." He exhales, lets the silence stretch again. "I chose *you*."

"Did you?" I laugh, my words hoarse and low.

"You know I did. She didn't really get hurt, ya know. She never loved you like that."

If he was here right now I'd knock his fucking teeth out for that comment. He has no idea what I lost when she left.

"I made a mistake, OK?" Jordan says. "Everyone makes mistakes. But I fixed it as best I could. I never did it again."

"That's funny," I counter. "You're still playing games with people."

"It's not what you think, Ixion. Why do you always assume the worst of me?"

"Because dude, that's all you show me."

"Really?" he asks. And then he huffs out a breath of air that says he finds my remark incredible. "You never ask for anything, Ix. If you did I'd give it to you. You know that."

"I don't ask because I don't need anything."

"Well, then I guess it's all gonna work out then, right?"

"Yeah," I say, eyeing Evangeline as she tucks that foot back under the covers. She must be cold. "I guess it will."

"We good?" he asks.

I say nothing. Because... good? Yeah, right. There's no way we're ever gonna be good again.

"Why did you even fucking take the job then?" Jordan snaps. "I mean, you could've said no."

I shake my head and sigh. "You just don't get it, do you?"

"Whatever," he says. "Later."

I press end. But the call drops with three beeps, not silence. Which tells me he hung up before I did.

"Whatever, indeed," I say back to the dark room.

Tomorrow is a new day. And Mr. Wells had better rest up for it. Because he's about to become a major player in my game. He just doesn't know it yet.

CHAPTER TWENTY-ONE

EVANGELINE

Sleep was fitful and not the least bit restful. Usually when this happens it's because I'm riddled with anxiety and can't shake it off. My heart beats fast all night, even though I'm doing nothing but lying still in a bed. My whole body buzzes with some kind of pent-up charge that has nowhere to go. And my mind races with thoughts of dying. I make plans about calling 911 to ask for help, then revise and make plans to just let myself die alone.

Thinking about it now—since that's not what kept me up last night—it feels very sad.

My heart wasn't beating fast last night. My body wasn't tingling with fear that I was dying.

I was calm to the point of lethargy. Satisfied. Which makes me huff out a laugh under the covers. I want his cock inside me.

Maybe tonight? Maybe he'll come to me again?

I try to think of what made him offer this... this *bonus* in the first place.

Compliance, I decide. He wanted a story about me. Why I was here. And he wanted it to be personal. He liked my poem. He likes honest emotion, maybe. I gave him something real and he rewarded me.

Maybe I'll keep doing that?

I swing my legs out of bed, eager to go downstairs to see if there's another note waiting. If he's got more demands. More ways in which I can please him.

And when I get to the kitchen I can't stop the smile even though I want to. My heart races as I walk over to the counter and pick up the notebook I was writing in yesterday.

Evangeline,

You want to know what I look like?
I'm short. Overweight. Balding and with acne scars. Not to mention a patch over one eye. That's why they call me X.

I laugh. Because I felt his body last night. He's not bald, he's not overweight, and he's not short. I might not know all the other details that go with those facts, but I don't need to. I'm not even sure I want to.

Anyway, I made a deal with you. You give me a story, I give you one back. So here goes.
The last time I saw Augustine we were in a large conference room, sitting in executive wingback leather chairs, glaring at each other from opposite sides of the table, silent, as our lawyers argued the finer points of splitting assets and money.
She had tears streaming down her face.
We were friends long before we were lovers, but the heavy cloud of anger and sadness hanging over that room was about as far from friendship two people can get.
I don't blame her for any of it. She was a hundred percent innocent. She had no idea what really happened that night.

And she'll never really know all of it because that whole deal was a damned-if-you-do, damned-if-you-don't kind of affair. Either way, I lose. So... whatever. Live and learn, I guess.

Now get dressed. You're leaving the house today. Wear whatever you want. Cover up as much as you need to. But be ready at eleven thirty. I'll have instructions waiting for you.

X

Well.

That was not what I expected.

Augustine? Who the hell is Augustine? His wife? Did they get a divorce? Sure sounds like it. But there's a lot more to this story than he just told, that's for sure. What happened to her? He did something, obviously. And what's this got to do with Jordan and their little camera game?

"Hurry up and get ready." The crackle of the intercom mixes with his words and makes me jump. "You're going out."

Out. Which I can only presume means... not the backyard. I look up at the nearest camera and say, "Isn't it a little soon for that? I mean I've only been here two days. I don't think—"

The intercom crackles with static. I wait for his voice. Hold my breath for several seconds. But it just goes dead again.

"I can only assume," I say, "that was you telling me 'too bad.'"

I stare down at his familiar handwriting on the note.

So... does this mean I will indeed meet the infamous Jordan today? Is that his plan? Will X send me somewhere so I can... *watch him?*

179

Am I a voyeur too?

Yes. I think I am. Because… because I'm going to get ready and do this. I'm going out.

I look down to hide my smile, because it sends a thrill up my spine. I don't even know why. I don't understand any of this. Nothing I'm doing at this house makes any sense at all. But the whole watching part. It's exhilarating for some reason.

Maybe it's because I've never had a chance to be the watcher. I was always the watched. I love standing at my window at home. Looking down on the people used to make me feel left out and sad, so I didn't stay there long. But it was interesting in a way I never realized. I was always so consumed with what I was missing, never understanding that watching had something to offer as well.

And now?

I'm being watched. Constantly. With no way out unless I give up and leave. The thought of missing my comeback performance has been—so far—enough to keep me here. But it's not going to be enough. Switching places though… watching might be enough to make me see this through.

If I give my watcher what he wants—total access to me, twenty-four seven—he'll give me what I want. I didn't realize it until he made his offer, but does that matter? What I'm going to do today—spy on someone, unaware of my watching eyes—is like a gift. And there might be another reward at the end of my day. Like last night.

"Thank you," I murmur, taking the note with me as I head back upstairs. "I think this might be just what I need."

I shower, dress in black slacks, a white shirt, and a black blazer. And then I bundle up in my coat, gloves, scarf, hat, and sunglasses. It's a chilly twenty-three degrees today, cold enough to warrant covering up all the exposed parts of my body. But it's not snowing. So still, I struggle with the idea of leaving the house. My instructions waiting downstairs are the only reason I've decided to go through with this.

There's a note on the counter when I enter the kitchen at exactly eleven thirty. There's a pamphlet as well.

I open the note and hold my breath as I read.

Evangeline,

The Denver Botanic Gardens is directly next door. I've left you a map to help find your way. Find the Tropical Conservatory. Grab a coffee at the cafe as you pass by. Inside the tropical greenhouse there's a treehouse. Go to the top and look down until you see a bench with a bright orange bush blooming next to it. Wait there. Jordan takes his Sunday coffee in that spot every weekend. Do not approach him, talk to him, or get his attention in any way.

Just watch.

I'll be watching you watch him.

And if you do everything the way I told you, I'll leave the blindfold under your pillow again.

X

I let out the breath I was holding and reach for the map. There's an X on it, indicating the house I'm in now. Apparently, this is some historic district and all the houses around me are equally as impressive as this one. X has actually drawn a dotted line, telling me exactly where to go.

I'm hot, too bundled up to be inside for long, so I go for the front door before I can think too hard about what I'm going to do.

Once outside, the cold feels good. It's overcast and there's a sharp wind that burns the exposed parts of my cheeks just below my sunglasses. But when I walk out the front gate and look at the map, then look left, I realize I am living next door to the Denver Botanic Gardens.

It's mere steps away. An old, weathered, dark concrete path leads into a canopy of bare trees that sway with the wind and bring me out into—I look down at my pamphlet—the Ellipse, an ornamental garden that is mostly covered in a thin layer of snow. But a bright tower of yellow glass and many smaller orange glass orbs decorate the centerpiece.

Which kinda blows me away, because I live next door and I never even knew this place was here. Granted, it's only been two days, but most people—*normal* people— would take notice of where they are in the fucking city.

And I missed it.

But I miss almost everything, don't I?

I continue along the pre-marked route, which is a straight pathway that leads to the greenhouses, but stop about halfway to gape at the pyramid building off to my left.

Once again I'm stuck by my ignorance. That such a beautiful building is so close—If I ever bothered to look out the window, I could probably see it from the upstairs master bedroom, and I never knew.

It makes me wonder how many other things I've missed out on because I was too afraid to step out my front door? Or look out a goddamned window?

The wind picks up and reminds me that I'm outside in the dead of winter, so I continue along the path at a brisk pace, heading towards the greenhouse.

I stop at the cafe as instructed and force myself to stand in line for a coffee. I'm sweating and not because it's too warm in here. There's too many people coming and going for the cafe to be anything other than tepid in temperature.

The people are the problem. It's not enough to realize what I'm missing by letting my fear dictate my life. My body responds the way it always does. With racing heart, shortness of breath, and the panic inside me building and building—

"Can I help you?" a young woman asks me when the person in front of me in line vacates her counter spot.

I don't even know what to order. I haven't been inside a cafe in… well, ever. Not as an adult. Not ordering coffee. I drink it at home, but I make it in one of those automatic machines by the cup.

"Ma'am?" the woman asks, lifting her eyebrows at my silence.

"Um…err…" I hate myself for stammering like an idiot. "Just a coffee," I say.

"Size?" she asks.

"Small," I offer.

"We don't have small," she says. "We have medium, large, and extra-large."

"Well, that's dumb," I say without thinking.

"So stupid, right?" she says, half laughing in a dry, ironic tone. "I mean, just call it a small." She rolls her eyes and I find myself smiling. "So small medium it is. What's your name?"

"My name?" I ask.

She picks up a cup and a black marker and says. "So I can put your name on your cup. I'm only allowed to take orders. Those geniuses back there fill up the cups." And then she snickers at her joke as she side-eyes her co-workers.

"Angela," I say, giving the name I use for Dan at Mott's.

"OK, Angela. Pick it up over there in like two seconds." She nods her head to the end of the counter and says, "Can I help you?" to the next customer.

I move aside quickly, baffled at the entire interaction.

My heart is galloping inside my chest. Which is ridiculous. She was a perfectly nice woman. Harmless in every way. And she was helpful and didn't make me feel stupid for not understanding how things work in the Botanic Gardens Cafe.

It's only then that I realize I had an actual conversation with a stranger. And I didn't *die*.

I force down a small chuckle at my own ridiculousness, just as a large man with a beard yells, "Angela!"

He doesn't even wait for me to come take my coffee. Just leaves it there on the counter and goes back to his work.

I slip in between a chatting couple, bumping them to reach my coffee, then almost panic again when the man looks at me with a disapproving glare.

Coffee in hand, I duck out quick and go back into the wind and the cold.

I like it better.

But the greenhouse is attached to the cafe. And the entrance I'm supposed to use, according to X, is the first one I come to.

I exhale, wondering if I'm up for this. I mean, that back there was good, but ended badly. And who knows how many people are inside the greenhouse? Probably a ton because it's winter.

I should've thought this through a little better before I agreed.

But then X's words are in my mind.

If you do everything the way I told you, I'll reward you tonight.

What does that mean? He'll touch me again?

Wetness pools between my legs at the thought.

What if he fucks me?

What if he doesn't? is my automatic counter-answer.

Which is enough to get my feet moving again. I head for the door, reaching for the handle, when it pops open and a family comes rushing out. Small children brush past me as a father follows, yelling at his kids, while his wife is left to maneuver the stroller through the already shutting door, alone.

I stand there, unable to move, as she manages to get her stroller out, glaring at me for not helping her at the same time.

I swallow hard, duck my head, and slip inside. Embarrassed, ashamed, and wishing I'd never come here at all.

"You're being stupid, Evangeline," I mutter to myself. She was obviously overwhelmed and only wanted a little help. And I stood there like an idiot and just watched. She probably thinks I'm a horrible person.

I look over my shoulder, wondering if I should apologize, but there's a crowd of people coming in behind me and I just need to get away.

Blindly rushing forward, I escape them only to encounter another crowd. Jesus. It's the middle of the fucking winter. Can't these people find some other public attraction to frequent?

Treehouse, Evangeline. I take deep breaths as I look up. The ceiling is glass—of course, since it's a greenhouse. But there are trees in here. It reminds me of the jungles in Thailand. I played violin at a birthday party for the youngest royal princess. And later she—middle-aged at the time, so not quite the image of a princess one might conjure up—took me into the royal gardens for a chat about tigers. I was obsessed with tigers after a trip to India when I was seven.

Nostalgia washes over me with the memories. I used to be so... outgoing. Social. Normal. What happened to me?

Lucinda has asked me this question many times since I made that first phone call asking for help. But I never had an answer. It was just... everything, I guess. I just got fed up. That's the answer I give Lucinda every time she asks. That Thai princess was part of it, probably. Playing at her party changed me somehow. It wasn't enough to manifest at the time. But it accumulated over the years. Slowly, my fame, my talent, and my young age poisoned me. Like a dripping faucet that drives you crazy.

I went crazy.

I've come to terms with it. And I didn't realize it at the time. Even a few months ago, crazy was a place other people went.

The treehouse is hard to miss. It's a large structure looming overhead, parts of it peeking out through palm fronds. And there must be a million ways to get up there, because the steps I ascend are almost empty.

Once at the top I walk along the railing, looking down, searching for the bench next to a large orange bush blooming with flowers.

How does this Jordan guy know his bench will be empty? There's so many people here. And so far, every bench I've seen was filled with families doing family things or old people doing old-people things.

And then… I hold my breath.

There he is. Sitting on the bench next to the flowering orange bush, one foot propped up on one knee, wearing a dark suit. Winter coat splayed out behind his shoulders like he shrugged it off as he sat down. His coffee must be empty—am I late? Did I take too long?—because it's sitting on the ground next to him.

There's a few children playing nearby, but he ignores them as he stares at the flora around him. Like he has a deep appreciation for plants.

I chuckle at that, which makes him look up and meet my gaze.

Shit.

I avert my eyes, but not before I get a good look at his. Blue. Piercing blue. The kind of blue that stabs you in the gut with their beauty.

I wait a few moments before looking down again, and when I do, he's walking down a path, deeper into the gardens.

I rush along the railing, trying to follow him. One look? *No.* One look is not enough to make up for all the panic that came with this trip.

I come to a set of stairs just as he disappears from view. I want to jump down those stairs, but there's people in the way, and I'm too afraid to push past, so by the time I get to the bottom and find the path he went down, he's gone.

No!

This is not how my first watching experience is gonna end. It doesn't even count!

I look around, wondering if X is watching me, wondering if I should go home now.

That thought is so depressing, I can't even consider it. So I just... stay. I walk slowly along the many pathways, my eyes desperate to find this Jordan man again. Oblivious to the bustling people around me. Tuning out the too-loud children with pent-up winter energy. Forgetting myself and concentrating only on the man who got away.

He was striking.

So handsome... my heart actually aches at the missed opportunity.

CHAPTER TWENTY-TWO

IXION

Evangeline returns home a little after two. Which surprises me. I didn't figure she'd stay so long. In fact, I counted on her bolting out of there at her first opportunity.

This twist intrigues me.

Is she so enamored with Jordan Wells that she can put aside her ridiculous phobia and face her fears?

Why?

Was it the suit? Does she like powerful men in suits? Men with money? Driven men who grab the world by the balls and never let go? Liars? Cheaters? Sick fucks who watch people?

I ponder that and wonder how people see me when I'm just being me.

Do they see the biker with leathers on the road going nowhere? Do they see the guy in the dead-end bar in the middle of BFE buying whole bottles instead of shots? Do they see the exiled fuckup who disappointed everyone and never got his second chance because...

What do they see?

I don't think I want to know the answer to that question.

I watch Evangeline on the screen as she fumbles with her outer clothes, tearing them off and throwing them onto random pieces of furniture as she makes her way to the kitchen where the notebook's waiting for her.

"No," she says, looking directly into the camera, her eyes wide, her voice shrill, and her... *anger* spilling out like water rushing from a dam that's overfull and ready to burst. "That wasn't even watching!" she screams, so loud I draw back from the monitor, surprised. "He left after five seconds! *No!*"

She picks up an empty vase on the kitchen counter and throws it at the wall, shattering the glass into a million shards.

I get up, ready to go out there and ask her just what the fuck she's doing. But I take a deep breath instead, push the button on the intercom, and say, "Clean it up."

"Fuck you!" she yells, opening a cupboard, grabbing a coffee mug, and throwing it at the same wall that is now marred with the impact of two things.

"Stop it!" I growl into the intercom. "What the fuck is wrong with you?"

She's wild. Her eyes dart to a platter propped up against the backsplash, and two quick steps later she's got it above her head with every intention of throwing it down onto the floor.

"Evangeline!" I yell. "If you do not stop this tantrum, I'll—"

"You'll what?" she seethes, looking up at a camera mounted in the corner of the kitchen. She whirls around, finds the camera mounted on the breakfast nook fireplace mantle, walks towards it, and knocks it off with a wild swing of the platter.

One of my monitors turns to fuzzy, white snow.

190

I see red. I rage with anger at her gall. "What the fuck?"

"Come out here," she demands. "Come out here and stop me!"

"What the hell is your problem?"

"You've got five seconds."

"Evangeline—"

"One."

"Put that—"

"Two."

"Plate—"

"Three."

"Down!"

"Four." She walks quickly to the next camera and swings, not even bothering to finish the count.

Another screen turns to static and snow. Then another. And another. She takes out every camera in the kitchen and moves to the living room.

Her rage builds, her eyes wild, her hair a mess, falling across her face as she swings, and swings, and swings.

I just sit in my chair and watch her destroy at least ten thousand dollars' worth of equipment.

Jordan is gonna be pissed.

She takes out every camera she can find. Which leaves me with two on the main floor, the one in the grand foyer chandelier—she can't find a ladder—and the one in the ballroom chandelier. Thank fuck. Because those chandeliers are probably worth twenty grand each.

When she realizes she's done all the damage she can, she stops and looks up the stairs. "Don't do it, bitch," I mutter to myself. "Don't you fucking dare."

She looks up at the foyer camera and smiles.

I lean forward in my chair, press the intercom button, and yell, "Stop!"

"Fuck you! You promised me! You promised! And he left after five seconds!"

She's nuts. Certifiably nuts.

"You're acting like a goddamned child!" I yell.

"I *am* a goddamned child!" She screams it. Top of her fucking lungs, *screams it*.

But her words stop both of us.

What?

She stands there, looking up at me looking down at her through the black mirror of the lens. Her chest heaving with her rapid, ragged breathing. Platter still clutched in her hands. Mouth frowning so severely, it turns her normally pretty face into something very ugly.

She starts to cry. Slumps down onto the floor, dropping the platter, which cracks into three or four large, anticlimactic chunks, and presses her face to the hard wood floor and sobs.

What the fuck just happened?

I sit back in my chair and wait. My view sucks. I have no angles to choose from. I can't see shit aside from this unsatisfying top view of her body, jerking with the end of her manic episode.

I let out a long breath, feeling exhausted along with her.

Now what? Should I call Jordan and tell him shit's going off the rails? Will they come take her away?

I chew on my lip as I think it through. Trying out all my options.

If I call Jordan… somehow, some way, what we did today is gonna come out and he's gonna be pissed. Not to mention what happened last night.

If I do nothing, she'll probably sleep on the foyer floor.

It occurs to me then—this is probably the inevitable conclusion to her completely overwhelming day.

Which means it's all my fault.

I press the intercom button and say, in the softest, most reasonable voice I can muster up through the crackle and the static, "Go upstairs and take a long bath, Evangeline."

She mumbles something that might be, "Fuck you," but I'm not really sure.

"I need to clean up."

"I want to go home," she says. And this time I hear very clearly.

"You can't," I say.

This makes her look up at the chandelier. "I can do anything I want! I'm the fucking whole reason you're here!"

"No," I say back. "I'm here because I want to be here. I could just as easily want to be somewhere else."

"You're no one!" she yells, tears running down her cheeks. "You're nothing. I'm the one who counts!"

"Are you even listening to yourself?" I ask her. "You really are a goddamned child. Sure as hell acting like one."

"Fuck you!"

"No, *fuck you!*" I yell back. "You spoiled little bitch. You just destroyed about fifteen grand in cameras! Do you have the money to pay for that? Because they're definitely gonna bill you for that stupid tantrum you just threw."

"I don't care. Let them take everything. I don't even care anymore." She gets up on her hands and knees, sways for a few seconds, like she might pass out, and then gets a foot underneath her and stands.

She raises her head to look at the camera. Her tears have left clean streaks through the filth covering her cheeks.

Silence.

"Go upstairs. Take a bath. And go to bed."

"And then what?" she asks. "Will you call them? Tell them what I did? Leave..." She whimpers out the word and tries again. "Will you leave me here alone?"

God. She is one fucked-up person inside that head.

"Do what I say, Evangeline. You're out of control, out of line, and out of excuses. You're a grown woman and you just threw a tantrum because some guy you don't even know didn't let you stalk him today."

Her breath hitches. Not remnants of her crying, but brand-new sobs. "It's just... that was the first time I've been out during the day in a long time." She sniffs loudly. "The first time I've been around people and didn't want to die. The first time I *wanted* to be out with people, X. I didn't want it to end so soon."

I exhale, not sure how to handle that part. I'm not a fucking therapist. I'm not even supposed to be talking to her, let alone setting her up on little excursions to fulfill some latent voyeuristic fetish she never knew she had.

"Well, you handled it badly," I say. "I don't even know what to think right now. Do I call this off? Have them come take you out?"

"No," she says. "No. Please. Don't do that. I'll fix the cameras."

I laugh. "Just go to bed."

"I don't want to be alone. You're all I have now."

Jesus Christ. What the fuck have I done?

"Please," she begs again. "Please don't call anyone. Please don't tell them."

Sighing, and not really sure where to go next, I press the intercom one more time. "Then do what I say."

Her body hitches from the sobs again. But she nods and begins walking up the stairs in silence.

I lean forward, panning the camera, then switching to the undamaged ones upstairs, keeping track of her as she reaches the top, turns left, and heads down the hallway. I wait for her in the bedroom, all five monitors in front of me showing the bedroom door open. Her crying is just soft whimpers now. She doesn't take a bath, she falls forward on the bed, hugs the pillow to her face, and cries harder.

I sink back in my chair and watch. Wait for her to exhaust herself and sleep. But thirty minutes later she's still crying and I'm torn between speaking to her again—to try to smooth things over—and letting her get it out.

Obviously that tantrum had some meaning behind it.

I am a goddamned child! she'd screamed. Some pent-up thing from when she was little, I guess. Pressure to perform, maybe? Lack of friends? I mean, her life has been pretty out of the ordinary. Special, for sure.

And terrifying too.

"What happened to you?" I ask the screen.

She turns onto her side and I zoom in, training the camera on her face. Her eyes are bloodshot and squinting, like it physically hurts her to keep them open. But still, she stares up at the chandelier camera, defying my last command to the very end.

Almost an hour later, with nothing more from her but soft sobs, she loses her battle. Turning onto her back, arms falling open like dead weight, lips slightly parted with her heavy breathing. She sleeps.

195

I leave the control room and go upstairs to see the damage first-hand. It's a mess. Motherfucking mess.

Quietly, I clean up the glass first, then start picking up camera pieces. Some of them actually can be repaired by splicing the wires she tore out back together. Others—the ones with cracked lenses—are trash. And that's exactly where they go.

I end up with three additional fully functioning cameras, one that only has video, but no sound, and one that only has sound, but no video.

I'll take it. Not like I have a choice. I can't exactly go buy new ones and install them without her seeing me.

But I have no eyes in the kitchen at all. Which will not do. So I take one from the hallway and remount it in the corner so I'll have a view of the island counter where tomorrow, the notebook will be waiting for her.

In fact, that jolts my memory and I grab the notebook from my control room and read her poem again.

Have you ever felt like a number?
Just a number on a line, at a time
when no one else is there to see you stumble?
Anonymous child with preposterous guile
and an innocence that wants to take you under?

Well, I have.
That was me.
Dressed up pretty.
Rolling waves of ribbon lace
and lights above me on the stage.

And then the nothing.
The great big nothing

as you walk away and try your best
to burn the joy you'll never know
like a brand on your mind
echoing like a cheer to the fear
of being everything you will ever be
at the age of eight.

I am just a number.
That's why I'm here.

A number. Boo-hoo, right? I mean, it's a little fucking entitled in my opinion. *I was born a child genius and my life was a fairytale. But I am a tortured princess. And I peaked at the age of eight. Watch me cry.*

Bullshit.

It's like she never grew up. Like she's still that small, privileged girl being carted around to play for kings and queens. Not some washed-up has-been who's too afraid to step outside without covering herself up from head to toe.

Hold on there, Ixion, the reasonable inner me says.

She did go to a very public place today. There were tons of people there, even though it's the fucking dead of winter. Or maybe that's why. Parents desperate to take their kids somewhere so they can have some semblance of a life outside their mundane suburban dream house.

And what better place to go in the winter than a greenhouse?

Yeah. That's my fault, I guess. Didn't think that through.

So one point for Evangeline for braving an invasion of nuclear families at a public park. And one point for allowing her intrigue to overpower her fear. But minus ten points for the tantrum.

She's eight behind, as far as I'm concerned.

When the place is as picked up as it can be—I mean, I'm not gonna fix the dings in the wall and shit. The rich assholes who normally live here can do that themselves. Or Jordan—I start for the basement stairs but end up at the bottom of the grand foyer stairs instead.

I should check on her.

You can check on her downstairs, rational me says.

Fuck rational me. I want to see her.

I climb the stairs, then climb again, until I'm standing in front of the double doors that lead to her bedroom. I lean in, listening, then cautiously open them, eyes fixed on her still body in the bed.

She must've gotten chilled, because she's under the covers now, that one defiant cold-seeking foot peeking out.

I smile. Partly because I do that too when I'm sleeping and get too hot. Partly because it makes her somehow… familiar. Like I know her now. I have this habit down. We're sharing a past experience. Sort of.

That's when I notice she's wearing the fucking necktie blindfold.

What the hell?

Did she do that—why did she do that?

Did she want me to come up here? Was she hoping I'd be watching, see her put it on, and understand that was her way of calling me to her bed?

I want to touch her.

Without second-guessing my urge, I walk over to the bed and sit down. She shifts position, but doesn't wake.

A few strands of hair are plastered to her cheek from sweat, or tears, or both. I reach over and pull them away so I can see her better.

"Stay," she whispers. "Please. I just... I just want someone to stay with me. I'm so tired of being alone. That's all I wanted from today. A chance to be with someone."

I sigh. Loudly.

"I'm sorry. This... I never wanted anyone to see me like that again. It was childish and stupid. And if you walk out..." She sighs. "I'll understand if you walk out."

I want to talk to her so bad, but that will fuck up the illusion. It's one thing to chat with her through a crackling intercom, and quite another to do it in person.

So I can't. I take her hand instead. Squeeze. She squeezes back and beings to cry again. "Sleep next to me," she says. "*Please.*"

It's not a request. It's a... it's a plea. For help, I realize. That's why she's here. She needs help. She's sick. Not dying. But yeah, she's *dying*. She's suffocating in her small world. She's withering like a fading flower. Like the last ember in a fire just seconds away from being extinguished. And even though I'm not the help she's looking for, I'm all she's got tonight.

So I kick off my shoes, lift my shirt over my head and toss it aside, and slip under the covers next to her.

Fingertips reach for me immediately, testing out the boundaries of my body. They flutter over my chest, trace down my ribs, and press against the taut muscles of my stomach.

I suck in air, hating myself for what I'm gonna do next.

Because I'm gonna fuck her.

I'm a dick for doing it because she's weak right now. She's depending on me and this feels like taking advantage of her.

And maybe it is.

But I want her and when was the last time I allowed myself to take something I wanted? When was the last time I didn't put someone else first?

Besides, she wants me too.

CHAPTER TWENTY-THREE

EVANGELINE

I have to bite my lip and hold my breath to keep the sobs inside. And it's not because I'm unhappy. I'm so relieved he didn't walk out it overwhelms me. I'm not sure what to expect when I reach for him.

That's a lie.

I know what I *expect*. I'm just hoping he disappoints me. Because I have conditioned myself to expect the worst in people. I expect to be treated badly. I expect to be left alone. I expect to be forgotten.

He doesn't push me away, but he doesn't take control either. When he doesn't try to dominate me the way he has been since I arrived—I want to cry harder, not less.

I suck in a deep gulp of air instead.

Calm down, Evangeline.

But I can't. The tantrum I threw downstairs is too fresh, the memories it brings back too raw, too humiliating for me to forgive myself.

So I concentrate on his body. The thump of his heart. The peaks and valleys of his ribs. The hard muscles of his stomach as he too takes a deep breath.

"I'm stuck," I whisper, pressing my face into his shoulder and closing my eyes. "I'm stuck somewhere in the past and I can't find my way out of it."

He lets out that breath he was holding and slips his arm underneath me.

Does he feel sorry for me? Is this just a job to him? Am I something he has to put up with to get something he needs? Money, maybe?

God. That's the story of my life.

I'm just everybody's little golden opportunity.

CHAPTER TWENTY-FOUR

IXION

I stop the second she opens her mouth and says the words, "I'm stuck."

I just stare at the ceiling, wondering how she knows me so well. Because I'm stuck too.

That's not why you're here, Ix.

No. I don't even know why I'm here. Jordan, I guess. The past I'm stuck in. Just like this woman curling her body into mine in the dark.

When I slip my arm underneath her, she molds herself into the shape of me. On her side, head on my shoulder, fingers now clutching my bicep, like she can't even think of letting go.

I have so many words that want to come out. Confessions of past transgressions. Grudges held close like something precious to be protected. Regrets that beg to be forgiven, but since I'm the one who needs to forgive, they stay with me. Like baggage, I guess. Whole suitcases overfilled with remorse and wishes for do-overs.

I weigh the value of letting go of the fantasy I'm cultivating and just… allowing myself to be *me* for once. Saying things I shouldn't say. Letting them spill out like water over a bridge. Not flowing under and escaping, but flooding it until it's impassable. Because so much water has already passed under that bridge and it never helped. Ever. So fuck it, right? Why not just flood the whole damn river? Bring it down. Fucking smash that goddamned bridge to pieces with a wall of water so high, my anger and resentment just go downstream like all the other garbage they're traveling with.

"They never loved me," she says, snapping me out of my insane analogy. Because if I blow up the bridge, I take her with me. "They only ever used me."

I squint my eyes, still staring up at the ceiling, trying to pick up the pieces she's scattering like breadcrumbs. Which is a horrible comparison, because the kids in that story are left in the woods to die by their wicked stepmother.

"My first memory is playing the violin."

Ah. OK, I get it. She's gonna puke out her feelings. Probably triggered by that hurricane of a meltdown she had earlier. I mean, what the fuck was that about? She lost her goddamned mind.

And you're in bed with her right now.

So fucking what? She wants me here. Why not take what she's offering?

"I don't know how old I was."

Jesus. I should just kiss her so she'll stop talking. I should not let her tell me these things. I don't care about any of it. I'd like to fuck her. And I'd like to get even with Jordan, but that's it.

Except, rational me points out, *you did ask her for her story yesterday. Practically ripped it out of her. And she sent that poem, which you read and discarded with no more thought given to what lies underneath than how it helps you play the game with Jordan.*

In my defense, I did just read it again. Paying more attention this time.

"Maybe two," she continues. "The violin didn't magically appear in my life. My parents bought it. This tiny little thing that could only fit the fingers and hands of a toddler."

I'm not a fucking therapist. I mean, this should be very obvious to any sane person. But apparently Evangeline Rolaine isn't sane.

"And I didn't know it then, but it was gonna save my life one day."

I think about that for a second. Wondering if it's figurative or literal.

"By the time I was eight I was a star. I had met kings, and princesses, and rock stars, and talk show hosts, and more members of Congress and local reporters than I could count." She sighs. "And by the time I was ten..."

The silence that follows lingers for a long time.

If I was talking to her I might feel pressure to prod her along. And I am, in fact, pretty fucking curious about what happened by the time she was ten. So *if* I was talking to her, that prodding might even be genuine.

But she never picks it back up. Her fingers begin wandering around on my chest again. Feeling my ribs like they are fascinating. And when she lowers them down to the waistband of my jeans, there's a moment when I have an urge to stop her. To say, "Nah. Let's just wait on that, OK?" Or, "You've had a rough day. How about we just go to sleep?"

But I can't talk to her, so I can't say any of that. And I've already decided to fuck her, and now she's practically asking for it.

So... But... Fuck.

CHAPTER TWENTY-FIVE

EVANGELINE

He stops me before I can get any further. His hand covers mine. Holds it still on the lower part of his stomach. "What?" I ask.

I want to take the blindfold off so badly. I want to see him. I want him to talk to me. And not over that static intercom, either. I want his unfiltered voice.

He slides my hand up to the middle of his stomach and keeps it there.

I sigh, because I can take a hint. He doesn't want me. Last night was just a tactic. A way to make me stay.

Tonight, after my display downstairs this afternoon, well, I can read between the lines as well as anyone. Tonight he's probably just thinking I'm crazy. And I need a babysitter. And—

His kiss surprises me. His lips are soft as they touch mine, his tongue sweet as it sweeps into my mouth.

But as soon as it begins, it ends.

He untangles himself from my embrace, gets up out of bed, and walks out.

I sit up, and for a half a second, my heart beats so fast I get dizzy.

That's the only thing that stops me. The fear of a full-on anxiety attack. Because I want to run after him. I want

207

to turn him around, look him in the eyes, see his face, and tell him to finish what he started.

I don't bother with any of that.

I give up instead. Flop back onto the pillows, leave the blindfold in place because I decide I kinda like being blind. I've been unable to see anything past my fear for so long now, what's the point?

"Fine," I say. "Fine. I get it."

That's all I have anymore. Acceptance. And Disappointment. This whole fucked-up life can just go to hell.

I wake up with the sun. The blindfold is tangled in my long hair, my eyes are tired from yesterday's tears, and the only thing I want is to go back to sleep.

The intercom speaker crackles like a warning, snapping me back to reality. I look over at it and wait.

So many seconds go by I almost think he's not gonna say anything. But then—"He eats lunch at the Mile High Cafe next to the capitol building. Eleven forty-five every single day he's in court. And every day this week he is. So…"

The crackling stops. Leaving me alone to figure that statement out.

My response is a laugh. "Downtown?" I ask the chandelier. "Are you fucking stupid? That's… that's like…" I don't really know how far away it is. But just a few nights ago it was insurmountably far. "I might as well just go home if I'm gonna go to the fucking capitol building."

"So go," he says.

"Asshole."

"You wanted to see him? That's where he'll be every day this week. Go. Don't go. Fuck if I care. You're just a job, Evangeline. I'm just a babysitter to make sure you don't do anything stupid."

"That's not what you are! You're a watcher, not a sitter. I don't need a goddamned sitter! You're supposed to be helping me. You're supposed to be—"

"I did help you," he says, cutting me off. "I got you out of the house, in a public place, among more people than you've been in the middle of in a fucking decade. And then you came home and broke shit. Like a fucking kid. No, like a *spoiled* fucking kid. Go see him. Don't go see him. I really don't give a fuck. But don't tell me I'm not trying to help you. Because I'm doing my best."

The crackle cuts off and the silence returns to the room like a ghost haunting its childhood home.

CHAPTER TWENTY-SIX

Watching her struggle with her decision for the next two hours would be kinda fun if it wasn't so depressing.

She finds the notebook I left her on the kitchen counter and writes in it for a while, even though I never asked her for another story.

I think I'm way too involved in this thing right now.

But I'm really fucking hoping she goes to see Jordan. Because I need to get the hell out of this house for a while. This place might be huge. Way too big for one person and her stalker living in two spaces so far apart, they might as well have different addresses. But the walls are closing in on me. As someone who likes to bail at every opportunity and just... fucking leave everything behind, being forced to stay put in this goddamned room is starting to take its toll.

I get dressed, just in case she surprises me, and then pull up Jordan's contact and press it.

"What now?" he asks. But he still answers on the first ring. Which kinda makes me smile.

"I'm fucking bored."

He sighs. I can just picture him running his fingers through his hair in frustration. "Ixion, I do not have time for you today. I have court in three minutes."

"Wanna have lunch?"

He scoffs. "No. I gotta go."

"Why?" I ask. "Why did you really come looking for me?"

"I don't have time."

"You know the answer," I say. "So just say it."

"Ix—"

"That was always your problem, ya know that? You want things and when you don't get them, you tear the world apart." *Just like Evangeline,* I want to add. But he won't get it. And I can't explain it. And fuck it.

"Fuck you."

"Yeah," I say. "Fuck me."

He hangs up without saying goodbye. Leaving me to stare at the phone as the call fades to the home screen.

They're made for each other, I realize. Jordan and Evangeline. Both a couple of spoiled fucking rich people who think sadness is a badge of honor and chaos is something you hand out like spare change to a homeless person.

"How do I get there?"

Evangeline's question snaps me back to the job. She's looking up at the grand foyer camera, standing in the middle of the stairs so she's more or less eye level.

There's no intercom in the foyer. Which is weird, I think. But whatever. Not my stupid design. So when I press the button and talk to her, it comes from every speaker in the house. The closest must be the office, because her head darts in that direction.

212

"There's a computer down in the basement office. Pull up a fucking map."

"Dick," she says. "You know what? The only reason I'm going is to get away from you."

"I'll be there too, Evangeline. You can't get rid of me."

"Watching," she snaps. "Like a creepy stalker."

"Yup," I say.

I follow her on camera as she finds the basement stairs, descends, and then wanders around looking at the games and the TV, then finally settles in front of the computer and starts typing. A few minutes later she's printing something and then she snatches it up and stomps up the stairs.

I should follow her on the cameras, but I don't. I'm too busy wondering what she wrote in that notebook instead. I want to grab it, but I can't.

Movement on the camera catches my eye. Evangeline is walking back down the grand foyer stairs, completely dressed. I'm talking hat, gloves, coat, sunglasses, scarf. The whole deal.

Then more movement as one of my monitors picks up a cab pulling up in front of the house.

But I smile at her tenacity. Her grit. Her gumption. Her *balls*.

So I get up, put on my coat, and follow her out.

CHAPTER TWENTY-SEVEN

EVANGELINE

There's a moment as I get in the cab, right after I hand the driver the printout with the address of my destination, when I wonder, should I just go home? I don't need my things inside the house. I didn't bring much. Wouldn't even miss that stuff.

But then I picture my sad life. The emptiness of it all. The loneliness. How desperate I was for a change last week and how I seem to be on a new path this week. And decide... not yet.

Not yet.

I can leave any time I want. Walk out, go back—or even just walk out and go forward. This isn't a chance to escape. It's an opportunity to grow. And now that I know there's a computer in the basement—how the fuck did I not know there was a basement? God, I'm so oblivious to the world around me—and now that I know I can call a cab any time I want...

Well, the urgency to find a way out of this messy plan seems to have dissipated.

I might even have hope.

Not the hope of dreams. I already had that when I agreed to this crazy scheme. But real hope. The dream of playing my violin again, of playing in front of an audience, of making money again, and being whole again, and letting go of the past and living again. Well, that's something quite different than actually taking steps towards that goal. Dreams are just that. Wishes.

But getting this cab feels like an accomplishment.

And yes, that's sad. Most people wouldn't see this as an act of courage.

But I do.

And anyway, I'm intrigued. I want to see this Jordan again. He was very attractive. I want to know more about this game he's playing with me. Why he's playing it. And even though X said I wasn't allowed to talk to him, who gives a fuck what X wants? This isn't about him, this is about me.

So I've already decided that if I see Jordan today, I'm talking to him. He's not gonna slip away like he did yesterday. I'm gonna ask him just what the fuck he's doing. I'm gonna ask him if Lucinda gave him permission to put X in that house. If they know what he's doing with me.

I have decided to take control.

So there. Take that, Mr. X.

Far too soon the cab pulls up to a curb and stops.

"Twelve seventy-five," the driver says. I hold up my credit card, ready to hand it over, but he says, "You have to use the machine." He nods his head at the thing mounted on the back of the headrest.

I fumble with that for longer than seems appropriate. But the device seems to be made for idiots and has been programmed to walk even the most clueless people through the act of paying for a cab ride, so about a minute later, I manage to conclude the transaction.

And then it's time to get out.

It occurs to me then... I don't have a way to get back. Jesus, I don't even know if I remember the address.

"Lady," the driver says. "You need to get out now."

I nod at him, take a deep breath, and open the cab door to the bustle of the strange city I've called home for almost ten years.

The second I close the door, the cab pulls away and I become just another person in his past.

I stare up at the sign. Mile High Cafe. There are a ton of people coming and going, all of them wearing business attire. Men in expensive suits, women in professional dresses. All ages, but mostly middle-aged. The courthouse is nearby. I can see the golden dome of the capitol building from where I stand. So these people probably all have an intimate relationship with the city that feels like a stranger to me.

"Don't wuss out now, Evangeline," I mutter under my breath. "You're already here. Just go inside."

It's a confident statement. Like going inside is so easy. Like going inside is normal. Something I do every day. Just go inside.

But none of that is true. And even though my head is trying to trick my body, my body isn't listening, because I'm suddenly breathing too fast, and my heart is beating too fast, and the whole world is moving too fast.

"How many?" the woman asks. "Just one?"

I realize the bustle of the crowd has pushed me into the door of the cafe and the woman asking me how many is actually the hostess. "Yes," I manage to spit out. "Just one."

She scans the room. Every table is full, and I feel stupid all of a sudden. Like... how did I not anticipate that the restaurant would be filled to capacity when it's lunchtime?

"Well," the young girl finally says. "There's a gentleman over there sitting alone. Do you want me to go ask him if he'd mind sharing with you?"

"Oh, no… uh…" I stammer out my objections. "I don't think—"

"He won't mind." And then the hostess laughs. "In fact, he told me when he came in if anyone needed a seat, he's happy to share."

She bustles off before I can answer, but I watch, in utter horror, as she approaches the man, points to me, and then they talk. *About me.* As they look. *At me.*

I turn to flee and bump right into a man's chest. Dark wool overcoat. Leather-gloved hands reach out to steady me. Firm grip on my shoulders. And when I raise my eyes to see who is blocking my way, I realize it's Jordan.

I whirl back around, and the hostess is there, grabbing a menu. "Come on," she says. "He's happy to help."

I follow her for no other reason than I cannot think of a single other thing to do. I just obey automatically. On autopilot.

Just get me away from the man I came to see.

The hostess stops at the table and pans her hand towards the empty chair. "Here you go. Have fun, you two!"

She leaves and I'm stuck there. I don't look at the man I'm supposed to be sitting with because I'm too busy looking back at Jordan. He catches my gaze, which almost sends me into a panic, so I sit down and turn my head away. Right into the direct gaze of my table stranger.

"Uh… hi," the guy says. "I'm Mike. And you are?"

He extends his hand, but all I can do is stare at it. So it's withdrawn just as fast. "Angela," I say, reverting back to my stand-by public persona.

"Nice to meet you, Angela. Do you work around here?"

I look at him, thankful I still have my scarf over my face and my sunglasses covering my eyes. *Just be normal. Just be normal.* I chant it in my head. "Yes," I lie. "At the courthouse. I'm new. First day."

There you go, I say to myself. *Good job.*

"Well, you're part of the crowd now." He laughs. "Everyone eats here at lunch. It gets pretty busy around this time. And I always eat alone, so I offer up my table when I can."

"Thank you," I say, remembering my manners.

"So what kind of food do you like?"

I chance a glance over at Jordan. He's still looking at me, so I play it off like I was just scanning the room, then remember I have a menu I can pretend to study.

"Sandwiches," I reply to the man's question.

"You should definitely get the club then. It's fantastic. They put a little avocado on there. Really, really good."

"What can I get you to drink?" a waitress asks.

I look up at her, ready to die from all this very sudden, very intimate attention, and blurt, "Water and I'll take the club sandwich."

"Coming right up," she says, taking my menu away with a smile.

"So…" My impromptu date seems to be chatty. And I think in my head, *Why me?* "You'll probably have to take your scarf off if you want to eat."

"Right," I say, slowly unwrapping my scarf. It would draw far more attention to keep it on than it will to take it

219

off. At least that's what I tell myself. But the whole time I'm sneaking glances over at Jordan, wishing I wasn't stuck talking to this guy instead of him.

"Do you know him?" the guy asks.

"Who?"

"That man you're staring at."

"What?" I laugh it off as I fold my scarf up and place it in my lap. "No. I'm not looking at anyone in particular. Just... you know. People-watching."

"Ah," he says. "I like to watch people too. That's why I come in here alone. You see all types. It's interesting."

I take another look at my date, intrigued by his answer. He's probably a few years older than me. Maybe early thirties. Light brown hair. Bluish eyes. Handsome. He's wearing a suit, but every man in here seems to be wearing a suit.

"What did you say your name was?" I don't even know how I get those words out, because as soon as I realize I've asked him a direct question, my heart races in a way that scares me.

"Mike," he says, smiling. He extends his hand again.

I shake it this time, but when I withdraw, he holds on to it. Which forces me to look him in the eyes to see what the hell he's doing.

"You can take off the gloves too, ya know. Gonna be hard to pick up a sandwich with gloves."

And he... he starts pulling on the fingertips of my glove. Removing it. Sliding it down my hand in a way that makes me hold my breath.

I pull away quickly, but the glove is off. My hand exposed. He reaches for me again, his fingertips gently squeezing as he says, "That's better. How about the sunglasses now?"

I jerk away, my hand unconsciously flying up to touch the lenses, as if to make sure they're still there. "No," I say. "I have sensitive eyes and I have to wear them when I'm in the sun."

He looks over to the window, is about to say something about the gray, overcast day, but then simply shrugs. "OK. Well, I'm done. And I gotta get back to work. Maybe I'll see you tomorrow?"

"Sure," I say, not knowing why I say it because I don't work at the fucking courthouse and I won't be back tomorrow.

"Nice meeting you, Angela."

I nod my head, but don't meet his eyes as he gets up.

"And lunch is on me. Don't worry about it. Thanks for the company."

"Yeah," I say, glancing up at him, then quickly averting my eyes. If I can't see him, he can't see me.

I want to roll my eyes at myself.

"Bye."

I nod, so he just leaves, resigning himself to the fact that I'm not gonna chat him up any further.

I stare at my one gloveless, exposed hand for a few seconds, then quickly put the glove back on. The scarf is still in my lap, so I wrap that around my face too.

Finally, all covered up again, I let myself breathe.

I am stupid.

"Did you want this to go?"

I look up at the question and find the waitress holding a plate with my sandwich.

"Um... yes, please."

She leaves to wrap it up and all I can think about is getting the hell out of here when I suddenly lock eyes with Jordan again.

He smiles at me. Gives me a little wave.

I look away and close my eyes, forcing myself not to panic. Why the fuck did I come here? What the hell was I thinking?

I stay like that, my head bowed, my eyes closed, until the waitress is saying, "Here you go," as she slips a gray cardboard box in front of me. "Your check is all set. Thanks for coming!"

I nod, take my box, and then get up, fully intending on escaping without looking at Jordan again... but—

I can't help it. And when I find his face, he's already found mine.

The doors open as a man enters, and I slip past him and out into the gray afternoon.

A moment of pure panic passes through my body as I realize I have no way to get home. I'm not even sure where home is, but then I see a cab, and I raise my hand like I've seen people do in movies, and it stops for me.

I climb in. And when the driver says, "Where to?"

I say, "The Botanic Gardens."

I get dropped off at the main visitors' center. Which happens to be close to the greenhouse I was in the other day, so finding my way back to the path that leads to the house isn't too hard.

When I finally get back inside, I collapse onto the grand foyer stairs and look up at the camera in the chandelier.

"Fuck you," I say.

But the house seems empty for some reason. Like... I can just feel his eyes are somewhere else. Not on me.

And even though I've been living with that same feeling for almost a decade, it feels lonely now.

I go upstairs, take off my coat, my scarf, my gloves, my shoes... and I climb back into bed, exhausted, and sad, and more unsure of myself than I have ever been in my life.

CHAPTER TWENTY-EIGHT

IXION

When I get back to the house I rewind the footage of her return. See the slump in her shoulders. The sadness and uncertainty in her expression. She is the perfect image of complete surrender.

I wonder what she thought of Jordan. I wonder what was going through her head when she found him staring at her.

Was it intrigue? Fear? Longing?

Whatever it was, this was a good day for me. And the night is about to get even better.

I remember the notebook in the kitchen and go upstairs to retrieve it and read what she wrote.

Did you ever feel like a diamond ring?
Just a ring on a finger, sitting pretty
on the hand that that makes you sing?
Preposterous child with anonymous smiles
and weariness dancing on your strings?

Well, I have.
That was me.
Invisible except for my ability.

So I said no and threw a fit
And yes, became a little sick
of the music and the stage
and all the things they made me play
until they sucked me dry
and left me standing there alone
small, but tall
and refusing to cry.

I am just a diamond ring.
That's why I'm here.

Hmmm. I have to read it like fifteen times. Not because I don't understand her metaphors, or literary interpretation of what a diamond ring is. But because I do.

I wasn't going to write more of my story, but maybe she just needs to know… well, that people have fucked-up experiences and they're OK afterward.

Except I'm not really a good example, am I?

Rational me pops up, taking my side for once, telling me, *Could've been worse.*

Could've.

You're still here.

I am.

You're helping her.

Just another stand-up guy, I guess.

Which makes me sigh. And roll my eyes. And pick up the pen and start to write.

I could start my story with boring details about how we all met,
what we all do, and how it all intertwined to make us what we are
today. But no one wants the boring backstory and I'm sure you're

far more interested in what she looked like. Or what he and I saw in her, or how we ended up fucking each other just a few years later.

She was a foul-mouthed tomboy who did her best not to look like she was modeling underwear on a catwalk while wearing wings, but failing miserably at it. But that was how it came off.

She is that girl. The elusive dream woman who can play poker and look like she's only there as a prop for her equally beautiful boyfriend until she kicks your ass and leaves you broke.

We had the same passion. Filmmaking.

Jordan was in undergrad at Stanford at the time. She and I went to UCLA. Alexander, the fourth wheel in this quasi-quad, was a consultant for the film industry. He, like Jordan, fell in love with Augustine the moment he saw her.

It's just a natural consequence of meeting her.

She fell in love with me.

But not the way they thought.

She dated them both. Sometimes together, sometimes not. It was always a game.

I was just her best friend. A guy she could—and would—come to, just to talk things through. Just to get a bad day off her mind. Just to have fun and not have the night end with drama or jealousy.

Alexander and Jordan shared her regularly for a couple years. And it was fine because Jordan was up at Stanford and the rest of us were in LA, and he only came down every once in a while and Alexander didn't mind sharing a few times a year if it meant he could have her to himself all those other nights in between.

But then Jordan got into UCLA law school and suddenly there he was. Every day, every night, every time we turned around, there he was.

And he said to me one night, "Ixion..." I can remember that night like it's happening right now. What we were wearing, what we had for dinner, what we were drinking. How he almost whispered

227

the words in the bar that night. He said, "Ixion, why haven't you ever…"

He never finished because just then Alexander and Augustine joined us, and drinks were flowing, and we were all talking, and laughing, and you know how it goes.

Why haven't I fucked her? That's what he wanted to know.

He asked me again a few days later, but looking back it all started that night. When they took her home and I didn't join them.

And my answer was, and still would be—if we were still friends, that is—"Because I have the relationship with her that I want."

I should've stuck with that.
Should never've let him talk me into it.
Should've just walked away.
But of course… I didn't walk away.

When I'm done writing I leave the book on the countertop for Evangeline to find when she wakes up.

She's stuck in her own privileged childhood.

I have decided that's her problem. Her mind didn't mature with her body. She never developed coping mechanisms as a teenager.

Why?

It's easy to assume. I mean, she was a child prodigy. Literally born a genius. Celebrated for her talent. Paraded all over the world to perform, applauded by the most important people imaginable.

Maybe never even told no.

That's the assumption, anyway.

But I've learned a thing or two about assumptions over the years. And it's almost never that simple.

I hold myself up as Exhibit A.

If you were looking at me from a distance, like... say... that sheriff back up in Wyoming, you'd see what everyone sees. Scruffy-faced, thirty-something man with no direction or purpose, who spies on people to make money.

If you were a little closer you might see the trust fund. The exile from the wealthy family. The aimless wandering. The loss.

But you'd have to be really intimate with me to see who I really am. What really happens inside my head. You'd have to be Jordan, for example. Because he's the only one who knows me.

It's a secret he'll keep, I have no doubt. It's not in his best interest for people to see the real me. Because then they might see the real him.

I ran into Augustine once. About four years ago. Few years after all that other shit happened, so she hated me at the time. She didn't even know I was there, probably. I had been erased, for lack of a more literal term.

I didn't say anything to her. Didn't offer up an explanation. Didn't defend myself or my actions. Because she wasn't interested. She threw me back the day we sat in that conference room with our respective lawyers and dissolved our business partnership.

Over.

I was the glue. That was the only thought that swept through my mind that day she pretended I didn't exist.

I was the fucking glue.

She just never knew it.

Jordan was there too. Smiling in that fucking suit of his.

The only thing that kept me from walking over to him and kicking his ass was the fact that he and Augustine weren't together. She didn't even look at him. I mean, she didn't look at me, either, and he wasn't the one she *hated*. That was me.

But it was clear, whatever they had was over. Long time ago.

They were on opposite ends of the party. It was her wedding. And why Alexander invited us… I can only guess because he never said. I just showed up, and I'm pretty sure that was what Jordan was doing as well.

Augustine never even looked at me.

"I'm not going back tomorrow," Evangeline says, obviously awake and walking down the stairs to the main floor.

I'd forgotten where I was for a moment. Lost in my last secret memory of Augustine. What's her last memory of me, I wonder? Not her wedding, that's for sure.

That day at the table? With the lawyers?

Or did she sneak in somewhere I was and see me from afar once?

I hope she did. And I hope it was a good memory. Maybe her wedding day? Maybe she did see me that day? Maybe Alexander told her I was there and she walked around, looking for me in the gardens?

Is it fate? Or irony? Or was it planned? The fact that Augustine got married at the Denver Botanic Gardens? The fact that Jordan put me here? Brought me into this new game of his. If all the world's a stage, then how do you ever know what's real?

"Did you hear me?" Evangeline yells as she reaches the kitchen. I watch for a moment as she spies the waiting book.

She looks down—hiding a smile, I'm sure of it, even though I don't have a good view in here anymore—and then she takes the book and walks away to read it.

I let her go and press Jordan's contact on my phone.

He doesn't pick up. But I leave a message, so who cares. And the message is this: "Did you get what you wanted out of her? And that's not sarcasm or cynicism. It's an honest question. Was it worth it? Because it wasn't for me."

I wait, like he's there or something. Like in the old days you could leave a message on the machine and wonder if the person just didn't pick up and was standing right there listening as you poured your heart out.

But this isn't those days. And no one has a machine anymore. So it's just voicemail. Just some digital cloud that hears your desperate message and gives no shits whatsoever.

I end the call and look back at Evangeline, who is sitting on the couch in the ballroom, facing the windows that open to the backyard. She's very absorbed in my story. It's only a few paragraphs, so maybe she's reading it twice?

I wonder if Augustine is happy with Alexander.

I heard they had a serious separation a few years ago, but got back together. Nothing since that.

Evangeline is talking again. "Where's the rest of it?" she asks, holding up the book. "I want the rest of it."

I press the button on the intercom and say, "Where's the rest of your story? I want the rest of that too."

She sighs. Loudly. Then says, "My story is a poem. It takes time to compose."

"I never told you to write a poem, Evangeline. A few scribbled words will suffice."

231

She just scowls at me. I can't tell if that comment makes her angry… or sad.

"Go compose it then," I say. "Leave it on the counter when you're done and then go upstairs and wait for me."

"Will you come up?" she asks.

I wonder if Augustine called Jordan when she and Alexander separated? I wonder if they got back together for those few months? I wonder if they talked about me?

"Why are you ignoring me?" Evangeline asks.

It's such an honest question. And the desperate tone in her voice mirrors my own feelings at the moment. So I say, "I'm just admiring you," and it's a lie, of course. Because I'm stuck in the past, just like she is.

But it's also sort of true. Because she *is* very beautiful. Especially when she's emotional. It's a tragic kind of beautiful. The kind that makes people look twice. The kind you see in perfume ads, or on a fashion runway with the too-skinny girls, dressed up as someone else, walking with hidden purpose that's really nothing but obvious anguish.

Dark. And hopeless. And emotional.

My answer soothes her to the point of softening. She looks at our book in her hands. She's sitting Indian-style on the couch, long, dark hair hanging to cover her pretty face.

And it makes me sad that lies… can be so soothing.

Makes me feel guilty too. Because it's way too easy to soothe people. You just say what they want to hear and they believe you.

Trust you.

It works on men too. I know. I've been that man.

But I was the glue, I remind myself. That part wasn't a lie.

232

And I'm the glue now too. I'm the only thing holding Evangeline Rolaine together at this point.

It occurs to me that this is a very serious role and I'm neglecting my duties. Neglecting her in favor of a past mistake. Forgetting why I'm really here. Not here, according to Jordan or her doctor. But here according to *me*.

I don't want to hurt her. I just... don't think I can help it.

"Write your poem," I say into the intercom. "And then go upstairs and put on the blindfold."

She looks up at the camera I had to rig up after her last tantrum, her expression one of total and utter confusion. Kinda like mine if I could see it.

"What?" she asks in a soft voice. But there's a hint of disbelief in her question. Like it's exactly what she wanted to hear next, but she can't believe she heard it.

"Do it." I whisper now. Let most of my words be muffled by the static and crackling of the intercom.

She takes a deep breath, squares her shoulders like she needs the courage, and begins to write.

That's when her phone, sitting on the desk in front of my computer monitors since she left it on that hallway table the second day she was here, beeps an incoming alert.

I pick it up, unable to read the message, but I think it's a voicemail. There are two icons with enough uncracked screen to press them, and neither are for the phone. But I press one until it starts to wiggle and rearrange the icons until the phone is in the right spot. Then I press it and play the message.

I listen to it three times, then call the number he left, plotting a new twist to the story we're telling.

233

Evangeline sits there agonizing over her words for hours. *Hours.*

So long, the arrangements I start making get made.

So long I run out of memories of Augustine to dwell on.

So long I get hungry and make a peanut butter sandwich and snap still images of her and then retouch them like I would back in school when I cared about how the fucking pictures turned out.

So long, I'm just about to scream that nobody gives two fucks about her stupid poem and to just get her ass upstairs so I can come up and fuck her.

But then she says, "OK," and stands up, walks to the kitchen, and leaves the book on the counter. She turns, but her hand remains on the cover. Which is just your run-of-the-mill notebook cover. No picture or anything. Just plain black.

And then she turns back. Like she might want to rip those words out of that book and stuff them down the garbage disposal so I never get to see what she wrote.

I'm just about to say something when she draws in a deep breath, turns, and walks away.

I don't bother following her steps up the stairs on camera. Or along the hallway to the second set of stairs. Or up to the bedroom. I don't even watch her take off her clothes, even though I never told her to do that, and slip the tie around her eyes like an obedient child.

I'm too busy thinking about the words in that book. Words she wrote but didn't want to write.

I just look up a few minutes later and there she is.

Lying on the bed naked. Her fingers between her legs. Her mouth slightly open as she rubs her clit. Her perfect breasts rising and falling with the fast beating of her heart.

She waits for me.

I make her wait.

I watch, forgetting about the past for once. Putting Augustine and Jordan behind me for a while.

And just be… present as I go upstairs, get her book, sit on the couch where she just was, and open it to the last page.

Did you ever feel forsaken?
Just a lifetime of waste
as people say they must've been mistaken?
Autonomous child now blasphemously wild
alone, and lost, and afraid of being broken?

Well, I have.
That was me.
Tired of all the publicity.
Choppy waves of tattered lace
and only shadows on the stage.

So I withdrew and stayed alone
withdrawing further from my throne
of greed and hunger
and all the ways they threw me under
until there was nothing left
but the fractured lights of night
and the disillusionment of wonder.

I have been forsaken.
That's why I'm here.

I think I stare at that poem for eternity. Several eternities. I read it nine hundred and twenty-three times. Or a dozen, at least. I scrutinize every word she chose for me. Every secret she just revealed.

And now I'm her. I hold the book up to the camera lens she is most definitely not looking through, and ask myself, who is not on the other side, "Where's the rest of it?"

I need the rest of it.

CHAPTER TWENTY-NINE

EVANGELINE

There are emotions flowing through me that I can't describe. There are no words for them. It's fear but longing. It's excitement, but sadness. It's desire, but anguish.

It's crazy. That's all I know for certain.

I am not a part of the real world. I am not here, or there. I am not living, or dead. I am something in between.

It scares me.

But I don't care.

It feels like hours later when I finally hear the creaking of the stairs under his heavy footsteps.

I stop breathing.

My hand stops playing with the sensitive skin between my legs. The wetness is already there, primed for him. *Please, God. Make him touch me.*

The door opens with a soft rush of air. The room fills up with his presence. Even though I have the blindfold on and I can't see anything, I feel him from across the room.

"Please," actually comes out of my mouth. Begging. I'm *begging* for his attention.

And then he's there, sitting on the bed next to me. His fingertips pinching my nipple. The heat of his body against the coolness of mine. I shiver, sending a chill up my spine, making the nipple he's still playing with bunch and peak and turn into a hard rock under his touch.

His hand rests on the inner flesh of my thigh and gently urges me to open my legs. I suck in air, and hold it again, because he makes me forget how to breathe out.

My body is squirming, still begging for more. I want him to cover me. Put his whole chest over my beating heart and cover me up. Make me melt into him and not be alone anymore.

But he does something better. He slips his hand up and down my inner thigh, lightly brushing my skin, and with each sweep, he takes it just half an inch further. Further down, until he's rubbing the inside of my knee. Further up until his knuckles bump against my clit.

I writhe with anticipation. Buck my back with expectations. I reach for his face, find a scratchy jawline, hold him like that. Imagining his face in my mind. My finger finds his mouth and his lips part. He sucks on me, his tongue caressing the tip of my finger, his teeth nipping at it, and I die. I swear to God, I die.

Then he holds my hand, withdraws the finger from his mouth, and places my palm on my own stomach. He slides it down, until it's back between my legs. But he holds it there, and when I begin to rub myself, he slaps my tit so hard, I gasp.

"No," he whispers.

And I want to scream, *Tell me what you want! Tell me what to do!*

And that scares me, because I never like being told what to do. Not since—

But he's leaning down now, his warm breath sweeping across my nipple as he takes it into his mouth and sucks. And bites. And I might lose myself in this moment.

I might just float into nothingness and be no one. Ever again.

Except… his mouth travels downward, his tongue gently licking the skin of my belly, until his face is buried between my legs, his scratchy jaw rubbing against the soft, tender skin of my upper thighs, and just the slightest movement of his breath near my pussy is enough to make me gasp.

A finger slips inside me just as his tongue licks my clit.

I might lose it. I might just come—

Two fingers inside me. Stretching me open as his face dips down, deeper, lower, until his tongue penetrates me the way I wish his cock would.

I can't control myself. I can't. I just moan, and whimper, and grab his hair, which feels soft and clean, and I want to take the blindfold off to see what color it is, but then I don't. Because I like not seeing him. I like not knowing what will come next. I like all this uncertainty. And I think… I think I like *him* too.

I never want him to leave me. I want him to slip into this bed and stay with me and we can—

He stands up and all the sensations stop.

I panic, nearly hyperventilating.

But then I hear the jingle of his belt, and the swoosh of a shirt going over a head, and the kicking off of boots that thud on the hardwood floors. And then his warm, naked body covers me. Just the way I wanted it to. And I hold his face in my hands as he kisses me. Deeply, and lovingly, and with longing that you don't expect from a stranger.

But he's not a stranger anymore. He's my stranger. He's my watcher. He's... *mine.*

So I say that. I say, "You're mine."

And he laughs, but it's not a laugh. It's an agreement. Or maybe a disagreement, because he's not mine, I'm his. And he knows this.

His knees kick mine open wide, and I hold them like that. Spread wide for him as he positions his body in place. His hard cock finds its way home to the opening of my pussy.

And I'm so wet, but when he forces the wide girth of his cock inside me, it hurts. But oh, God, does it hurt in all the right ways.

My legs wrap around him, squeezing him to me, and I wonder... what kind of a sick person must I be to let a stranger fuck me like this?

And I think he's thinking the same thing.

But neither of us stop.

We just need to be held, and caressed, and yes, fucked. And I don't know how I know he needs it as much as I do, but I know. He's lost too. He lost himself, like I lost me. Or something, the way I lost my childhood. Or someone, the way I lost my family.

So I say, "I'll be that," to him. And I don't exactly feel him stiffen, and I definitely don't hear him agree.

But we agree. I know we do.

As soon as that thought enters my head, he pushes himself deeper inside me. And even though I'm blindfolded underneath this man's tie, I close my eyes anyway. Because it just feels too good to keep them open.

He goes slow after that. We both do, because we're in this together now. Fully invested in the watched-watcher dynamic. Fully committed to whatever this is. Sick fantasy, or inevitable solution, it doesn't matter because it's *ours*.

So I just enjoy it. And I think he enjoys it too. Because he begins to moan a little, just a little, just like me. And he starts kissing my neck, the way I'm hungrily teasing the skin of his bare shoulder with my mouth.

His hands slip under my ass and squeeze as he flips us over so I'm on top.

I don't even know how to process that change of position.

It stills me for a moment. And I sit on his hips, straddling him. The heaviness of my breasts eased by the grip of his hands. His cock still inside me as my hips begin to move a little. My hands pressing on his hard, muscular chest.

And the urge to lift my blindfold and look at him is almost overwhelming. My hand actually flies up to my face—

But his hand is there to catch it. Like it was meant to be there all along. And he says, "Shhh," and lowers it back to his chest.

So I give in. And go with it. And let him lead from below.

His hips begin thrusting upward, taking me for a ride as his cock slips in and out of me as I rise and fall with the motion of us. Then his hand is gripping my ass again, and for a second, I think he's gonna flip me over again, and even though it never happens, I mourn the imaginary loss of my top position. Until his finger slips into my asshole and—

Holy. Fucking. Shit.

It feels so good. Like, too good to be happening.

He pushes against the tight muscles that prevent his entry, making me gasp, making me whine with pain. But then a second later his finger is inside my ass, and his cock is inside my pussy, and I feel him from both sides.

I come.

I can't help it. I just let go, and there's a wailing, pleasure-filled scream coming from my mouth as he fucks me harder from underneath. I coat his cock with my slick release, making it easier to thrust himself up inside me.

I respond in a way I didn't think possible. Didn't think I knew how. But I fuck him back with abandon. Because there are so many more things I want to do with him tonight. I want to suck his cock. I want it so far down my throat, I choke on it. I want to lick his balls, and grab him with my fist, and pump him up and down. I want to sit on his face and rub my pussy all over his chin. I want his hands around my throat, holding me from behind, forcing me to be still. To be owned. To be his as he takes whatever he wants.

"I want all of it."

He laughs, still pounding me. It's a small, gruff, deep-throated laugh that sends a chill of pleasure through my body as my pussy slides up and down his shaft. He wraps his strong arms around me, pulls me down into his chest, and holds me there. Tightly. For just a moment.

And then he throws me off, scrambles around, and holds my face in the tight grip of his thumb and forefinger until I open for him and taste his hot, salty come shooting across my tongue.

He groans and I want to come again just from the sound of him.

Dear God, he makes me feel like an animal.

He collapses off to the side, breathing hard, but smiling. I can just tell he's smiling so I smile too.

"I want to see you," I say.

He says nothing. Just leans over, kisses me, not even caring that his come is all over my face, and whispers, "That would ruin everything."

A moment later he's up off the bed. And even though I want him to stay, I think he's right. I think... there are so many ways to ruin this and only one way to make it right.

With the blindfold.

So I let him go. I don't take off my blindfold. I don't even get up to wash my face. I want his claim on me all night.

CHAPTER THIRTY

IXION

It's a peculiar thing to feel reluctance about a woman I'm involved with. I mean, typically I don't feel anything at all.

Not true. I feel satisfaction in the moment of climax.

But I feel a reluctance to leave Evangeline after we're done.

I do leave her. Feeling things and doing things don't always coincide in my mind. So I do leave her.

But I don't want to.

And then, when I get back down in the basement, I have a strange premonition that I'm taking this too far. That what I'm doing is crossing a line. Hers, for sure. But his too. And if I go through with this, it's an ending of sorts. With her, for sure again. And him too.

Not that we didn't already end things. That happened a long time ago. But he moved on and I sorta... didn't. I sorta stayed behind. Sorta... dwelled. And let it all fester and build into an anger I had no idea I was holding inside me until I saw his face when he came to bail me out of jail.

And now I'm pissed. And I'm sorry, too. Sorry that Evangeline is a part of this. Sorry that I'm playing his game with her. Sorry if she gets hurt. And then I wonder...

Maybe there's another way to get what I want?

So I stay up for a while looking for information. Watching the footage. Reading her story, her poem, and her Wikipedia page, over and over again.

Wanting more because I know the answer is out there.

I mean... can she really hate me if I fix her in the end?

Why do I care if she hates me?

I dunno. I do. So I sit down to write, and even though it takes a lot longer to get it right this time, I put in the effort. Her poem is like a challenge. A way to turn her past into art. Or something like that.

By the time I'm done, it's nearly six AM and I never went to sleep. I tell myself, no big deal. I've stayed up days at a time before.

But I lose the battle as soon as I get back into bed after putting the book on the counter for her.

CHAPTER THIRTY-ONE

EVANGELINE

I wake before dawn. Rested and filled with hope and maybe even a little satisfaction. I want more of last night, so after I shower, I put on a clean nightgown and go downstairs, not really expecting the book to be waiting for me, but it is. And I don't even know what that feeling coursing through my body means.

Is it elation? I don't know.

I just pick up the book, run back up the stairs, and get into bed to continue the story where he left off.

The first time Jordan kissed me I punched him in the face. The second time I was drunk, and we had a girl in between us, so I didn't really care. The third time he sucked my cock afterward.

I stopped talking to him for months after that. It was senior year of high school and even though I'm not gay, and I've always known I wasn't gay because I really like pussy, I'm really not bisexual either.

I mean, yeah, OK. I'll fuck with Jordan if there's a girl involved I like. But anyone else? No. I'm not into it.

I was just into him. That's it.

And trust me when I say that has passed. I'm not interested in spit-roasting you, Evangeline. I don't like to share anymore. I'm not letting you spy on him with the hope that we'll eventually fuck you together.

Then why, I wonder?

When Jordan moved to LA for law school he completely fucked with the dynamic. We were all feeling it. Even me, and I wasn't involved with Augustine in that way.

But then Alexander got tired of it. And Augustine and Jordan weren't exactly finished yet. So he bailed and they continued, but as I said, Augustine never loved him. She loved me.

And maybe it's her fault after all because it was her idea to bring me in to replace Alexander.

Friends with benefits. Does that ever fucking work?

I'm not jealous of Jordan. I wasn't jealous then and I'm not jealous now. He doesn't have her either. So fuck it. We came out even in that respect.

I'm not jealous of Alexander, because even though he was the man she chose to marry, she loved me first.

I was always her number one and I didn't need to fuck her to be that.

I just was that.

Well. I didn't see that coming. I picture the man at the greenhouse yesterday. His handsome face. His expensive suit. His piercing blue eyes. And I wonder what X looks like?

He feels magnificent on top of me. Inside me. When I touched his face last night, I could almost see him.

His story is like… a peek inside the lives of beautiful people. This arrangement is scary and intriguing at the same time. And even though he said in no uncertain terms that he was not after a spit-roast—I'm not even sure I know what that means, but I can take a guess—it's hot. I can't deny it, the whole thing is fucking hot.

I wait for his instructions, because there was no note about what we're doing today. So I write my next entry. My story almost complete. And when ten o'clock rolls around and he's still not talking to me, I make a decision.

CHAPTER THIRTY-TWO

When I wake up, she's gone. Nothing but a note waiting on the counter for me.

It says,

X,

I'm going out. But don't worry, I'll be wearing the blindfold for you tonight, not Jordan.

Evangeline

I get dressed and then I'm gone too.

CHAPTER THIRTY-THREE

EVANGELINE

I know that to most people, what I just did was not monumental. I walked out of a house. Under no one's instructions and with my own purpose. It's something small children do all the time.

But for me... it's exhilarating. I feel the change since I've been in the house with X. Since we've been trading stories.

I want to know who he loved so much it destroyed him. And I think he wants to know who destroyed me too.

Everyone wants to know that. Well, they used to. When people gave two shits about my life. I'm pretty sure I'm nobody again. Pretty sure no one cares now.

Lucinda has asked me more times than I can count. Did they abuse me? Yes. Did they hurt me? Yes.

But not in the way people think.

And I don't feel like telling her because I don't think she would understand.

X would though. I have decided to write it down for him and him only. I will make him burn it, and forget it, and when I leave this house, leave him behind, I'm going to leave the past behind too.

I feel different now.

I'm not sure if it's confidence. Maybe not that. But it's… a willingness to see past my limitations and look forward to my challenges.

I want to play that show.

I think I'm going to do it.

There's a reason I didn't call a cab at the house and instead cut through the city by way of the gardens. There's a bank of pay phones near the entrance. I had a few coins in my purse, but I'm glad I have a credit card when I get to them, because they don't take coins.

This world, I swear. It moves way too fast for me.

I get my card out, swipe it like I do in the cab, and then press the numbers I looked up on the internet before I left this morning.

"Dr. Chatwell speaking," she says.

"Lucinda," I say.

A pause. "Evangeline? Did you—"

"No," I say quickly. "No, I'm not quitting. I just wanted to call and tell you… thank you. I think things are going very well. I'm even meeting someone for lunch today."

"What's going on?" she asks. "You're not supposed to—"

"Lucinda," I say, sighing at her reaction. "I make the rules, OK?"

She lets out one of those scoffing laughs. The incredulous kind.

"And if I want to call and tell you thank you, then I will."

She's smiling. I can tell. "Who are you having lunch with?"

"I can't say. You wouldn't approve."

"What?" she asks, slight panic in that word.

"That's all I'm going to say. That's all I want to say. Talk soon. Bye."

I hang up the phone, listen to the beeping the computer inside makes as it completes my transaction, then hike my purse up onto my shoulder, adjust my sunglasses, and walk out the other side of the gardens and back into the city.

I catch a cab a few blocks down, get dropped off in front of the courthouse, and contemplate going inside to see if I can find Jordan before he finds me.

I decide against that. It's not the fast beating of my heart, either. It's not the feeling of too many people, even though that feeling is there. It's because I'd like to be early today. I don't want to share a table with some stranger who wants to talk to me. I want to watch Jordan when he comes in and not be distracted.

He's handsome and I want to study his face. I want to imagine what it would be like to talk to him. Date him. Fuck him.

So I get to the coffee house at eleven forty. The lunch crowd is just starting to pick up but there are several open tables. I ask for one in the back, in the corner where I can hide in the shadows. I take my scarf off as my heart begins to gallop inside my chest, but I did that yesterday, so it feels a little familiar. I leave the gloves and sunglasses on.

I order the club with avocado without looking at the menu and feel like a local. Which makes me smile. Not because I'm tricking anyone. But because it's true, after all. Practice makes perfect. And it's just as easy to lie to other people as it is myself. Which is kind of a relief.

I spend the next twenty minutes watching the door, so eager to see the man I came for. And when the minutes tick off, and he's late, I have a sick feeling in my stomach that this whole idea is stupid, and I'm stupid, and I will sit here all afternoon, by myself, and never get the reward I'm after.

To watch, instead of being the one watched.

But then he's there. At twelve o nine. Pushing through the crowd, leaning into the ear of the hostess, who points him to the counter, where he walks up with the confidence of a man who has nothing to fear and orders a sandwich.

He's not staying, I realize. If I want to talk to him, I will have to make a move. I put both gloved hands on either side of the plate holding the club sandwich I won't be eating, and begin to rise.

"Angela!"

My head swivels at the name and I sit back into my chair, surprised that Mike, the interloper from yesterday, is making his way to my table.

"Ha!" he says, pointing to the empty chair on the other side of the table. "You saved me a seat. See, one good deed yesterday gets me a seat today." He says that as he unwraps his scarf, takes off his gloves, shoving them into his coat pocket, and sits down.

Jesus fucking Christ. I sigh. "Hello," I say. "I didn't expect to see you again."

"I'm here every day," he says, looking up at the waitress to say, "I'll have what she's having," pointing to my plate. The waitress nods, and then Mike turns back to me. "So, how's work today?"

Jordan is paying for his lunch. He's going to leave in like two minutes.

"People treating you good over there?" Mike nods his head, indicting the government buildings across the street.

"Fine, yes." Jordan is checking his watch. And when he looks up, he's staring right at me. He smiles, then gives me a two-fingered wave. Almost... a salute.

I put my gloved hands on the table again, one on either side of my plate, and this time, I stand up.

"Hey," Mike says, covering one of my hands. "Do you want to go out some time? You know, like a real date or something? Dinner? Maybe drinks after work tonight?"

I stare down at Mike, unsure what to say. I don't think I've ever been asked that question before.

"What?" he asks. "Why do you look so surprised? Don't tell me people aren't beating down your door to ask you out. You're so beautiful."

"No," I snap. Rudely. And then I sigh, because I don't want to be rude to this man. He was nice to me yesterday. And I really needed his help at the time. He kinda saved me, in a way. "I'm sorry," I say. "I didn't mean for it to come out like that. I just... I don't date people from work."

Which is a lame excuse because obviously I don't work with him.

But he shrugs it off. "It's OK."

"I have to go," I say, fishing into my wallet to find a twenty-dollar bill and placing it on the table next to my uneaten sandwich. I turn around, find Jordan gone.

My heart skips a beat. Then I see the back of his winter coat, passing through the front door.

I rush after him, intent on getting what I came for.

Which is stupid. I realize that. Because I have no idea what I came for. Did I expect him to... what? Fuck me in the bathroom?

Why? Why does that thought even come to mind?

When I get to the door, a whole crowd of people are entering, and I have to say, "Excuse me," several times as I push past them, oblivious to their reactions, and when I get outside I look around. Wildly. People pass me, staring, their watching eyes glued to mine. Entrancing me in the poison of their gaze.

I don't have my scarf on. They can see most of my face. Which sends my heart racing again, but for all the wrong reasons. And by the time I hastily put it on, Jordan has disappeared.

Again.

Fuck.

CHAPTER THIRTY-FOUR

I'm waiting for her when she comes home, my cameras trained on the front door like a cat watching a hole in the wall for a mouse.

She is rumpled. Hair tousled, breathing hard, cheeks red from the cold, and beautiful in all her disheveledness.

I feel like maybe this is the real Evangeline. That this stupid goal of spying on Jordan has taken her somewhere she's been before, but hasn't been back to in a very long time. Like it's giving her power.

Why? I have no idea.

But I think... I think I really like the powerful music maker.

She takes her coat off, throws it on the floor, then her gloves, and her hat, and her sunglasses. She looks up at the chandelier. At me, looking at her through the black bulb. "What the fuck?" she screams. "Why can't I just catch a break? I mean, I'm out there, putting myself out there, and he even looked at me! Waved! And this stupid guy who thinks... I don't know what he thinks... is distracting me, asking me out on a date! A date?" She shakes her head, like the idea makes no sense to her. "I just want a few moments to spy on Jordan. Is that too much to ask? Where else does he go? You have to know. Tell me. I feel like I'm making an effort here and the universe is just laughing in my face!" She squints her eyes up at the camera bulb. "Are *you* laughing at me?"

I chuckle. But say nothing. Not even a push of the intercom to let her know I'm listening.

"I know you're listening," she says, eyes fierce, expression defiant and vulnerable at all the same time. "Say something."

I take a sip of the coffee I got while I was out. Enjoy it.

"X," she says. "Are you there?"

X. Just hearing her say my name makes me want her. It's so close to what Jordan calls me. *Ix. X.* So close.

"I'm going upstairs," she says.

"Good," I say, but only to myself.

"I'm gonna put the blindfold on," she says.

"Perfect," I say.

"I'm gonna wait for you."

"I'm gonna make you wait."

She starts walking up the stairs, then turns about halfway up to stare at me again. "You'll come, right?"

My heart skips.

"You will," she says, trying to convince herself. "I know this probably isn't easy for you. And you probably have a million better things to do with your life right now than babysit me." She pauses. "But I'm glad we're doing this. I... I think I like you."

And with that proclamation, she turns her back to me and disappears.

I am so stunned at her admission, I don't even follow her on the cameras. I just sit there in front of the monitor, wondering... wondering how I got here. And wondering what I did to deserve this chance.

Because that's what it seems like all of a sudden. Not that I'm here helping her, but she's here helping me.

The stories we exchange are sad, but beautiful too. They're desperate, but bring a sense of peace.

It makes me wonder if she's getting better because of me? Or Jordan?

I'm dying to know the answer to that question.

Especially since I'm starting to figure out why I'm really here.

And it's not her.

But I want it to be her.

I don't make her wait too long. Not because I'm feeling generous or anything. But because I think I need her tonight. I think I'm going enjoy this a lot. Because I sense that she's not as fucked up as she thinks and our time together in this house is drawing to an end. It hasn't even been a week, but we're almost done here.

Almost. But not quite.

So I get up, take off my clothes, check the mirror and wonder if I should shave. Decide no. I want to eat her pussy and I want the stubble on my jaw to scratch the sensitive skin on her inner thighs raw.

I want her to remember what we do at night when, tomorrow, she leaves here again looking for the man who isn't me.

When I climb the stairs leading up to the third-floor bedroom I realize I didn't check to see if she was wearing the blindfold. She could be waiting in there to ambush me. Eyes open. She'll know everything if she is.

But I open the door without knocking anyway. Trusting her.

She's lying down on top of the white down comforter, legs straight, arms at her side, the tie wrapped around her eyes just like she's supposed to be.

Trusting me too.

She exhales as I stand over her. Sensing that I'm close, maybe fearful I will leave if she moves. She stays absolutely still.

"Touch me," she breathes.

I want to talk to her so badly. I want to say so many things about what she's been writing in our book. I want her to know I'm listening. I'm here. I want to help her.

And I want to know what she thinks about me. The things I've told her.

Her hand reaches out, finds my bare leg. She sucks in a breath, surprised that I'm naked. But then her palm flattens on my thigh, her fingertips stroking me softly.

I close my eyes. Lost in her touch. The moment. Not caring that everything we're doing here will end soon. I have her for now and that's all that matters.

My knee sinks the mattress next to her hip. The other leg swings over her body until her legs are between mine. There's a crinkle in her forehead, like she's closing her eyes tightly underneath the silk tie, not wanting to see the truth, but eventually, she'll have to. She's gonna come to terms with her life. Maybe I'll come to terms with mine too?

I stare at her face. Her tongue darts out, swipe across her lips. Wets them.

The smile on my face is between her legs a moment later. Licking. My tongue probing between the lips of her pussy until I find her clit. I take it gently between my teeth. She whines, then lifts her hips up, pushing my face deeper. She tries to open her legs, give me better access, but I hold my position, not yet ready to give her what she needs, still enjoying the tease.

"Take my blindfold off," she says.

I stop.

Her hands finds my head, urge me to continue. But I just stare up her body. Past her peaked nipples, to her sweet face.

I shake my head no.

"Please," she begs, still pushing on my head. Hips still moving. Like she wants to grind my face on her pussy.

I ignore her verbal request and sit back, taking both her hands in mine as I pull her up as I lie back. She gets what I'm doing. She gets me. So as I lie back, she scoots up, and even though I won't let her take off the blindfold, I will grant her nonverbal request. Her legs settle on either side of my head as she lowers her pussy down onto my waiting tongue.

I close my eyes and lick her. Tongue sweeping back and forth, stopping at the nub of her clit to flick it until she arches her back so far, the tips of her long, dark hair brush against my hands holding onto her ass.

She lifts up just a little, giving me more access, and then begins to rub her pussy against my unshaven jaw.

She will have a rash in the morning. And I'm gonna make sure she thinks about what I'm doing to her all day long.

She's inhaling, exhaling. Long, breathy pants that get louder and louder as she slides her pussy against my chin. My tongue tickles her clit, making her squeal, and then her hands slap down on the bed above my head and she really begins to fuck my face.

I push a finger into her asshole, remembering how much she liked that last time, and decide I will fuck her in the ass before she leaves this house for good. I will take her every way I can think of before I let her go.

She comes in my mouth, my tongue lapping up the gushing wetness of her climax. Her legs straighten, flatten against the outside of my thighs as she slides down my body.

For a second her blindfold slips and I think, *Shit*.

But she adjusts it. Puts it back into place, still sucking in air like she will never get enough. Her body trembling slightly, her muscles fatigued from suspending herself over my face.

I flip her off me, pin her to the bed, and then allow myself one more transgression...

I say, "Now it's my turn," in a whisper so low, it barely counts as words.

CHAPTER THIRTY-FIVE

EVANGELINE

"Yes," is the only answer I have for him tonight. I will do anything to keep this man with me right now. I know he's going to walk out. He always walks out. Leaves me here in this strange bedroom that I now think of as our room alone. And he's gonna do that again tonight. Maybe forever. Maybe I'll never truly know him beyond the sex and the words on the page that come after. But right now, it's enough. More than enough.

He flips me over in such a rough, quick manner, I gasp, fear shooting through my body, but then...

Oh. *Jesus.*

He's on top of me. His mouth kissing my back. His leg kicking mine open, spreading me wide to give him access. His hard cock pushes against the curve of my ass, then his hand is there, guiding it between my legs, rubbing the wetness I made for him.

He slips inside me, stretching my pussy open with his wide girth, lowering himself, pushing himself deeper and deeper until he touches something inside me that makes me bite my lip and stifle a scream.

He stops. Waits. Leans his face down into my neck, and whispers, "You OK?" in my ear, his soft breath just a tickle against my skin.

I don't know why two stupid words in the middle of sex with a stranger mean so much to me. But they are *everything*.

I swallow down tears and nod my head. "Yes. Don't stop."

He goes slow after that. Still pushing himself deep inside me. His hips rocking on my ass cheeks. His arms balancing himself, pushing into the mattress on either side of my head. I can smell him. It's the smell of snow, and the city, and all the things I've been missing these past twelve years.

And even though we've been rough with each other all the other nights we've been together, we are calm tonight. Like this is more than sex.

I know it's not true. I know why he's here. I know what he's doing. But for some reason it doesn't matter. He's still here.

Which is more than I can say for anyone else.

"I want to see you," I say.

He leans down into me again, his mouth on my neck, kissing and nipping at my earlobe. And maybe that's all I really want. His consideration as he struggles to deny me so he can keep his secrets.

"I do see you," I say, coming to a conclusion. "And I don't need eyes to do it. Because I have your words. And they don't lie."

He huffs a breath into the long strands of my hair. A laugh, I realize. But he's not laughing *at* me. What I said makes him happy. It's a happy laugh.

"Come," he whispers. "Come for me again, Evangeline."

And when he says my name, I know him.

It excites me. And he begins to move faster now. His grinding more pronounced. His movements more exaggerated. His cock slipping in and out of my slick pussy so easily, he has to thrust it further and further inside me to get the friction he needs.

He fucks me hard enough to push me up the bed, until my head is bumping into the soft upholstered headboard. My palms flatten on the fabric to give him the resistance he needs.

I arch my back, pushing my ass up and into his fast-rocking hips, and when his fingers slide under my body and find the little nub of my clit, electricity shoots up my stomach. He strums me the way you strum an instrument. He plays me. It makes me think of music, and applause, and all the good things that came with being child Evangeline.

His other hand grabs my breast, squeezing so hard I cry out. This time he knows it's not pain, but pleasure, and he doesn't stop to ask me if I'm OK.

He just knows.

"I want to come inside you," he says. "And I don't care what happens."

I whine so loud, my yes echoes off the ceiling.

No one in this room gives a good goddamn about consequences.

We come together. For the first time in my life, I come at the same time as the man on top of me. He bites my neck, sticks his fingers in my mouth, pushing them towards the back of my throat. I suck on them, imagining the way I will suck his cock tomorrow night before I let him fuck me. And enjoy wave after wave of climax rushing through my body.

He falls off to the side, breathing hard. Like a man after sex. Something I knew once, but lost. Something I want again, with him.

"X," I whisper, turning my blind face towards his spent body.

"Come here," he says, pulling me in close to him, wrapping his arms around my body. "Come here and be still. No talking," he whispers. "Just be still with me."

I fall asleep, I guess. Safe in the arms of my stranger. My watcher. My protector. Because that's what he feels like.

When I wake it's still dark. The middle of the night, I think. But the little moon nightlight is on and there's a note on the bedside table.

It says... *My name is Ix, not X. Call me Ix from now on.*

I smile as I clutch the note in my hand. I have his real name. It's a weird name, for sure. But it's not X, and it's not Stranger, and it's not Watcher. I look up at the camera. I don't know if he can see me in the dark, but I can see him. In my mind. In my dreams. In my future.

"Ix," I say to the camera. "Very nice to meet you."

CHAPTER THIRTY-SIX

IXION

God, this woman. Where has she been all my life?

My phone rings. I know who it is. Jordan has been calling all night. When I got back to my little room there were already several messages and texts. All saying the same thing. "Call. Me. Now." In that commanding tone of voice (even in the texts).

I answer, because why not? "Yup," I say into the phone. I'm sort of impressed at the amount of indifference I can conjure up in a single syllable. I almost feel like I'm channeling Jordan. Because right now, I do not give one flying fuck about him.

And that's a first. In a long-ass time. Fucking Jordan has consumed my life, I realize. Ever since shit went wrong with Augustine I've been... dwelling.

"What the fuck is happening over there?"

"What'd ya mean?" I ask. Evangeline just found the note. And I'm obsessed with zooming in on her face, trying to reach her expression as she reads it. Jordan is blabbing on about something, but I tune him out.

She smiles. Then she looks up at me. Says, "Ix. Very nice to meet you."

"What the fuck was that?"

"What was what?" I say automatically.

"Was that her? Talking to you?"

"What do you want? I'm fucking doing my job, man. I'm watching her right now."

"Did she call you Ix?"

"Dude, you're hallucinating. Why are you calling me?"

"What's happening over there?"

"Nothin'. Why?"

"She called her therapist today. On like… a *pay phone*."

"Did she?" I ask, sorta laughing about that. "Well, she broke her phone the first day she was here. Smashed the screen to bits. And even though she asked me for a new one, I didn't get her one. What'd she say to her doctor?"

"She thanked her. And said she was meeting someone for lunch. Who the fuck was she meeting for lunch?"

"Well," I say, turning away from the monitor. Fuckin' woman is way too distracting. And I'm getting the impression that Jordan is feeling me out about something. Something I don't want him to feel me out about. "That's nice, I guess. This weird-ass treatment plan is working then, right? She left the house."

"Where did she go?"

"Dude," I say. "I'm not sure that's any of your business. You're not her doctor."

"I'm your employer."

I laugh. Kinda loud. "Fuck. You."

"I know what you're doing," he says.

"No, I really don't think you do. Because if you did you wouldn't be on the phone with me right now. You'd be here, in my face, asking what the actual fuck."

"Stay the fuck away from this woman, do you hear me?"

"Or what?"

"You're fired. Pack your shit—"

"No," I say. So calm. So steady. "No. She needs this, Jordan. So put your petty bullshit with me aside and do something for someone else for once."

I hear his incredulous laugh just before I end the call and turn my ringer off.

Let him come over. I'd love to have another face-to-face with Jordan Wells.

When I look back at the monitors Evangeline is lying back down and if I look very hard I think I can still see a smile on her face.

I take out our book and read her last entry again.

I'm tired of the poems.
I'm tired of the pretty words
all dressed up to make it shine and take the trophy of first prize.
I'm tired of the dream I never dreamed,
for it wasn't mine and no one cared if they stole
my youth, or my talent, or my soul.

I was just a number.
A diamond ring made to sing
then forsaken and left shaken.

My father sold me. Like a thing that can be sold.
I am not a thing.
He is not a king.
And I'd rather die in the dark than be told
this is my purpose in life.

Jesus. *Sold?* I shake my head and hope that was a metaphor for how her parents used her. Because clearly they did use her. But I can't shake the bad feeling creeping up on me. Like something just happened but I missed it. Or something's coming and I can't see it.

Stop being stupid, Ixion. It's a fucking game. And you're both winning, so who cares? Just write your next entry and leave her the book. What she does with it after that is up to her.

I pick up the pen but just hold it over the page, unsure of what to say next.

A text dings on my phone and I almost ignore it, because all I want to do is think about the girl upstairs and what I need to tell her next.

And after I read that text, I wish I had ignored it.

Because this changes everything.

CHAPTER THIRTY-SEVEN

EVANGELINE

In the morning I can't get down to the kitchen fast enough. My feet trip over themselves trying to skip down steps. I bounce into the hallway, sliding around the corner, eager to get back to our story.

Our book isn't there.

"Ix?" I ask the ceiling. "Where's your story? This is the end. You can't deny me the end."

It's a joke, said jokingly. Because of course it is. Because there's no way he'd do that to me. Because I know him so well now. I know almost all his secrets and this was the last secret. The final piece of information that will open him up to me completely.

But there's nothing but silence echoing back in my head.

So I wait. I make coffee. I eat the almost-spoiled raspberries left in the fridge, and I wait.

But he never says anything. No notes materialize. I even get up and walk around the house, conveniently disappearing from the kitchen to give him a chance to come out of whatever secret room he's hiding in and leave me the final chapter of our story.

I even get dressed, go outside, and swing on that stupid family swing for a while, hoping that when I go

273

back inside, our book, the story of us, will be there waiting for me. And next to it a new note. An apology. *Sorry for making you wait.*

But it isn't. He didn't write that. There is no apology. There is no book.

It's like… he's forsaken me.

Why?

I have an urge to write. Every morning I've been writing back to him. I have the poem nearly composed in my head. It's murky, and sad, and reveals secrets that I was, for once, ready to reveal.

I was going to give him the last piece of my puzzle too.

But he never shows. And I can't write the poem anywhere else but in *our book*. That's the only place it belongs. The only place it could possibly exist. So it sits up there in my head like a black cloud hanging over me. Like a threat. Like a menace. Like this is an omen of something very, very bad.

And unlike the last time he made me angry, I have no urge to break things. It's like I don't have the energy I once did. Or the… anger. Or whatever it was that was fueling my darkness.

I am ready to step into the light but the light is gone.

The stupid clock is gonging off the hours and when it gongs off eleven tones in a row, I make a decision.

Fuck it.

I'm going to meet Jordan.

I get dressed. Put on my scarf, my gloves, my hat, my coat, my sunglasses. I call for the cab and I wait outside for it to come.

I actually *wait* outside.

And when it does come, I get in and find it to be stifling hot because stupid Denver is having one of those sunny days in the dead of winter, like it's prone to do. Maybe, if I don't play my show and get over this bullshit, I will move somewhere colder. Somewhere the sun refuses to shine?

I fantasize about this. Someplace far. Like Alaska. Or Iceland. Someplace where the darkness is welcome.

But then I recall some lesson from childhood. That the sun never sets in the summer in those places. And then I feel like the whole fucking world is against me for some reason.

Why?

I have to take off my gloves and my scarf because I'm sweating underneath all this garb. And even though I really want to take my hat off, I don't. And not because I want to stay covered up, but because my hair is a mess. I didn't really pay much attention to it when I was leaving and... and today I *will* talk to Jordan and I don't want him to see me as the woman with the fucked-up hair!

I pay the stupid cab driver using the stupid machine on the back of the headrest, and get out of the cab, slamming the door behind me, and stand there, looking up at the stupid coffee house and the people outside, and I wonder, maybe for the first time, why a guy as beautiful as Jordan comes to this stupid place every goddamned day?

Are there not better places? Less busy places? I mean, is the goddamned club sandwich so goddamned good here that these people can't find somewhere else to eat one?

I push my way inside, probably rudely, but I don't care. I've been coming here all week with a goal in mind and every day I've been denied. And this day, of all days, is not a day for denial.

I can't take it. I really can't.

So I stand there, combing the place, looking for Jordan, and who do I see?

Fucking Mike.

But I take a second look at fucking Mike. Because fucking Mike is already sitting with someone. A woman who is not me, obviously. And fucking Mike glances at me, then averts his eyes.

Averts his eyes.

Like I am someone not worthy of being seen.

I seethe. What the ever-loving fuck is going on with this day?

"Just one today?" the hostess asks me.

"Yes," I manage to say, somewhat civilly, I might add. "Table for one." I say it loud. Loud enough that Mike over near the window hears me and once again glances in my direction, but then quickly looks away, pretending I'm not even here as he talks to the woman across from him like they're together or something. When I know good and goddamned well he's got no girlfriend because just yesterday he was trying to get me to go out with him.

Huh. So that's his game. He's with someone who *will* go out with him for drinks after work. Good. Good for him. I'm not here to see him, anyway. I'm here to see Jordan.

"Right this way," the hostess says.

So I follow her, and she takes me all the way to the back, in the shadows, where a goddamned tree in a pot is blocking my view of the door. And I really want to say, *Hey, can I have another table? You know, like a good one?* But I realize there's no other tables. This is the last one. And I'm probably lucky I didn't have to cajole Mike into letting me sit at his table as a third wheel.

So I shut up, sit down, and order the stupid club with the magic avocado and wait for Jordan to appear.

But he doesn't.

An hour later, I'm still there, my club sandwich reduced to a bit of bread crust, and the lunch crowd has all gone back to work. Alone. As usual.

"Is there anything else I can get you?" my waitress asks.

"No," I say, no longer manic with purpose, but defeated with disappointment. "Just the check."

Which she has ready, pulling it out of her apron pocket and setting it on the table, like I've been sitting here too long and she's been waiting for me to disappear so she can seat someone else.

I pay and go outside, ready to just get in a cab and go the hell home, and... there's no cabs. Not one in sight.

So I start walking towards the Botanic Gardens, because at least I live next to a major landmark and there's signs everywhere, hoping for a cab. But every single one of them passes me by. Because of course they do. This is like everyone-needs-a-cab day and they all have passengers already.

By the time I stumble through the gardens nearly an hour later, I'm dead tired.

But hopeful.

Hopeful that Ix is at home, waiting for me, perhaps out of his mind with worry.

But when I key in the code to the gate I feel despair washing over me. And when I get inside and look up at the chandelier bulb, I know. I feel it in my gut.

He's not even here.

I drop my purse on the floor and only then realize… I left my gloves and scarf in the cab on the way over to the coffee house.

I walked all the way home uncovered except for sunglasses and a coat. And I didn't even notice.

This should make me feel good. That finally there is something in my life that trumps my stupid fear of being watched.

But I wasn't even seen today.

I was nobody.

Mike didn't even see me.

Ix has left me.

And all I want right now is to be seen by him.

I go upstairs. All the way upstairs. Take off my clothes, lie on the bed naked, and then fish the blindfold out from under the pillow and tie it around my eyes.

I will wait, I decide.

I will wait just like this until he comes for me.

I wait a long time. Hours and hours. And in that time my mind goes wild with the things that have been happening here. Both under this roof and at the coffee house.

The suspicions form in my head, the clues leading me down a path. Several times I make up my mind and several times I change it.

But no matter how hard I try, the idea lingers.

Ix isn't who I think he is.

CHAPTER THIRTY-EIGHT

IXION

By the time I leave Chella's tea house it's dark. I didn't mean to stay so long. Didn't even mean to go. Her text last night was vague, but it was enough to plant ideas in my head. Enough to make me question everything.

I didn't mean to say so much to her. We're not exactly friends and I barely know her, but she knows enough. More than most. And she had a bit of information she wanted to share with me. Just in case I wasn't aware.

I was not aware.

Her information ripped my world apart in too many ways to describe, so I don't bother summing it up in my head.

It's just...sad. Sad that people can be so manipulative. So self-centered. So fucking filled with lies that they can't even tell the difference between honesty and deceit.

I'm careful with Jordan's Mercedes as I pull into the carriage house, even though I want to crash this motherfucker into the side of the house. Even more cautious as I peer over the gate to the garden, afraid Evangeline might be outside.

But she isn't.

Even after what Chella told me today, I'm not mad at Evangeline. That girl doesn't have a dishonest bone in her body. She had nothing to do with Jordan's stupid fucking game. She's not even a player. Just a piece to be moved around the chessboard.

Like me.

Fuck that, I'm not a piece, I'm a player.

In fact, this is my fuckin' game.

Isn't it?

Am I delusional? Crazy, like I thought Evangeline to be?

She's not. But neither am I. Especially after what Chella told me today.

Fuckin' Jordan. Now I remember why I hate him. Why I left and never looked back. Why I never wanted to come here in the first place.

I was suspicious, but not suspicious enough, apparently.

I walk down the path that leads to the back steps, take them two at a time until I'm at the bottom, and key in the code to get inside.

A huge feeling of relief washes over me as I close myself up inside. And for a second, I wonder if that's how Evangeline felt all those years she locked herself up inside? Did she feel that relief when she came home?

If so, I can relate. I want nothing more than to block out the world right now. Just be alone in my aloneness.

Her body, lying prone on the bed up in the master bedroom, makes me look at the monitor. But the blindfold she's wearing makes me deflate with anguish.

She's waiting for me.

I can't do it tonight, Evangeline. I just can't. There's too much bullshit rattling around in my head. And if I go to you, you'll know. You'll feel it. I'll ruin all the good I've done and I can't. I just can't fuckin' do it.

But of course I can't tell her that. I can't tell her anything. I could do the little intercom crackle, but that would invite more discussion on the matter. It would open it up and I want to keep everything closed right now.

I can't.

So I just sit in the chair and watch, like I'm supposed to, and pick up the notebook to finish the story.

I don't get far because she sits up in bed. "I know you're here now. I felt something. The rumble of a car nearby. The vibration of a door closing inside this house. I know you're here. And you had better come to me right now and tell me why. Why did you leave this morning? Why didn't you finish the story? I had a poem for you! All written up in my head and I had nowhere to write it."

Fuck.

"I went to see Jordan and he didn't show up."

Fuck again.

"But you were there, weren't you? *Mike*."

What the fuck?

"Was it fun? Watching me wait? Was it fun when you paraded another woman in my face? Was it *fun*"—she stresses the word hard now—"when I had to leave alone? Did you know I walked home? All the way home?"

She's visibly shaking. And the image of her, wearing the blindfold, is disturbing.

I reach for the intercom, press the button, and say, "Take off the blindfold and go to sleep. I'm not coming."

"Fuck you!" she yells. "If you won't come to me, I'll go to you."

She stands up, blindfold still on, and walks across the room like she can see without eyes.

She can't. She trips over the rug and falls on her hands and knees.

281

"Evangeline," I bark into the intercom, my voice booming, louder now than it's ever been in her presence. "Take off the blindfold and go to bed."

She just shakes her head as she gets uneasily to her feet. She stumbles over the rug again, but this time catches her fall with a hand on the bedside table. She feels along the wall, her fingertips now her eyes, until she comes to the door.

She pulls it open.

She stands at the top of the stairs.

And then she steps down.

CHAPTER THIRTY-NINE

EVANGELINE

I slip, my heel skidding off the polished wood stairs, and land on my ass. The hit is hard, and bruising, and I slide down several more stairs before I catch hold of the railing and stop the fall.

Somewhere in the house, somewhere far away, I hear a door bang open, as if hitting a wall. And for some stupid reason I cannot fathom, I wonder if the doorknob made a hole in the sheet rock.

Footsteps echo after that. Coming up from below— so he's in the basement. I hold on to the railing as I make my way down to the second floor, my fingertips gripping the wood tightly.

That fall really fucking hurt and I'm going to have a giant bruise on my ass tomorrow.

"Go. Back. Upstairs."

He's panting out the words, very out of breath. Which is why they come out like three separate sentences. They're not mean, though. Not a command. More of a request. One I choose not to take into consideration.

"Come with me then," I say, pretty calm for the circumstances. "I don't want to be alone today. It was a rough day. I'm tired. I need..." I draw in a huge breath. "I need to be with you."

"I had a hard day too. I'm tired too. And I need to be *alone*."

I realize… this is the first time I've really heard his true voice. Without the static of the intercom or being whispered so low into my ear it almost didn't count as speech.

It's deep. And rough. Like his jaw under the touch of my fingertips that left the tender skin between my legs sore with a rash. Like the chiseled muscles of his stomach. The sculpted shoulders rounding out his arms.

But… I can't help but shake the feeling that hearing him is very bad. Like he's giving up a part of himself he should still be saving. Like…

"Then let's spend the night together," I say, desperate. It takes every bit of self-control not to lift the blindfold away from my eyes and look at him. But that would spoil the game for sure. It really will be over and I'm not ready to stop playing. Not yet.

"I can't," he says.

"It was you, wasn't it? You're Mike."

"I'm not Mike. Don't be dumb. That guy is just another sad, in-it-for-the-money player. Fuckin' tool. Just like Jordan."

"Jordan didn't show today," I say, voice quivering. "I sat there and waited for him. He never came."

Ix lets out a long breath, like he really is tired. "I'm not surprised. He had a lot going on."

I am desperate to keep him here. I feel compelled to say something that will convince him. Change his mind about whatever it was that ruined his day and make him spend his night with me.

I consider my options. I don't have many, but I refuse to spend tonight alone. I need him. *Something*. I cannot stand to be invisible now. Not after being seen by him for so many days. So I say, "Give me your story and I'll go back upstairs."

"I didn't write it."

"Liar," I whisper. "That's a lie, Ix. I know you wrote it. The only reason you've been writing it down at all was to get to the end. And this was supposed to be the end."

"Evangeline," he says. I can almost imagine him pinching the bridge of his nose in frustration. "I can't tonight, OK? It needs to be revised. So tomorrow."

"No," I say. "I'm going home tomorrow."

He pauses. For several seconds. So long I start counting. And when I get to ten, he takes a deep breath. "Why?"

"Because we're done here. I'm cured, I think."

He huffs out some air. "You didn't even play the violin yet."

"I didn't come here to play the violin," I say. "And I don't need to play it. I'm a prodigy. I know what I know. You don't lose something like that."

It comes out bitter and defensive.

"You don't sound so sure," he says.

I shift my weight onto my other foot. My hip is sore from the fall and I really want to sit down. But I refuse to go back upstairs and hide away in that bedroom.

"I want you to take me upstairs and stay with me or I want your ending. You don't revise an ending. If you have to revise it, then it's a lie. Are you lying to me?"

He pauses.

And that... *that* is what makes up my mind.

I stumble down the hallways towards him. I know he's at the top of the stairs. And when I crash into his hard body, feel the softness of his t-shirt, I get such a sad feeling, I pull away, spin, and then my foot hits the top step and I fall.

CHAPTER FORTY

I catch her by the arm, jerking it hard enough to make her cry out in pain, and just barely prevent her from toppling over and falling head-first down the stairs.

"Stop," I say, my heart beating fast at the near-fatal accident that almost happened. "Just fucking calm down and stop."

"No," she says, jerking her arm away. She turns and I see a massive bruise forming on her hip. It's ugly. Already deep purple and swollen. "I'm going downstairs."

"Then take off your fucking blindfold," I say, reaching for it.

Her hand grabs mine. Hard. Well, I mean hard for such a tiny hand. "Do not," she seethes, "remove my blindfold."

"Why are you doing this?" I ask. "Why are you being so fucking difficult?"

She opens her mouth to say something. Then pauses to take a breath and tries again. "It's not over yet," she whispers. "I want more time here."

"No one's kicking you out," I say.

"No, but you're leaving, I can feel it. So either help me down the stairs or get the hell out of my way."

She shoves me to make her point and then her foot is hovering over empty space—

I pull her back a second time. "Fine," I hiss. "Fine. I'll take you down the stairs. Just… be fucking careful, will you?"

"I will." Her voice is soft through her smile.

She steps very carefully as I lead her. Much more carefully than she was before. And the fear I had begins to fade. She will not fall and break her neck. She will not stumble into a hundred-year-old window and cut herself to pieces. She will be fine.

Unless, that is, I fuck her up again.

I hesitate when we get down into the grand foyer. "Where do you want to go now?"

"Outside," she says. "I want to sit on that swing with you."

"Evangeline," I growl. "You're completely naked. It's nineteen degrees outside. We're *not* going outside."

"I'm kidding." And then she giggles. Like… actually *giggles*. As if trying my patience was the cutest thing she's ever done in her life.

I smile. Reluctantly.

Maybe not so reluctantly.

I'm going to miss her.

"You seem to think I need to practice, so take me to that violin. You might as well be the first person to hear me play in a decade."

I stay absolutely still. Probably even hold my breath.

"Ix?" she says. "Did you hear me?"

I nod. Exhale. Then clear my throat and say, "Yeah. Yup. It's down here. Stay close to me. I don't want you to fall again."

Her small hands wrap around my bicep, squeezing like she never wants to let me go.

I'm so sorry, I want to say. *I'm so sorry you're part of this game. If I could take it back, I would. But I can't.*

But I can't. Because I'm a coward. And not only that, I'm playing as well.

I'll make it up to you. I promise.

There are no more incidents as I lead her down the hallway to the library. And I can't help thinking back to that first day I came here. How wrong I was to assume that her instrument would be the most interesting thing in this house. I pictured her unable to leave it behind when in reality she had almost no interest in it at all.

My intuition—my infamous intuition—failed me.

How many other things have I gotten wrong?

"Do you want to stand in front of the window?" I ask. Because I feel like... I have no idea who she is right now. I can't even begin to predict what she wants out of this night.

"No," she says. "I want you to sit on the couch. It's yellow, right? Crushed velvet? Something my mother would hate because it's too... romantic."

I stare at the yellow couch and remember back to her first night here. When she was in a blind panic. When she raced to the bathroom to hide. When she came out, wandered around, and then crumpled to the floor after she saw the violin waiting for her. How she slept, shivering with cold, desperately trying to cover herself with a blanket that would never be able to cover enough. How she never came back to this room again.

How wrong I got it.

How badly I have already fucked this up.

289

How she might take the gift I'll give her, but never forget why I gave it.

"I like it," I say, referring to the couch. Because I do. It's not something my mother would've liked either, and it hurts a little to think that. Because it means we're different. That I was always different.

"Get me the violin," Evangeline says, standing right in the place I put her in the middle of the room.

"OK," I say, prying her fingers from my arm before walking over to get it. When I pick it up I'm reminded of how light this instrument actually is. Mostly hollow, mostly air, nothing but thin wood and thinner strings. I take the bow and a little container of resin Evangeline will surely want, and bring it all over to the couch.

"Good," she says. "Now sit."

It's not an order. Not a command. Not a request, either. It's just… what she wants.

So I sit, because I want to give her what she wants tonight. And she sits on my knee, perched off to the side a little with her back straight, and her legs closed, and her hands reaching out.

I place the violin in them and it's like… she inflates. Immediately. Her chin lifts to accommodate the instrument, her shoulders square as one set of fingers find the strings and the other set holds the bow. She sucks in a breath, like she's about to play a flute instead of a violin.

"Now listen," she whispers. "Don't miss the gift I'm giving you."

When that bow touches those strings the room is immediately full. The tone starts out deep as she begins some once-well-rehearsed Evangeline Rolaine version of a scale. Her fingers fly, picking up and coming down on just the right string, as her bow slices through the air in just the right way. And the heavens open up inside this almost-empty room as she proclaims that in this singular, elegant way, she owns the entire fuckin' world.

She is poetry incarnate.

The beauty she creates makes me want to die from joy. The notes reverberate off the wood-paneled walls. The music takes over my mind, and my body submits to her spell, and there is no way anyone who hears her music could ever miss the fact that this girl, frightened as she was, lonely as she was, sad that she was, is nothing but a genius.

And with that realization I understand... she no longer needs me.

CHAPTER FORTY-ONE

EVANGELINE

I feel his sigh the moment the music starts. I feel him give in. His whole body relaxes even as mine tenses up and it's an analogy, really. How two people can be in the same room, experiencing the same thing, and discover two very different feelings lurking inside them.

I am nothing but power when I play. I am who I am. Completely whole. Thoroughly complete. Absolutely, conclusively *filled up.*

All the years between then and now melt away. None of them matter anymore.

There is no fear of watchful eyes. There is no sadness of dreams never realized. There is no remorse, or regrets, or shame, or guilt.

There is only us. Here. Now. Together.

Me, and my music.

I stop that thought as soon as I have it.

Because that was my problem in the first place. The possession the music holds over me. The enchantment I have with myself.

I am singular when I play. A small girl who rules the entire world. I am nothing but one and I don't want to be one anymore, I want to be two.

He did that for me.

He gave me back my life.

He made me see that I am not alone, I am not the center of the universe, I am not the culmination of millions of lives, lived over thousands of years.

I am just one soul in a sea of souls, all looking for their purpose.

And it's not fair that I was born with mine. It's not fair.

I know that. Have always known it. But I didn't care.

And I was used, and I was cheated, and I *was* nothing but my parents' golden opportunity.

But I let them do that.

I liked it.

And there's always a little more responsibility one can take, even if they are eight. Or ten. Or fifteen. Or immortal, like me. Because even after I die, I will live on.

It's not the world's fault I am who I am.

It's mine.

I can either learn to live with the responsibility or suck people dry with my expectations.

I don't want to be a taker. I don't want to exsanguinate the world with my power. I don't want to die alone, lonely, and leave the world nothing but the memory of music.

I want to share my gift with him forever.

So I force myself to slow down. The improvised powerful scale that fills the room to capacity turns into a sweet, soft melody that begs to be heard.

I make myself small. I make myself part of the world around me instead of overtaking it. I meld into something altogether new as my bow now caresses the strings like a long-lost lover.

Ix lets out a breath. Like he was holding it in. Like the music I make was forcing him to do that. The power of my talent holding him captive.

But he's free now.

Practice does make perfect.

His hands wander to my breasts, which wiggle slightly with the swaying motion of my body as I play. He pinches my nipple and I can feel his excitement growing against my bare thigh.

I stay slow and small. Let him become big and hard. Let him fill up the room with his masculine strength.

Draw from it.

Smile.

"Yes," I say. "Touch me everywhere. Take anything you want."

"You don't want to give me that power," he says. His voice is low, like the notes coming from my fingers.

"I really do," I whisper back.

I slip into Ave Maria, my favorite song as a child. The first one I ever played on stage when I was four.

Ix's hands stop everything and the room, though filled with music, goes still. I close my eyes as my body moves, and he begins again, the song powerful, but what's happening between us even more so.

His fingertips slide up and down my ribs. Soft, sweeping motions that send a chill up my neck and come out in the notes that float in the air.

"God," he whispers, his touch wandering down to the curve of my hips. My legs part, like he commanded them to. But really, it's nothing more than my own invitation.

Which he accepts by parting the lips of my pussy, finding the wetness accumulating just for him, and begins to play me like I'm playing the violin.

CHAPTER FORTY-TWO

IXION

I can't stop myself. The beauty in this room is overwhelming. Not just the song she's playing. It's not just Ave Maria coming from the soul of one of the world's most talented violinists, it's her too. Her sweet face, her innocence, her large, soft breasts, the shape of her waist and hips and the tickling touches of her long hair as it brushes across my arms as she gives me what I wanted since the first time I met her—I just didn't realize it.

Herself. With no expectations. Blind and willing.

Her pussy is wet, her clit swelling under my touch the same way my cock is now filled with longing.

Her legs open wider, the weight of her body on my legs silently driving me wild.

I can't wait any longer.

Reluctantly, I take my touch from her to me. Open my belt, open my pants, and fist my cock as I pull it out.

She shivers. Like she knows what I'm doing even though she's blind. "Yes," she murmurs.

I don't need her encouragement, but I do like it. Leaning back into the cushions to get a better view forces her to shift her weight. I pump one hand up and down my cock as the other returns to her open and exposed pussy. If she could only see herself. How beautiful she is. How perfect. If ever there was a moment that needed to be caught on film, this is it.

But a wave of regret washes over me. Because no latent image could ever capture the stunning brilliance of her in real time.

She turns her back to me, but not in a dismissive way. Because she edges her ass up my lap until my cock is between her legs. She lifts her hips, her fingers still playing the soundtrack to the lust building inside us.

She hovers over me, her pussy rubbing against the tip of my cock.

I can't wait any longer. She is urging me to take her and I just want to please in this moment. I want nothing more than to give her what she wants.

My cock slips inside her, but she pulls back, looking over her shoulder, and stops playing. "No," she whispers. "I've had that before. Take me in a new way, Ix. Be the first ever to take me in that way."

I have to blink, several times, as the realization of what she's asking for manifests.

Her ass. She wants me to fuck her in the ass.

"Are you sure?" I ask, my voice thick with husk and growl, betraying the hunger inside me.

"Yes," she says. "Yes."

"Then stand up," I say.

She obeys, resumes playing the soft, slow song as she rises off my lap. I kick her legs wide, her bow still sliding across the strings, and then sink to my knees, pull her ass cheeks apart, and lick her. My fingers drag the now pooling readiness from her pussy to her asshole, and I slowly stick my finger in.

She never stops playing. But she whines, and grunts, and when my finger is all the way inside her, she whimpers, "More."

She is so wet now, so eager for what's coming next, that her asshole is well primed when I sit back in the chair, place her on my lap, and press my cock up against her tight muscles.

Her music turns wild and frantic, her bow skipping across the strings, her fingers jumping on the neck.

And then I enter her.

She moans. A whimpering moan that's equal parts pain and pleasure. I hike her legs open, totally exposing her, and pull her back into my chest, my hands cupping her perfect, round breasts, and squeeze them, just as she clenches her muscles and squeezes me back.

Dying. I am dying of pleasure.

I close my eyes, let my hands wander back between her legs, strumming her clit, as she becomes more comfortable with my cock inside her ass, and begins to move—just a little, just enough to drive me crazy.

One hand goes to her hip, urging her to fuck me harder. Urging her to let me even deeper inside her, while my fingers push up inside her pussy, stretching her wide from both ends.

"Oh, my God," she moans.

And she never.

Stops.

Playing.

"I want to see you," I say, urging her to turn around. "And I want you to see me. Take off the fucking blindfold."

"No," she says, her song slow again. "No. Not yet."

299

So I have to settle. I have to settle for fucking her in the ass, her back to me, her song filling my ears, her long hair teasing my chest as it lightly crashes onto my skin like feathers in a wind storm.

But there are worse ways to settle.

"Come," I say, my thumb finding her slit as I push my fingers deeper. "Come on my fingers right now."

She lets out one long breath, her body stiff for a moment, her bow stuck mid-air, her fingers still... and then she melts into me. Gushing relief spills out of her, coats my fingers, spilling past them, and drips down onto my cock.

I have to bite my fucking lip to stop my own climax.

She falls forward, drops the violin on the floor, and places her hands on my knees as she pants through the waves of pleasure that overtake her body.

I make myself wait. It can't end yet. I'm not ready.

She takes all the decisions away from me when she stands up, my cock slipping out of her ass, and then turns around, gets on her knees between my legs, takes my cock in her hand, and lowers her mouth to it.

No hesitation. No overthinking. No resistance at all. Willing to lose herself in the moment. Willing to do anything and everything to keep this dream going.

I die.

I die over and over again as she licks my tip, wraps her lips around my swollen head, and then pushes my cock deep into her throat.

There is no way I can't come. No chance I won't explode.

I grab her hair, guiding her mouth, pushing her down onto my cock until her nose is almost flat against my stomach. She gags, gasps for breath, and then tilts her head up like she's looking me in the eyes.

I want to rip that blindfold off and see her. Really fucking see her.

But she's reading my mind, or maybe she's telling me no, she can't continue like this, I'm suffocating her with my cock, because she shakes her head.

I lift her face off me and come all over her mouth.

Her hands crash onto my chest, pulling at my t-shirt, clawing her way up my body until she's sitting in my lap again, her legs straddling mine, and she kisses me on the mouth.

I kiss her back. Long, and hard, and desperate. I hold her face and she says, "Not yet," when I think, *Take off that fucking blindfold.* "Not yet."

"If not tonight? If not now... then when?" I say. "When?"

She just shakes her head again, her body becoming soft, and then slips off to the side, pulling me over with her, until we're nestled up to each other, her ass pushing against my cock, her back pushing into my chest, like we're a couple.

I smile.

Because tonight, we are.

We sleep. I'm not sure how long, because it's still dark outside when I pick her up in my arms and carry her up to her bedroom. She moans, and even though that stupid blindfold slips off her eyes, she never opens them. It's like she's afraid to see me.

Which is perfect, right? Just fucking perfect. Because I am desperate for her to see me. I am desperate to be seen. And she wants to keep me invisible.

Once she's settled in bed, I kiss her on the lips. She wakes just long enough to kiss me back, her fingertips threading into my hair, grabbing me, making me feel wanted, and then lets go, rolls over, and sleeps.

I reluctantly leave her. Go downstairs, find our book and begin to write the end I started and couldn't finish.

Because this is it. Our stories have been told, her fear has been banished, and my job here is done.

I leave our book on the kitchen counter where she expects it to be, then take myself back downstairs, enter the secret room, and stare at the ceiling until the sun comes up.

CHAPTER FORTY-THREE

EVANGELINE

I wake up smiling even before I remember why I'm smiling. How have I only been here six days? This feels like my life now. Like everything I was doing before I came to this house with Ix—God, I'm still getting used to that—was fake. A dream. Or some kind of alternate reality. And now this is reality. I'm awake and I might even be… happy.

I get up, throw on my nightgown and robe, run down the stairs, and I'm just about to walk into the kitchen to get our book when a loud chime fills the house.

I whirl around and stare at the hallway leading to the grand foyer.

It's the doorbell, I realize.

I travel the hallway on tiptoe—which is stupid because I'm barefoot and still in my nightgown—and peek around the corner like a child who is supposed to be in bed. There's someone on the other side of the wavy, leaded glass in the front door.

The bell rings again, so I tiptoe closer.

I'm almost certain whoever is on the other side can see me, so I take a deep breath, clutch my silk robe around my body, and open it.

"Evangeline Rolaine?" the man asks. He's wearing the tidy blue uniform suit of a well-known local delivery service.

"That's me," I say, surprised I have a voice. Surprised I even opened the door, now that I think about it. I'm very exposed. No scarf, no gloves, no hat, no sunglasses.

"Sign here, please," he says, thrusting a tablet at me. I sign with my finger, then hand it back as another man comes up the front walkway with several large packages.

"Would you like us to bring them inside?" the first man asks.

I nod, trying to understand what's happening, and then move out of the way so they can enter the foyer. "Here is fine," I say, pointing to the exquisitely upholstered bench under the mirror. "And I'm sorry, but I don't have my purse—"

"No need," the second man says, arranging the packages neatly on and around the bench. He smiles at me. "The tip has already been taken care of."

"Who's this from?" I ask.

The first man says, "There's a card, ma'am. Do you need anything from us?"

"What would I need?" I ask, genuinely curious.

"We were instructed to ask if you required anything, ma'am."

"No, thank you," I say. "I'm good."

They both bow their heads at me as they back out, closing the front door behind them.

How strange.

I walk over to the packages. There's about half a dozen, each with a small card attached to the bow, and each card has a number on it. One through six.

They are all different sizes. One is the size of a large shoebox, three are the size of my hand, one is very large—at least three feet long and very wide—like it contains a whole other world under that paper and ribbon. The last one is very thin and flat. And they are all wrapped up in matte black paper, adorned with yards of golden fabric ribbon, and each has an elaborate golden bow.

One—the largest box—has a regular-sized card attached to it as well as the smaller one with the number.

I pluck the card off the paper—it comes off easily, like special care was taken so the paper wouldn't rip—and open it up.

Dear Evangeline,

Today is the day you break free. Don't be afraid of going after what you want. You deserve the world and the world deserves you.

Unwrap the packages numbered one through four. Don't open the last two. Those are for later.

I won't be watching today. A car will come to collect you at exactly eleven thirty. You will be dropped off, you will go inside and satisfy your curiosity however you see fit, and then you will return home in the same car.

Ix

I'm holding my breath. I don't realize it until I let it out in a gush of air and feel a little dizzy.

Alone. I am to go out today alone. Is it much different than yesterday when I left here without instructions?

Yes, it's very different. I don't know why, but it is. And for a few seconds I allow my heart to beat fast. I allow the sweat to form on my brow. I allow my hands to shake and my legs to tremble.

And then I look up at the chandelier and say, "OK."

I walk over to the gifts, lay the box marked One down onto the foyer rug, and kneel. My fingers can't help but feel the rich, golden ribbon. It's not smooth satin, but has a raised damask pattern woven into the silk. Very special, I realize. And very expensive.

I pull on it, expecting it to resist, but it doesn't. The knot falls apart easily, like it was meant to do that, and soon it's just a puddle of gold near my knees.

The box has a lid meant to lift off. Again, without resistance. And when I lift it, there is a swoosh of air which makes the black and gold tissue paper inside puff up with a display of splendorous pageantry.

My fingers are eager now, pulling the delicate paper aside to reveal a dress.

"Oh, my," I sigh, lifting the dress out of the paper so I can hold it up to the light filtering in from the high, arched windows above the door.

It's white. Winter white, not summer wedding-dress white. Almost cream. And it's clearly cashmere, because it's so soft, my fingertips want to pet it. I stand up, holding it against my body. It's been tailored to my shape, because even though the skirt is long, it's not too long.

I shrug off my robe, slip out of my silk nightgown, and step into it, just to make sure.

And even though the bodice is low-cut, it's not too low-cut. My breasts fill up the cups on either side of the v down the middle, and make a spectacular show of cleavage. The a-line waist hits me just above my hips, and the hem swings just above my calves.

The intercom crackles just once, letting me know he's watching.

I twirl for him, laughing, feeling like a child again. I had so many pretty, pretty dresses as a child. I wore them to spectacular places.

For a moment I'm disappointed that my destination today is the coffee house. This dress... this dress was meant to take me somewhere *spectacular*. The halls of a palace, or the desert gardens of a sheikh in winter.

But I remember there's more inside the box. So I rush over and pull out a winter coat. Tan, the perfect color to compliment the winter-white dress. Double-breasted with large black buttons, a wide belt, and brown faux-fur trim on the hood and cuffs. It's A-line, like the dress, with a long loose ruffle just above the waist for added flair.

Underneath the coat are tan leather gloves. Which make me laugh, because I left mine in the cab yesterday and even though I'm not sure if I care about exposing my hands, I will surely need gloves to leave the house on a such a cold winter day. There's a scarf too. But not a thick one to cover my face like I usually wear. Silk. Cream with a intricate tan pattern.

There's even a new pair of sunglasses. Not big and round and meant for hiding, but sheer, and sleek, and chic.

The second box contains over-the-knee suede boots the same color as the coat. Heels high enough to make me worry, but I dismiss that fear. I'm done with fear.

There's more to unwrap. It's like Christmas and I feel like I'm young again.

I go back over to the bench, find the package marked three, and sit back down on the rug to open it. The skirt of the dress pools around me like a puddle of snow.

The ribbon gives in as I tug, just like on the other boxes, and when I open the lid on this one there is... a necklace.

I can't stop the huff of surprise that escapes my lips. Because this is no ordinary necklace. It's diamonds and sapphires intricately woven together on a strand of silver, or white gold, or platinum, that would make a queen feel special.

"Oh, Ix," I whisper. "This is..." I shake my head. "Too nice for a coffee house."

The crackle of the intercom urges me to keep going. So I lay the box aside, get up to get number four, and sit back down in a pile of ribbon that looks like spun gold.

The fourth gift is earrings to match the necklace.

He bought me an entire outfit. And it's perfect. It's... *me*. So very, very *me*.

I didn't even know who I was before coming to this house with Ix, but these clothes on my body add up to the image I've always wanted for myself.

No longer the child prodigy, but a grown, competent woman.

I daydream about how gorgeous I will look wearing this ensemble.

"What time is it?" I get up, rush to the kitchen to find the clock, and realize I only have an hour before the car will come collect me.

I shower, blow-dry my hair, and lightly apply a little makeup. Not too much. Today I don't want to hide. I want to be me.

I put the dress back on, slip the boots up my legs with a sigh, and fasten the necklace around my neck and the earrings on my ears.

For the next ten minutes I just stare at myself in the mirror, amazed at how different I look. How well I have grown up. How beautiful I am, even without the violin.

"Do you think I'm pretty?" I ask the camera above the bed. "I think I'm going to like you, Ix. When I finally meet you properly. I think I'm going to like you a lot."

The door chime pulls me away from my own reflection. I put the coat on, fasten the wide belt at my waist, pull the gloves over my hands, put on my sunglasses, and walk downstairs, ready for this day to begin.

The driver is at the door wearing a dark suit and dark sunglasses. He says, "Good morning, ma'am," as he extends his forearm.

I take it. Unafraid. And let him walk me to the car, open my door, and hold my hand as I slip into the backseat that smells like rich leather and honey.

There's tea set on the console between the two luxurious leather seats. A small pot made of white china. One cup. A tiny dish filled with golden honey and an equally tiny honey dipper sits off to the side.

I decide why not indulge? It's been so long since I had this kind of luxury in my life. Luxury I could afford to enjoy. Luxury I felt I deserved.

So I pour a cup of tea, drip long viscous strands of honey into the amber liquid, and sip, fully content in the stillness of the smooth ride as we make our way through downtown.

We stop and I look out, surprised. "Where are we?" I ask the driver.

"This was the destination, ma'am." He gets out, opens my door, and holds out his hand to help me out. He says, "I was told to give you this note."

For some reason the small, folded piece of white paper in his hand makes my stomach clench up with fear. "What does it say?" I ask.

"I don't know, ma'am." I take it, and he says, "The car will be here when you're ready to leave."

I look up and realize we're parked in front of what might be a hotel valet area. There's a large revolving door, but no sign above. It looks... empty. "Is this—"

"No, ma'am," the driver says. "There." He points to the shop next door that does have a sign, which reads The Tea Room. And then he bows his head a little and walks back around to the driver's side and gets into the car.

I'm alone. Again. And I don't like it.

Hesitantly, I open the folded note and read.

Evangeline,

Go into the tea room and tell the hostess you're looking for Jordan Wells. She'll tell where to go next.

Ix

I don't think I want to do this. Something inside me is screaming, *No!* A gut feeling that whatever is waiting for me inside that shop, it's not what I'm looking for.

But I came all this way. All the way from frightened girl to confident woman, and I don't want to run away now. I don't want my future to slip through my fingertips. I don't want to go back into the past.

So I draw in a deep breath, walk over to the door, open it up, and step into the tea room.

Inside it's quaint. Lots of tables, mostly full of chatting women sitting in overstuffed chairs. It's bright—

far brighter than any room I'd have been caught alive in one week ago—and smells delicious. Like fresh baked goods and summer afternoons.

"Ms. Rolaine?"

I turn my head to find a tall woman with long, dark hair—about my age—looking at me with an air of familiarity. "Yes," I say. "I'm Evangeline Rolaine."

I don't think I've introduced myself to anyone in public since I was fourteen. Managing it excites me, because it's a huge step forward. But it also scares me. *Why does she know my name?*

"They're waiting for you back here." She smiles and turns, her long hair swishing from the quick movement.

"They?" I ask, but she's steps ahead of me now, so I feel like the only thing I can do is follow.

I'm very glad Ix left me the sunglasses, and I'm also extremely happy that they're not the large, dark, round ones I used to wear, because these don't look like sunglasses you have to take off indoors and those did.

I leave them on as I maneuver my way through tables and people, until we reach a set of double doors at the back.

The panic sets in as she reaches for both doorknobs and pulls them open to reveal a man. Standing tall and still in the middle of the room. Hands clasped in front of his body. Uncertain smile on his face.

But I have no idea who the man on the other side of the door is.

"What's going on?"

"Oh, my. Evangeline." I turn to see Dr. Lucinda Chatwell off to my left, walking towards me with her arms outstretched. "You look so… different. So beautiful."

She pulls me into her, grabbing both my hands and kissing me on the cheek as I awkwardly embrace her back.

"What's going on?" I ask again. "Who's this?" I ask, motioning to the man in the room.

"This is my partner. Ixion said you were ready to leave the house and you wanted to meet Jordan before you left."

"What?" I shake my head and blink my eyes, like I'm dreaming and just need to wake up. "This isn't Jordan. I know him. I've been watching him all week. In the gardens next to the house and at the coffee house for lunch."

"What?" They say it at the same time.

"Jordan. This isn't—"

"What are you talking about?" Lucinda asks. "This *is* Jordan Wells, my partner. He's the one who found Ixion. That's the name of your watcher. Ixion Vanir. When he called me last night he said—"

"He called you last night?" I ask. "And he set this up?"

"Yes," Lucinda says. "What's wrong? Why—"

I tune her out as all the puzzle pieces all into place.

X. Ix. Ixion. My watcher. My stranger.

He was the one meeting me all week. It was him in the greenhouse. It was him in the coffee house. It was him the whole time.

"Where is he?" I ask.

"Who?" Lucinda asks. Jordan just stands there looking as confused as I feel.

"Ixion," I say, trying out his name. He wanted me to look at him last night. He wanted me to see him. And I said no. I wanted to stay blind. "I have to go," I say, rushing back the way I came. The woman who took me to the private tea room is blocking my way, also wearing an expression of confusion on her face. I push past, then weave through the tables and people—all the while Lucinda is calling my name.

But I don't turn back. And I'm not running away, either. I'm running towards something.

Ixion.

This is why I had such a bad feeling all morning.

No. No. No. No.

I push through the front door and run to the car, Lucinda follows me out, calling my name, but I slip into the backseat and tell the driver, "Take me home. Right now. Quickly! Quick!" I say it again when he looks at me in confusion. Lucinda opens the door, but I put up a hand and stop her from getting in. "No," I say. "This is not over yet." And then I push her back, close the door back up, and lean into the front seat. "Drive! Now!"

I chew my lip as we weave our way through downtown traffic, the familiar gut-wrenching, all-too familiar fear I've known for the past ten years overtaking me again. I need to get inside. I need his eyes on me. I need... *him.*

He can't leave me like this. He wouldn't.

But when I get to the house and rush through the front door, the first thing I see is the missing bulb up in the chandelier.

He's gone.

I had a chance to know him. Really know him. And I turned him down.

And now he's gone.

"You never told me the end of the story!" I scream, whirling around, looking for more cameras.

That's when I see the last two gifts still sitting on the bench where I left them this morning.

I sink to the floor in the grand foyer, the piles of golden silk ribbon surrounding me like a pond of summer, tears welling up in my eyes.

"I don't want them," I say. "I don't want *presents*. I don't need more clothes. I don't need jewelry, I don't need any of this stuff! I just want to talk to you! I'll take off the blindfold. I promise." I'm pleading now. Begging to the empty air.

And because he's gone, there's no reply.

No crackle of the intercom to urge me on. No sense of his all-seeing stare.

I am alone. Unseen. Unheard. Hidden from the world.

And it's ironic, after all those years of wanting to be invisible, right now I can think of nothing I want less.

The front door is still open. The wind is whipping through the house, making me shake with cold, when a shadow falls onto the floor in front of me.

I look up, hopeful, but see only Lucinda standing there, her body a silhouette of darkness against the bright winter sun.

"What's going on?" she asks. "What happened here? Did he touch you? Did he hurt you?"

I shake my head as a tear falls down my cheek. "No," I whisper. "He was gentle, and good, and I want him back. Can you bring him back?"

I see that Jordan—the real Jordan—has also come. He steps out from behind Lucinda and says, "He left. About an hour ago. Called me up and said the job was done, I should go to the tea room to meet with Lucinda and you, and that was it. He hung up. I tried to call him back after you ran out... but..." He shakes his head. "He won't answer."

"Where did he go?" I ask. "Where does he live? I need to find him!"

He shrugs. "I don't know, Evangeline. Somewhere up in Wyoming, I think. I found him in jail a few weeks ago."

"You *what?*" Lucinda asks. "What the hell is wrong with you, Jordan? Why the hell did you hire a man who—"

"He's a friend, OK?"

"Then why don't you know where he lives?" I ask, getting to my feet. "If he's your friend, then where is he!" I yell that last part. "Is this part of your stupid game? Am I just another piece to play with?"

"Evangeline," Lucinda says in her stupid, calm doctor voice.

"No!" I scream. "No! You people put me here with him and now you think you're gonna take him away? No!"

"I'm sorry," Jordan says. "When Ix disappears, well, he just... goes. He's just gone."

The three of us stand there, staring at each other. Lucinda looking like she really needs me to accept reality. Jordan looking guilty, about what I don't know, but I want to find out. And me... God, me... I feel so... alone.

That word in my head makes me wilt. "I want to go home," I say in a soft, small voice that reminds me of the woman I was before I came here. "I want my apartment, with the curtains drawn, and the city far, far away."

"Why?" Jordan asks.

"Why what?" I snap.

"Why go back when you came this far? Ixion was never part of your future, Evangeline. He never was. He wasn't supposed to talk to you or... whatever else he did," Jordan says, starting to put the pieces together. "He broke the rules, OK? You need to forget about him. Believe me, he's forgotten about you. That's what he does best."

I seethe at that characterization of Ixion Vanir. I glare at Jordan. Stare him straight in the eyes. Let him see me as I draw myself up, square my shoulders, lift my chin and say, "You don't even know him. You don't even know me. But I know you," I say, pointing my finger at him. "He told me everything about *you*."

Jordan shrinks back.

"Yes," I say, nodding. "And if he left here, it was because of you. Not me."

We stare at each other for several seconds. I pull away first and that's when I see the last two gifts. The one marked Five is about the right size. And when I walk over and pick it up, it's the right weight too.

"What's that?" Lucinda asks.

I glance at Jordan as I pull the ribbon apart, tear the paper off, and hold our book in my hands.

"The end," I say. "This is the end I was waiting for."

I grab the other gift, walk out of the house, get back into the still-waiting car, and give the driver my address. I don't open the book. I sit quietly as I'm taken back to my home. And when I walk through the front door of my building, I stare straight at the concierge and say, "Hello," as I pass. "I'm going to need you to let me in my apartment. I seem to have left my purse behind."

He stares at me, then offers up a quick, "Hello, Miss Rolaine. I'm glad to see you again," as he pats his jacket for a key card and follows me to the elevator.

"It's good to be home," I say, as the elevator door opens and we get inside together, the unopened present in one hand, the book in the other. And when the doors open, and when I'm let in, and the door is closed behind me, I walk to the couch, set the unopened gift down, and collapse into the cushions with the book in my hand.

If I read it, it's going to be end of everything.

It's going to be the end of us.

I open the book and turn to the page where we left off.

CHAPTER FORTY-FOUR

IXION

I was done. *I enjoyed sex with Augustine, but it wasn't the sex that made me love her. I didn't need her body, just her mind. Likewise with Jordan. I wasn't in love with him. He's a good-looking man and we had some fun, but I'm not interested in being in a relationship with a man.*

Besides, they didn't really need me. They fucked, and most of the time I just watched. Sat in the chair across the room, stroking myself as they went at it. And even that wasn't necessary.

I wasn't necessary.

Except it turns out I actually was.

I was the glue that held them together. I was the necessary part that made their machine run. Augustine loved me the way I loved her. We were friends first. Business partners second. Lovers came a very distant third in our relationship.

Jordan is smart. He understands people. Most of the time better than they understand themselves.

He had that advantage over us, I guess. He knew us better than we knew ourselves.

When he came up with his plan, he knew she was longing for Alexander again. He knew I was done. He knew it was already over.

But he also knew she loved me. Not him, but me. Not Alexander, but me. I was the glue that kept her and Jordan together.

Alexander was the one who kept them apart.

Jordan told me… wouldn't I like just one shot at her alone? And he asked her, wouldn't she like me, with her and only her? Just one night, just Ixion and Augustine? One night to do whatever we wanted. Whatever our hearts told us to do?

I was going to say no. I didn't expect her to say yes.

But she did.

CHAPTER FORTY-FIVE

EVANGELINE

It ends there?

No, that can't be the end! That's not a fucking ending! What the hell, Ix?

I stand up and the last package rolls on the couch cushion. It's too small to be another notebook, but I pull on the gold ribbon and tear at the black paper anyway, eager and hopeful that I will find the answers I was looking for.

It's… a phone. My phone with a new touchscreen. And there's a voicemail alert blinking at me.

Ixion's voice is clear and calm when I press play.

"Hey," he says. "Bet you're wondering what the fuck, right? What happened next?" He sighs. Silence for several seconds as he works through whatever's on his mind. "Me too," he finally says. "I think about it constantly now. I know what happened. I know what he did. I know what he *didn't* do. I know that most of what came next was just… bad luck."

He pauses again. My mind is racing with questions.

"I took responsibility. Jordan was in law school, was about to graduate, about to take the bar exam and join his father back here in Colorado to carry the torch and all that bullshit.

"The point being... Jordan had a future. And yeah, I'd do anything for the guy back then. I loved him in my own way. He's been my best friend since we were little kids. Partners in crime, we used to joke. Never knowing it'd really turn into that twenty-some years later.

"You can't be a lawyer if you have a felony record. He didn't ask me to do it. I just felt compelled. I feel compelled a lot. It's why I am where I am and... and it's partly my fault, anyway. Because I lied to everyone. To Augustine, mostly. But everyone. So fuck it, right? Fuck it. Bad choices lead to bad outcomes and fuck it."

He pauses again. Maybe to collect himself. Because I can hear the hard swallow like we're just inches apart.

"You should stay away, Evangeline. Play your show, live your life, and forget I ever happened. Trust me, it's for the best."

CHAPTER FORTY-SIX

IXION

This time I'm not drunk. I hear the rotors of the helicopter landing outside. The jail in this town is pretty small. Just a substation, really. And the only dude on duty is, of course, my friend Sheriff Gramps. He's been grinnin' at me all day. Like somethin' bad's coming.

And he's here. Because that helicopter outside doesn't belong to the Wyoming law.

It's Jordan.

Again.

Comin' to save me from myself, I suppose.

The front door swings open—I can see it from my cell, which isn't even locked—and Jordan Wells walks in wearing a navy-blue peacoat, three-thousand-dollar shoes, and a watch that probably costs more than Gramps makes in a year.

He brings a bitter winter wind in with him that sweeps into the little building like a vortex, twirling loose papers around and lowering the temperature by ten degrees immediately.

He slams the door closed behind him and the bits of papers settle on the floor.

Gramps looks pissed off about that.

I watch through one cracked eye as Jordan takes the place in, tracking everything like he's a goddamned detective or somethin', and then his gaze rests on me.

"Can you give us a minute, Jake?"

Gramps, who must go by the name of Jake, nods, shrugs on his coat, grabs a pack of smokes off his desk, takes a package from Jordan as he heads out the door—probably a bribe—once again, evoking the wind that stirs things up before it settles them down.

"Why am I such a fuckup?" I say, not even bothering to sit up as Jordan enters my cell. "Just my natural talent, I guess."

"You bashed that guy's new truck in? *Again?*"

"No," I correct him. "This is the first I've bashed in the *new* new one." I laugh at my joke.

"It's not fuckin' funny, asshole. He's not letting you off this time. Gonna press charges. Why the fuck do you do this shit?"

"Because," I say. "When I got home from Denver I remembered why I did it the first time."

"And why was that?" Jordan is seething with anger. Nobody asked him to come up here, so I don't really give a fuck.

"Because he beats the fuck out of his wife," I say. "And this time he did it in public. In front of me. And no one in that stupid town wanted to interfere because he employs most of them out at the feedlot he owns. That asshole only stopped hitting her when I bashed in his brand-new headlights on his brand-new truck. So fuck him, he got what he deserved. And if he wants to press charges, well, I'm more than happy to testify how she ended up at Thermopolis General Hospital last night after he knocked her unconscious."

Jordan blinks at me. "What?"

"It's a long story that starts with Rachel, the woman's sister, hiring me to kick her brother-in-law's ass that night I got drunk a few weeks back. I was already in the bar. Already pretty fucked up. And she had the bat with her, just in case I didn't have a gun. Which I did, but took the bat anyway. I got more common sense than that. And it ends with me bashing in his new truck instead of his face. You know, because I'd probably have killed the guy and murder's a long stretch in the pen."

Jordan blinks again.

"Too long, really." I sigh. "I mean, I'm looking for a vacation, ya know? Not a permanent stay."

"You're fucking crazy," he says, finally finding his voice.

"Yeah." I sigh. "That's what they say. Ixion was the original bad boy of Greek mythology, right?" I smile at Jordan's expression, which is a cross between disgust and respect. "Might as well live up to the name."

"You tricked her," he says, referring to Evangeline now.

"I gave her what she needed."

"You pretended to be me. Don't bother denying it, she fuckin' told me the whole story."

"I let her see what she wanted to see."

"You're lying."

I hold out my hands, a *mea culpa* gesture. "Hey, that's what I do best, right? Get you outta trouble. Maybe I should've gone into law?"

"I didn't ask you to take responsibility for what I did."

"You didn't have to, Jordan." His name comes out of my mouth with a hiss. "You didn't *have* to."

He shakes his head. "I'm sorry. How many fuckin' times can I say it?"

"As many as it takes to mean it."

He huffs out a breath of air that's half laugh, half loathing. "I did mean it."

I stand up so fast, have my hands around his throat so firm, get my face right up in his so quick the shocked expression is lost on me because we are...

Eye. To. Eye.

"You're the liar," I seethe. "You wanted me because Augustine wanted me. Not you. *Me*."

He pushes me back so hard, I stumble and crash into the wall. "I made a mistake," he says. "I would've taken responsibility for it."

"It was a fuckin' felony!" I yell.

"So what!" he yells back. "So what? I never asked you—"

"I was your fucking glue, Wells. I held you two together. She never wanted you. She wanted Alexander."

"Yeah." He laughs. "And look what that got her. Look where she is now."

"Oh, I know exactly where she is now, asshole. Chella called me two nights before I left Denver. And you know what she told me?"

Jordan shakes his head. "That's not why I brought you home."

"Bull. Shit!" I fuckin' scream it. I point my finger in his face, using every ounce of self-control I have not to choke the life out of my former best friend. "You've been playing a game with me since we were kids. You don't know how to stop. You're a fuckin' addict, Jordan. And your drug is deceit."

He swallows hard. Unable to deny it. Which just pisses me off even more.

"You came here to bail me out why?"

"That's not why," he says.

"Why?"

"I didn't know she was in Denver until you were already back."

"You're a fucking liar. You can't stop. You're lying to yourself now. You knew Augustine was in Denver. That she was looking for me! She told Chella. She looked you up the first day she got there. You two had lunch. She asked about me and—"

"You'd already moved in the house when that happened, Ixion. Ask Augustine yourself if you don't believe me."

"No," I say, shaking my head. "Fuck her. And fuck you."

"It's not her fault."

"No," I say. "It's not. It's my fault for lying to her about you. It's my fault for covering your tracks. For taking your fall. You wanted us, right? Me, and you, and her. And you thought everything was gonna be great. Until you realized she was only there because of me."

"That's not—"

"She wanted Alexander for his stability, and she wanted me because the love we have—had—" I correct, "—was pure. You were just part of the *game*, Jordan. Just another player. And it drove you crazy when she said she was going back to Alexander. So you put those cameras up in my apartment. You filmed us. And then you got caught. And instead of telling her it was you, you let me take the blame."

"I never asked you—"

"YOU NEVER HAD TO!" I yell it so loud, my head begins to throb. "You'd have been charged with a felony. And then what, Jordan? What law degree? What career? What life would you have had?"

He just stands there, unsure if he should argue his point further. But then he gives up and shakes his head. "I only came here to beg you to go to Evangeline's show. That's all. I haven't even talked to Augustine since that first day she contacted me. Evangeline asked me to talk you. She asked for your phone number, but I didn't want to give it—"

"Without my consent," I sneer. And then I laugh. "You know what the worst part is?" I ask him.

"I'm fucking sorry, OK?"

"That crash that killed my family? That crash that made me richer than God because I was the only one left to inherit the family money?"

"Ixion," he whispers.

But I keep going, because there's no stopping me now. I've been holding this in for years. "That crash happened before I could tell my father the truth. So my entire family—my mother, my father, my *baby sister*—they all died thinking I was a sick fucking voyeur. That I made a sex tape with Augustine without her consent and then sent it to Alexander to try to break him and Augustine up for good."

"I'm sorry," he whispers again. "I'm fuckin' sorry."

"I didn't even get to go to the funeral because I was in jail." I'm not screaming now. It hurts too much to do anything more than whisper that last part. "She only dropped the charges because she felt sorry for me."

"Just tell me how I can fix it, Ix."

"Fix it?" I laugh. "You can't bring people back from the dead, Jordan. There is no do-over for death. And you know what the most ironic part about all this shit is? Alexander knew, you dumbass. He knew what we were doing, so your plan made no sense. She just... she just *never loved you.*"

"I know that," he says. "I don't know why I did it."

"You did it because you still believe that bullshit. Total Exposure, right? That's the little nickname you gave Evangeline's game?" It's such a brass-balls move. A slap in the face. All I can do is laugh. "Get the fuck out of here and don't ever look me up again."

Jordan lets out a long breath of air. Defeat. I think that was him admitting defeat.

Good.

He lost his fuckin' game. Finally. He's getting exactly what he deserves.

He turns away, his back to me, but stands there for a few seconds, just shaking his head. "You saved her," he says.

"Yeah," I growl. "*I did.* Not your stupid game. It was me who saved Evangeline. I was the one who helped her, not *you.*"

He glances over his shoulder at me. Eyes narrowed. Frowning. "And who the fuck... do you think... sent *you* to *her*, Ixion?"

What?

"Me," he says. "I'm not what you think."

He leaves my cell, crosses the small sheriff's station, opens the door, lets the wind in, and then walks out of my life.

Gramps, AKA Jake, enters a few minutes later, stirring up the room one more time. But instead of going back to his desk, he comes into my cell and hands me...

The book.

"Where'd you get this?" I ask, staring at the black cover in his outstretched hand.

He nods his head to the door. Indicating Jordan. "He slipped it to me when I left you two alone." And then he sets it down on the cot. "Ya know," he says, sighing deeply, like he's been doing this job way too long. "You're not even under arrest, son. Dude's getting charged with attempted murder this time. You can just go home. You played your part, Ixion. We'll handle it from here."

I played my part, all right.

The low thrum of helicopter rotors shakes the ceiling. Gramps and I stare at each other until the noise fades. And then he says, "Go to the show."

"What?"

He nods at the book. "I was bored outside, so I read it."

"*What?* You asshole!"

"She needs you," he says. Then he shrugs one last time before turning his back to me. "And you need her too."

I stare at the book, then give in because there's not a chance in hell I wouldn't read what she has to say. I pick it up, settle back down on the cot, and open it up to the last entry.

Have you ever felt adored?
Not for your talent, but because you struck a chord
that resonated like light in the night?
Held in the gaze of a stranger

330

totally exposed, completely enclosed
tightly embracing the danger
one feels when they are loved?

But through it all you find
that you are more than they defined
and there is something bright
like light in the night
for the years ahead.

I have felt adored, Ixion.
And of all the people on this earth, only you were able to do
that.
That's why I'm here.

Jordan has added something to the book as well.
A VIP pass to Evangeline's show tonight.

CHAPTER FORTY-SEVEN

EVANGELINE

Mei Ling Chao is standing in my living room.

I am due to leave for my first performance since I was a teenager in twenty minutes, but I don't care if I'm late. Mei Ling Chao is *standing in my living room*.

"Can I get you some tea?" I ask. She looks ill. I know she has cancer, so that's probably most of it. But she looks nervous too. "And please," I say, motioning to the nearest chair. "Sit."

She has a large package with her, which she holds onto tightly. Almost lovingly. But she lowers herself into the chair and smiles at me, keeping the package in her lap. "Yes, I'd love some tea. Thank you."

"One sec, OK?" I say. I'm reluctant to leave her. Like… if I take my eyes off her she might wither away to nothing.

"I'm fine, dear," she says in her old, grandmotherly voice. "Go. Make the tea. I'll still be here."

"OK," I say, wiping my sweaty hands on my dress, then immediately regretting that decision, since this is what I'm wearing on stage in less than an hour. "I'll be right back."

My whole body hums like it's been charged with electricity as I make my way into the kitchen. My heart is

333

racing and I feel a little out of breath. A little bit like the old days when I'd start to get a panic attack, but that's not what this is. I'm not panicking. I'm nervous for the performance and excited too, because ever since that night I played for Ixion, the music has returned. It came home to me that night and filled me up, and changed my life. Again.

My hands shake as I make tea, wondering what this new feeling really is.

Then I realize… it's *awe*.

Mei Ling Chao is in my home.

When I've got the tea pot and cups on a serving tray, I take them back out to the living room and set it down on the coffee table. I smile at her as I pour her cup, and she helps herself to honey and milk as I pour one for myself too.

When was the last time I had a guest in my house?

God, I don't even remember. Maybe never. And Lucinda pounding on my door demanding entry doesn't count.

"You're my first guest ever," I tell her as I take my seat on the couch

"Am I?" She laughs. "Well, it's an honor, my dear."

I don't know why I feel like crying, but I'm very close to tears. "No," I say. "I'm the one who's honored. Truly. This is the best moment of my life. Just seeing you. And right before I take this huge leap back into the life I thought was over… It's…" I shake my head and can't continue.

"You're going to be spectacular tonight," she whispers.

I nod and then the tears are there. Welling up in my eyes and threatening to break through.

"I have a seat right up front."

"You do?" I ask. Mei Ling, practically on her death bed, has travelled a thousand miles to see me play. Something she can do just as well as I can, and she came anyway. She's here for *me*.

"I bought my ticket the moment they went on sale," she says. "I had my nephew on the internet, ready to purchase at midnight." Tears are welling up in her eyes now too. "I always knew you'd be back, Evangeline. And that's why I've been keeping this for you."

She holds up the package in her arms and presents it to me.

I take it out of instinct. Pulling it into my lap and just... staring at her. Unable to understand what's happening.

"It's missed you," she says.

And that's when I realize what this is. What I'm holding. Before I even rip the paper off, before I open the case and see my most prized possession for the first time since I sold it all those years ago. The one thing that saved me when I was living through my darkest moment, desperate for money, and freedom.

My Stradivarius.

I shake my head, tears flowing freely down my cheeks now.

"I spent almost all my money on it. But it was worth it. I knew you'd be back."

I take the violin out. Carefully. So very, very carefully. And then I realize what she just said. "I can't possibly take this," I say. "I can't pay you for it. I'm broke too. You should sell it," I say. "It's worth... it's... it's priceless, Mei Ling."

She laughs. It's a sweet laugh. One I wish I had heard more. "It's already been paid for," she says.

"What?" I whisper. "Who? Who bought it?"

"It was bought for you, dear. It was an anonymous sale. I don't know who actually paid for it. And I wouldn't have sold it to anyone if they hadn't mentioned it was a gift and I could present it to you myself. But it's been paid for, so don't you worry about me. I've already set up trusts for my sisters and their families with the money. They will all be taken care of after I'm gone thanks to your secret benefactor."

I don't know what to say. I just sit in my living room, with a living legend I have admired and emulated my entire life, and weep.

She gets up, hard as it is with her health and age, and walks over to the couch to sit down next to me. She holds me as I cry. Strokes my hand, pets my hair, assures me everything is gonna turn out just fine.

Mothers me.

And I cry harder.

CHAPTER FORTY-EIGHT

IXION

I charter a jet to Denver. It takes me several hours to get myself together and drive out to the airstrip in Sheridan, so I don't arrive in the city until almost seven PM. I get to the performing arts center in Downtown a few minutes after eight. But there's no music yet—was she waiting for me?—so they let me in the doors, clutching my VIP pass in my hand, and direct me to the stairs, because I have a balcony seat.

I expect Jordan to be there, at least. Or Lucinda. But it's a private box, so I take my seat just as the lights dim and the cacophony of voices dulls to a murmur.

The deep scarlet curtain opens and the entire theatre immediately becomes silent.

Evangeline walks onto the stage with no gloves. No hat, no coat, no scarf, no sunglasses.

The entire room erupts in a standing ovation.

I stand with them. Smiling.

She looks up at me, right at me. Like dead in the eyes.

And I stare back at her.

She's holding the Stradivarius. Cradling it in her arms like a baby. She wipes a tear from her eyes, whispers, "Thank you," to the crowd as they continue their applause. And then nods to me.

I nod back.

And when her bow touches those strings… the whole theatre cries. Tears of joy over the beauty of her gift.

I sit mesmerized. Barely able to remember to breathe. Still. Eyes only for her. And maybe for the first time since I gave up my life for my best friend, I feel… whole again.

She's wearing the dress I left for her that last day. The whole ensemble. The diamonds and sapphires sparkle under the bright lights.

She keeps her eyes closed most of the time. But every time she opens them between pieces, she's looking up at me.

And I understand why I'm up here in the box, and not down below with Lucinda and Jordan and a few other special guests she's invited.

It's so she could *see me, seeing her.*

It's so the spotlight that erases the crowd right in front of her won't erase me.

I am the only person in this entire theatre she wants to see.

So I watch her. I watch her shine the way I knew she could. I might even cry when she stops, and wish for more.

When it's over—and man, it's over way too soon—she accepts her flowers. She takes her bow, and then a curtsey, just like she used to when she was little, and says, "Thank you," in a small, but very sincerely appreciative voice.

I don't know what to do after that. So I sit in my box for a while. Eyes on the people down below. Jordan, Lucinda, Chella and her husband, Smith. And Dan. That guy from the used books and record store.

"Ixion?" a voice whispers behind me.

338

I shake my head, unable to believe it's really her. But when I turn, there she is.

Augustine. Older than I remember. Sadder too. And alone. "I just want you to know—"

But I put up a hand and cut her off as I stand up. "Another time, huh?" I say it without malice. Just matter-of-factly. "This night isn't yours, Augustine. It belongs to someone else. So... just another time, OK?"

She sucks in a breath, but nods her head as I pass her, pulling the curtain aside so I can enter the hallway and find my way backstage.

There's only one person I need tonight.

And she's got nothing to do with my past.

CHAPTER FORTY-NINE

EVANGELINE

Mei Ling sits with me in my dressing room after the performance. Just her. Only her. I know Ixion came because he was up in the box I saved for him. I watched him watch me as I played my way through a spectacular comeback show.

And he has the pass to come back here and see me.

But he's not here.

"He's coming," Mei Ling says, patting my hand.

She is more of a mother to me in this moment than my own mother was my entire life. And I have known her less than a day.

It's a very sad realization. To understand that your parents never loved you. They only loved the opportunity that came with you.

I think this was my problem. And even though Ixion was the one who broke the prison walls I'd built around myself, it was Mei Ling who led me back out into the light.

I was going to play the show before she showed up, but I wasn't going to enjoy it.

She changed everything.

A soft knock at the door has my heart beating out of my chest with excitement.

The door opens a crack as the stage manager pokes his head in and says, "Ixion Vanir to see you, Miss Rolaine."

I stand, smooth my dress with both hands, and nod. "Please, show him in."

Mei Ling gets to her feet, but I turn and say, "You can't leave yet."

She smiles at me and says, "I'll be right outside if you need me." And then she leans up to kiss me on the cheek and turns away just as the door opens again and Ixion Vanir appears.

He smiles at Mei Ling, who takes his hand and gives it a squeeze. "Thank you," she tells him.

Ix shrugs, like this is all just a normal part of his day, but graciously replies, "You're welcome," as Mei Ling leaves us to figure things out, closing the door behind her.

"It was you, wasn't it?" I say, pointing at my long-lost violin.

Ixion smiles at me. It's a familiar smile, but strange too. I saw that smile in the greenhouse. In the coffee shop. But this is the first time he's smiled at me being... *me*. And not the scared little girl who couldn't stand the heat of a gaze.

The first time he smiles at me being him, too.

"Hey," Ix says. "What the hell am I gonna do with millions of dollars anyway? My apartment up in Wyoming goes for six hundred and fifty dollars a month and my Jeep still runs, so not in the market for a new car yet."

"How did you know she had it?" I ask.

"Dan called your phone and left a message. Said you'd asked about the violin and he knew who had it. I might've been prying into your personal life and found that message. And then I might've called Dan back and told him to wrap that shit up, we were taking it home."

I shake my head and look down at my feet, but quickly recover and meet his gaze as I say, "I never want you to stop looking at me, Ixion."

He nods back. "Well, I guess you're in luck. Because I don't think I can. I think you might be stuck with me, Miss Rolaine. And even though I have a shitload of money, I'm not really much of a catch. I was in jail this morning, ya know."

My laugh escapes as a huff of air. "Jordan told me. Told me what you did, too. Beat the shit out of a truck. Twice."

He shrugs. "Asshole had it coming. I'm not really a creepy spy, Evangeline—"

"I know that," I say, cutting him off. "Jordan told me all that stuff too. You're an investigator, right?"

He nods. "I do watch people, that part's true. I expose them, just like I did you. But it was never my intention to hurt anyone."

"You didn't hurt me, Ixion. You saved me."

"No," he says. "That was all you, Miss Rolaine. You were always the one with the plan. I just supported you."

"It's what I needed," I say.

"Me too."

"And now… now what?"

He swallows hard, like this question makes him very nervous. "Tell me what you want. And I'll give it to you."

"No," I say. "I've taken more than my share in this lifetime. I want to give you something."

He laughs.

"I'm serious, Ixion. Tell me what you want."

He sighs now. A long breath of air escapes him. Like he's getting rid of things. Like he's considering my question. And finally, after many long seconds of silence, he says, "I just want you. No games. No cameras. No lies. Just you."

I walk towards him. He opens his arms and embraces me. Kisses me on the head, then the cheek, then the lips.

Our kiss is brand new.

And when we step out of my dressing room door our life together is brand new too.

Totally exposed for who we really are underneath all the fear, and regret, and mistakes.

And ready to live with it.

JORDAN

"So listen," Chella says. "I have an interesting job for you."

We're sitting in her tea room, having tea, of course, just catching up after the shitstorm called Augustine blew through town and upended everything about my life. She's still here, still not talking to me after I admitted it was me, not Ixion, who filmed her and sent the footage to Alexander all those years ago.

Still driving me fuckin' nuts.

Augustine already knew. Alexander told her the truth after they got married. But hearing those words from my own mouth... well, that's something completely different.

So I've been in a funk ever since I came clean, and Chella, annoyingly perceptive person that she is, picked up on it. I can only imagine that's why I was invited to tea today.

"Does Smith know you're doing this?" I ask her.

"Smith," she huffs as she rubs her very pregnant belly. Chella is the most adorable pregnant woman I've ever laid eyes on. "He's all about helping people. You know that."

"So he doesn't know," I say.

"I mean, look," Chella says. "I can't help it if he's too busy to really pick up what I'm throwing down, right? I tell him all kinds of things, Jordan. Everything I do, I report at dinner." She opens her hands, palms up. "I am an open book."

I laugh. "So Smith hears what Smith wants to hear? Is that what you're saying?"

"Exactly," she beams. "Like, I told him I have this friend who might like to spice up her life." I raise an eyebrow at that. "And she's looking for a game, OK?"

"What did Smith say?"

"He said, 'Game's over.'" And then we both laugh. "And that's it. Right? So I told him. Basically spelled it out as far as I'm concerned. And he just heard what he wanted to hear."

Fuckin' Chella. "This shit is gonna catch up with you, ya know that, right?

"What shit?" she asks, innocent, bewildered look on her face. "I'm just trying to help a girl out. You know, kinda like you do." And then she winks at me.

"I dunno," I say. "I'm kinda sick of games. Maybe I should just... be a fuckin' lawyer? Ya know? Stop all this bullshit. Settle down with a girl or something."

"Just one?" she teases. "And no men?"

I roll my eyes at her. "My point is, maybe it's time to just butt out let people live their lives."

"Where's the fun in that?" Chella laughs. "And besides, people need this, Jordan. Like this girl I know. She's a really cool chick, right? Got her shit so together... I mean, her life is sewed up *tight*."

"Sounds kinda boring," I sigh.

"Exactly! She's *dying* of boredom."

I shake my head and give in. "What kind of game is she looking for?"

"Well, there's the thing, OK? She's not exactly looking for a game. But she totally needs one. She just doesn't know it yet."

"*Chella*," I say, my tone cautioning.

"Trust me," she says, "I know what I'm doing. She needs this, Jordan. Just give her what she needs."

I shake my head. "You know I can't do that."

"Listen." She says, putting up a hand to stop my objections. "The game is called... The Pleasure of Panic."

"You got a name for it already?" I ask, kinda chuckling at her audacity.

"It's good, right?" She laughs. "So much better than Total Exposure. Say it with me, Jordan. *The Pleasure of Panic.*"

"So this girl you're just looking to help out—she needs...?"

"Take a guess," Chella says, her Cheshire Cat smile wide and wild. "You'll never guess."

I can take a good guess at what The Pleasure of Panic Game might look like.

And if you wanna play along with me and this unsuspecting girl... well, you can get that book right now at your favorite retailer.

END OF BOOK SHIT

Welcome to the End of Book Shit. This is the part in the book where I get to say anything I want about the book, or the process, or whatever. It's just me, rambling on like a… rambling person.

So right now, as I write this, it's January 10, 2018 and I'm sick as a fuckin' dog. And I was gonna record this EOBS now for the audiobook so you could get the full effect, but somehow I didn't think my audio publisher would find that cute. So whatevs. Telling you I'm sick is really just a warning for what might a pretty incoherent EOBS. Just sayin'.

Anyway – so hey, it's 2018 bitches! How about that? Why don't we have flying cars yet? Like, this is the future!

So I'm in this little author group on Facebook and I'm pretty new to it, so I think this is my first new year with them. They have this thing where we pick a word for the year to concentrate on. Like it could be… FOCUS or PRODUCTIVITY stuff like that.

349

Well, my word for 2018 is BOLD.

I've done lots of bold things in my life.

One. Raised two kids as a single mother.

Two. Went back to school as a non-traditional student.

Three. Went to grad school.

Four. Started my own business.

Five. Said no to a job offer to become a full-time author.

When people think of what it means to change their lives, BOLD is the word that should come to mind. Risk, too. But risk as a lot of negativity attached to it. All those things I listed above were also risky, but BOLD is an action word. Bold is something I can be. Risk isn't. Right? Risk is a reason not to start if you ask me.

So the theme of this book is BOLD, not risk. I don't think Evangeline took a risk, because honestly she had nothing to lose. She was already gonna lose everything. And even though Jordan thinks you can lose something twice, I'm kinda with Chella on this. It's an outlook, I think.

Your perception is what makes a decision bold instead of risky.

So for 2018 I've decided to be BOLD. I've taken on a new writing partner (Johnathan McClain). We're trying to sell The Company script to Hollywood. We're releasing seven books together in 2018. I've now got a PR person, and entertainment lawyer, and a photoshoot in LA coming up in four weeks.

All of these things are outside my comfort zone so yeah, they're a bit risky. But really, can I lose if I never had those things in the first place?

I don't think so. And I think that makes a huge difference when it comes time to decide if you should take a RISK.

Since Total Exposure is my first book of 2018 I would like to encourage all of you to be BOLD with me this year. Be more like Evangeline. Do something you've always wanted to do. Find an old friend and reconnect. Start up a hobby you left behind long ago, or get a new one. Check one thing off your bucket list.

Take chances.

Live big.

Be loud.

Play the game, you guys. You can't win if you don't play. And if you fail, for fuck's sake, celebrate that failure. It's the failures that make you a better person. Failures are what teach you things. Failures stick with you, shape your future decisions, and make you take a different course next time—IF YOU LET THEM.

So if you've been reading my books for a while you probably know that a lot of my early stories are centered in and around Fort Collins, Colorado. That's because Fort Collins was where I made the biggest change of my life. That's where my kids and I ended up after leaving my boyfriend behind to be a single mom. I was in school. I actually got accepted to Colorado State University on a free-ride scholarship for first generation students. I was the first person in my family to complete a bachelor's degree.

My first few months at school were horrible. Every day I'd come home from class and just cry. I was older than everyone else by almost ten years, I had responsibilities they didn't, worries they didn't, and no money at all. Like none.

On top of that I was studying to be a scientist. I wanted to go to vet school and math was never my strongest subject. In fact, I'm only average at math. So chemistry, and physics, and calculus were really hard for me. I had to drop those classes the first time I took them because I was failing. All three of them. Not at the same time. These failures happened in different semesters, thank God.

The first one I had to drop was chemistry. I tried taking that the first semester I went back to school at a community college, before I transferred to CSU, and I was like WTF is this shit? Because I had never taken chemistry in high school. It was all very new. Plus, I was like twenty-eight or twenty-nine at this point. So everything I did take in high school was practically obsolete.

I dropped chemistry that semester and picked it up again the next semester. That time I had a better idea of what was expected in order to pass the class. At least I was prepared for what was coming. Sometimes I just need a failure to grasp how to succeed. If that makes sense. A little exposure goes a long way as far as I'm concerned. Going in blind is always harder than being prepared.

Same thing happened in Physics the following year. I just had no clue what that guy was talking about. The theory was interesting but the math was too hard for me. So I dropped it. That was my first semester at CSU and I was pretty overwhelmed with all my BOLD changes.

By the time I tried to take calculus for the first time, I'd gotten this class-dropping thing down. I mean, look, I was a great student in all my other classes. I regularly got straight A's. Just these three classes were challenging. So like first week into calculus I realized this grad-student TA who was teaching the class was an idiot. He was reading from the textbook for fuck's sake. I was never going to learn calculus from this kid.

So I dropped it and took over the summer at a local community college instead. You know, where they had real teachers. I got a B+ in calculus, bitches. And I even understood it. And that only happened because I learned that failure was instructive and made a BOLD decision to stop wasting my time in that CSU class and find another class that would help me learn. Of course, I worked my ass off for that B+ in calculus. I went to the tutoring center every day before class for like 3 hours and made that guy explain everything to me like I was a child. He didn't care. It was his job. And he was good at it.

Teachers make all the difference. That's something I realized that year too. Because the next semester, when I had to take statistics, I got an A without even trying because that guy, who was also graduate-student TA, knew what it meant to be a teacher.

If you want to learn something, find a good teacher.

That's probably the most important thing I learned from my undergraduate experience as a non-traditional student.

If you want to be BOLD, find a BOLD person to emulate.

That's why I decided to make Johnathan McClain my writing partner. He is so bold. He just puts himself out there and goes with it. One hundred percent of the time. He's got big ideas, and he's talented, and he knows people.

When he and I were first figuring out how this partnership would work we were talking about what we wanted out of it. He had his list and I really only had one thing on my list.

I wanted to learn something new.

Mostly that was how to work with another person and be successful because I'm a little bit antisocial.

Working well with others isn't easy to do when you've been doing it alone for a while, so it's been challenging for me. But worth it. Totally fuckin' worth it.

Selling the idea of a Company TV show is worth the days when working with new people overwhelms me. Writing new books with another person is worth it, even though I'm still learning how to do that. Taking the steps necessary to get a PR person and an entertainment lawyer are all things I would've never done if Johnathan hadn't encouraged me.

He's a good teacher.

And I'm teaching him something new this year too. How to write and romance, for one. :) How to interact with fans. How to do all kinds of things that he hasn't done before.

So he's being bold too, whether he knows it or not.

I'd like to encourage you to be BOLD with us this year, you guys. Make changes. Make new decisions. Find new friends who can teach you things.

Yeah, all that's risky, for sure. Risk comes along for the ride when you're bold.

But even if you fail at what you set out to do, you can still take something away from it. You can still learn something new about yourself or the world around you.

You can still learn that dropping a class and trying again is always an option.

I hope you enjoyed this book. It's probably not what you thought it was gonna be, but... really... that's what I do best, right?

Thank you for reading, thank you for reviewing, and if you want the next book, The Pleasure of Panic, you can find all the links to buy it at www.jahuss.com/Jordans-Game-Series/

Julie
JA Huss

ABOUT THE AUTHOR

JA Huss never wanted to be a writer and she still dreams of that elusive career as an astronaut. She originally went to school to become an equine veterinarian but soon figured out they keep horrible hours and decided to go to grad school instead. That Ph.D wasn't all it was cracked up to be (and she really sucked at the whole scientist thing), so she dropped out and got a M.S. in forensic toxicology just to get the whole thing over with as soon as possible.

After graduation she got a job with the state of Colorado as their one and only hog farm inspector and spent her days wandering the Eastern Plains shooting the shit with farmers.

After a few years of that, she got bored. And since she was a homeschool mom and actually does love science, she decided to write science textbooks and make online classes for other homeschool moms.

She wrote more than two hundred of those workbooks and was the number one publisher at the online homeschool store many times, but eventually she covered every science topic she could think of and ran out of shit to say.

So in 2012 she decided to write fiction instead. That

year she released her first three books and started a career that would make her a New York Times bestseller and land her on the USA Today Bestseller's List eighteen times in the next three years.

Her books have sold millions of copies all over the world, the audio version of her semi-autobiographical book, Eighteen, was nominated for an Audie award in 2016, and her audiobook Mr. Perfect was nominated for a Voice Arts Award in 2017.

She also writes book and screenplays with her friend, actor and writer, Johnathan McClain. Their first book, Sin With Me, will release on March 6, 2018. And they are currently working with MGM as producing partners to turn their adaption of her series, The Company, into a TV series.

She lives on a ranch in Central Colorado with her family, two donkeys, four dogs, three birds, and two cats.

If you'd like to learn more about JA Huss or get a look at her schedule of upcoming appearances, visit her website at www.JAHuss.com or www.HussMcClain.com to keep updated on her projects with Johnathan. You can also join her fan group, Shrike Bikes, on Facebook, www.facebook.com/groups/shrikebikes and follow her Twitter handle, @jahuss.

Made in the USA
Middletown, DE
17 July 2018